BATMAN

THE KILLING JOKE

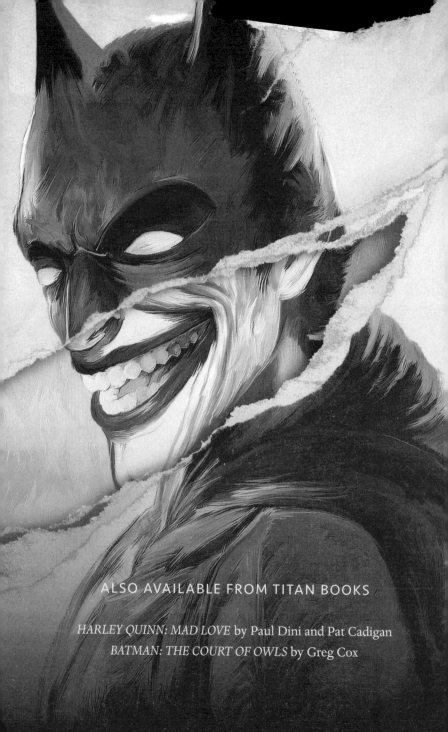

ALSO AVAILABLE FROM TITAN BOOKS

HARLEY QUINN: MAD LOVE by Paul Dini and Pat Cadigan
BATMAN: THE COURT OF OWLS by Greg Cox

BATMAN

THE KILLING JOKE

CHRISTA FAUST AND GARY PHILLIPS

Based on the graphic novel by Alan Moore and Brian Bolland

Batman created by Bob Kane with Bill Finger

TITAN BOOKS

BATMAN: THE KILLING JOKE
Paperback ISBN: 9781785658129
Ebook ISBN: 9781785658112

Published by Titan Books
A division of Titan Publishing Group Ltd
144 Southwark Street, London SE1 0UP
www.titanbooks.com

First paperback edition: February 2019
10 9 8 7 6 5

TIBO41853

A CIP catalogue record for this title is available from the British Library.

Typeset by MannMade Design. Based on a design by Crow Books.

Printed and bound by CPI Group (UK) Ltd, Croydon, CR0 4YY

To all who have taken the journey into the worlds of Batman

NOTE FROM THE AUTHORS

Our story is set when *The Killing Joke* was published, 1988, but this will not be stated explicitly. While we have sought to preserve the context of the original Moore–Bolland story, as with the retro-influenced *Batman: The Animated Series* from the '90s, and the current *Gotham* TV show, our novelization will be a mash-up of anachronisms—boxy Ford LTDs and Malibu SS muscle cars tooling around, GCPD blimps patrolling the skies, Art Deco high-rises, hidden laboratories with voltage coursing through glass tubes and big dials on machines, the thawing Cold War, people smoking indoors and, most importantly for our story, emerging technologies foreshadowing the positive and negative aspects of their impact on our culture.

1

The black cat crept along the narrow top of the brick wall, its wet fur glistening as rain fell on nighttime Gotham.

A powerful beam of light swept down from above, momentarily illuminating the feline's depthless eyes, which twinkled in the harsh glare. The light swept past, a thrum of muffled turbines accompanying the moving illumination. The searchlight came from one of several Gotham City Police Department patrol dirigibles crisscrossing the wet sky.

•

From up above Gotham seemed quiet, but the officers in the blimp knew this was deceiving. As one of them piloted the rigid aircraft, another wore earphones connected to a console that controlled what was essentially audio surveillance equipment. The state-of-the-art electronics were channeled into a unit attached to the blimp's undercarriage. While very much in the experimental stage, the gear could detect such occurrences as a voice raised in distress, a scream, or a gunshot, often before there was visual contact.

A third officer, Nancy Payton, used a pair of military grade binoculars that looked more like something out of that science fiction film she'd seen on television. These were connected by heavy cable to a control unit, and had several electro-mechanical additions to their bulky frame. The lenses utilized a modified infrared light, the better to peer into the darkness.

All of the equipment bore the logo of a division of Wayne Technologies.

The blimp continued soaring across the night sky, just beneath a roiling layer of clouds lit from beneath by the silvery lights of the city. Down below, a large black vehicle glided through the dark slick streets over which the dirigible had just passed.

•

The grim figure behind the wheel was protected from the downpour by a rounded bullet-resistant glass canopy that allowed him a full 360-degree view of his surroundings. He was known to the denizens of the city, and beyond, as Batman. His was a fearful reputation as a detective and a seeker of truth. Some called him a vigilante, others a hero. Few dared to cross him.

His vehicle, the Batmobile, was a one-of-a-kind wonder, from the carbon fiber armored hull to its custom-built, fuel-injected V12 engine, a 980-horsepower iron monster capable of achieving some 230 miles an hour if the need arose. The battering ram on the prow of this land ship was a stylized version of Batman's cowl. The sleek vehicle ran low to the ground, but there were heavy duty hydraulics installed that, at the flip of a toggle switch, would enable the car to rise up, whether to avoid obstructions in a high-speed chase or to engage in an evasive maneuver.

Given the nature, some might say obsession, of his work, Batman routinely modified the various potent gadgetry he had incorporated into the blue-black behemoth. There were ports that slid open, allowing blinding white light or explosive spheres to shoot out. A pair of spring-loaded forward-facing Browning machine guns could pop out on either side of the hood. These were particularly effective in disabling opponents who wore armored exoskeletons, and for less formidable targets they could be switched to non-lethal "sleeper" rounds.

The Batmobile also boasted side-mounted electro-stun disc launchers, and a prototype laser device capable of cutting through as much as eight inches of steel. That was a recent addition. The vehicle even possessed compressed-air launchers that could shoot wickedly barbed grappling hooks from either side. When a hook became attached to a wall or any structure stable enough to act as an anchor, the car could instantly be powered into a sudden 180-degree turn.

The automobile was as legendary as its owner, and the secrets of its armaments were jealously protected.

Little escaped the masked figure's attention. Out of the corner of his eye he saw a man weaving about on the sidewalk, leaning forward to grasp a lamppost to steady himself. Batman slowed, and his first impulse was to stop and render aid, but then he saw the man bring himself upright.

He wore a carnival clown grin on his face.

Batman frowned beneath the cowl. Another foolish individual high on drugs, likely the one known on the street as "Giggle Sniff." It was a new concoction that had come to his city, one more way to addle the mind and destroy the body. Medical types were still assessing its long-term effects, but the implications of its symptoms were inescapable, especially to the Dark Knight.

At times his crusade, to cleanse Gotham of such poison as an example, seemed overwhelming. The power-mad Ra's al Ghul had suggested a simple solution—*burn it all down and start over again*. That approach lurked in a corner of Batman's mind, and at times he wondered if the leader of the League of Assassins might be right.

No, he thought, dismissing the idea yet again, determination steeling his resolve. *Gotham* can *be saved*. Even if it took him the rest of his life. And tonight he was taking what he hoped would be a bold step on that journey.

The growl of the engine was almost imperceptible as the buildings sped past. Before long he was on the outskirts of town, where the landscape flattened out and the wind blew even more fiercely among gnarled trees older than the city itself.

Massive wrought-iron gates appeared in the powerful beams of the headlights. Batman pulled to a stop at the entrance to Arkham Asylum. Even in daytime, the place was dreary and foreboding, even more so in this weather. Opening the canopy that was more like the cockpit of a fighter jet than a car, he unlimbered his tall form and stepped into the rain. Kevlar-woven cape trailing behind him, he strode toward those gates, his tread surprisingly light for a man of his heft.

He was the product of years of intense training in an assortment of disciplines, having studied with masters throughout the world as a teenager then as a young adult. He learned martial arts such as hapkido and wing chun, chemical analysis, safe cracking, and acrobatics that included what was called *traceurs*, running up then backflipping off walls, contorting himself into seemingly bone-breaking positions. He perfected heart and pulse control learned from a hidden sect of yogis all said to be more than one hundred years old.

Yet none of that would help him this night.

•

The gate wasn't locked. He unlatched it to swing open with a screech of old metal. Knowing he was being watched from all sides, he strode toward the foreboding stone structure with lights shining in its windows.

Two men awaited him at the front door. As he came closer thunder boomed and a jagged bolt of lightning sizzled the air overhead. The flash of charged light against the asylum's rough-hewn walls and stilted roofs only made it seem more menacing, as if it hadn't been built, but emerged from the underworld, exiled and unwelcome.

In the early years of the 1900s its founder, Amadeus Arkham, had presented himself as a pioneer in the field of psychiatric treatment. Arkham's mother Elizabeth had suffered from mental illness and had died an apparent victim of suicide. This had spurred him to renovate his family estate and devote his resources to helping others, that they might not suffer as she had.

Yet the place had been built on a lie. Amadeus Arkham had ended his mother's life, cutting her throat to end her suffering. Then he'd repressed the memory, hiding the truth from his own orderly mind. The subsequent murder of his wife and daughter had shocked him into remembering, sending Amadeus down a spiral of madness until finally he was committed to his own institution.

The history of Arkham Asylum was steeped in blood.

Batman was here to confront his greatest foe. Their own

bloody conflict seemed endless, with more collateral victims than he could count and no good end in sight.

There had to be a resolution.

Reaching the front door, he gave a curt nod to the two men standing side by side as the rain beat down steadily. One was Tim Carstairs, a uniformed GCPD patrolman who Batman had encountered a few times before. The other held a Styrofoam cup of coffee. This was the police commissioner, James Worthington Gordon. Gotham's top cop was dressed in a tan trench coat, his off-the-rack brown suit and striped tie visible underneath. Dollops of water dripped from the brim of the uniform's cap and the Commissioner's fedora.

The Commissioner possessed a misleading appearance. White haired, sporting a white walrus-brush mustache and glasses, he might just as easily have been a harried high school principal who'd gotten turned around on the highway and had stopped to ask for directions. Yet Batman knew him well from their years of association. Beneath that mild-mannered exterior was a man who, in his younger years as a plainclothesman, had risked his life and the health of his family to confront and weed out the corruption that choked the police department like kudzu.

His was a disciplined resolve that had remained strong as he rose through the ranks.

2

Gordon took another sip of his tepid coffee and handed the cup to his subordinate. He pulled open the door, which moved on silent hinges, and Batman stepped inside without saying a word. Gordon followed.

They'd had a conversation earlier by phone, and something in his gut told the Commissioner he should be here when the man in the mask arrived. He couldn't exactly put his finger on why, but he hadn't made it this far by ignoring his cop's intuition.

The reception area was well lit, but the hallways beyond were jumbles of angular gloom. Sitting at the receptionist's station was a woman with short-cropped blonde hair. There was a sign on her desk.

You don't have to be crazy to
work here—but it helps!

She held an unlit cigarette in her hand and gaped as Batman stood over her. Mutely she pointed down one of the halls, where the shadows of prison bars cut obliquely across the walls like glimpses of the internal landscapes of the inmates' minds. This, Gordon knew, was the maximum-security wing. Batman strode past.

The woman picked up her cigarette lighter, then stopped before sparking it to flame. Smoking was forbidden here, but who enforced such rules at Arkham? The stale scent in the air told a different story. Perhaps the sight of Batman had suggested to her that she address her vices.

If only that worked on everyone, Gordon mused.

Gordon started after the caped man. As he did, he paused momentarily to touch the peak of his water-soaked hat. A courtly gesture to the receptionist out of step with modern times, but there you had it—he was a man with one foot in the past, but understanding time stood still for no one.

He followed the dark form down the corridor, Batman's footfalls a whisper to the slap of Gordon's shoes against tile. Periodically halogen lights gleamed overhead, so that their shadows were dark and crisp on the sickly yellow walls. They passed a metal door marked with a name and a number.

WESKER, A.
0770

There was a window cut into the door with three bars. Gordon turned his head slightly to see into the cell and noted Arnold Wesker sitting on his bed. He was doing a crossword puzzle, most likely in the *Gotham Gazette*, one of the two dailies in town.

Wesker's was a classic case of dissociative identity disorder.

Alone, he was a quiet man of modest means and ambitions— but he had a talent. He was quite adept at throwing his voice in his use of his ventriloquist dummies. Unlike most such acts, however, the little pals sitting on his lap took on personas of their own. Nor were his ambitions the same as other performers, entertaining at kids' parties or on the stage between the burlesque acts.

Through the forceful personality of the wood-and-wires construct he called Scarface, Wesker planned and pulled off daring heists and murders. He dressed the dummy in '30s style gangster attire and outfitted it with a working miniature Tommy gun. While there were many social norms Wesker alone was too timid to cross, Scarface had no such limits.

"Bats."

The word was startling in the silence of the hallway. It came from the once matinee handsome Harvey Dent. They had turned a corner and passed his cell. Dent had formerly been the district attorney of Gotham City, a hard-nosed yet fair prosecutor who was being groomed to run for the mayor's office. But a tough public official like that made dangerous enemies. During a very public trial the gangster Sal Maroni threw sulfuric acid into Dent's face, permanently and hideously disfiguring one side of his countenance. The incident drove Dent insane.

After sessions with Dent, Arkham Asylum's chief psychiatrist Dr. Joan Leland speculated that his personality had been fractured due, in part, to an abusive childhood. At any rate, following the incident "Two-Face" had been born. The Gotham villain would flip an old silver dollar coin, one side scarred, the other pristine, to choose how to carry off a scheme, or even decide the fate of an individual—sometimes permanently.

Again, Batman didn't break his stride. Dent stood at the door, his hands on the bars of his cell as he watched them pass. Gordon glanced at him, though. So much promise, so much disappointment.

The two drew close to their destination, a cell numbered 0801 and indicating, tellingly, "Name Unknown." A second uniformed police officer stood there on duty, arms crossed, slumping against the door, a bored look on his doughy face. *Badoya*, his name tag read. He had an old-fashioned ring of keys fastened to his belt loop. His nose looked as if it had been broken at some time in the past. The cop came alert as the two visitors arrived and unnecessarily saluted his boss, the Commissioner.

"If you would," Batman said. The cop out front and this man were not the usual guards. If he were to speculate, he'd say both were part of the around the clock duty assigned to the Commissioner, and that Gordon had put them in place for his arrival tonight.

Normally there would be an orderly on duty whose function was to unlock the cell doors. Yet even by Arkham standards the occupant with the chalk-white complexion required extra precautions. For the Joker had plagued Batman and the city for many years with his deadly machinations. The giggling mass murderer was responsible for a body count that hadn't been— *couldn't* be tabulated, but it was monstrously high.

Or it could be that Gordon was more concerned with what the masked man had in mind with this meeting, thus putting his own men in place.

The officer unclipped the key ring, selected the right key

and unlocked the thick door. Badoya and Commissioner Gordon waited in the hallway as Batman stepped through. In the shadowy cell he looked for all the world like a giant bat.

•

The door softly clanged shut behind him.

He stood there for a moment, surveying the spartan ten-by-twenty-foot cell. A simple overhead light hung from the ceiling over a metal table that was built into the concrete wall. The Joker sat, most of his features hidden in the gloom beyond the beam from the light. He was playing a game of solitaire. Behind him a bunk bed, also connected to the wall, was unmade.

As Batman grasped the back of the only other chair in the room, he wondered what sort of dreams haunted the man. Did he even sleep that much? Judging from the reports, the answer was no.

Then again, if the masked manhunter got four hours' sleep in the early morning hours, it was as if he'd taken the day off and slept in. In the Joker's case, he considered, that unbalanced mind was always too busy working out some fantastic endeavor that would cause mayhem and panic. Batman and Gordon had discussed at length the fact that most of the Joker's crimes were motivated, not by profit, but by pure effect. Many of them were as insane as their creator.

Once he had used a derivative of his Joker venom to mutate the fish in Gotham Harbor. He and his henchmen turned them pasty white with features like his own; red-lipped stretched death's-head grins. After an initial panic the fish turned out not to be poisonous as the Joker sought to patent the process, thinking he would get a cut for all of the fish sold in Gotham.

Another time he sought violent revenge on five former members of his gang who in one way or the other had betrayed him. This forced Batman to protect people he'd ordinarily be hunting. Still another time he'd built three-story-high jack-in-the-boxes and positioned them in several locations around Gotham City. When the huge grinning clown heads popped out on giant springs, shards of glass spewed forth from their smiling mouths. Dozens of people had been injured, often blinded when the glass slit their eyes. More than a few had died.

The Joker sometimes called such schemes "gags."

Big joke.

Yet here he sat, calmly playing a card game, his namesake card prominently displayed. There was an empty card box on the bed marked "Apex Playing Cards."

The masked man moved the chair over to the table and sat opposite the cell's occupant. So far, the Clown Prince of Crime hadn't acknowledged his presence, but that wasn't uncharacteristic of him. In truth, nothing about him could be called "characteristic." The one constant with the Ace of Knaves was his unpredictability.

Ranting one moment, then coolly calculating the next. Whatever weird, delusional logic guided him, it was his alone. He allowed no one a glimpse behind the wall of his madness. Numerous attempts had been made to ascertain what was going on inside of his head, in the hope that they might derive a methodology that would help him. Those efforts had failed.

Nevertheless, Batman acknowledged, here he was.

The triangle of light bathed the table and cards in a yellow glow. Their torsos and hands clearly visible, both men remained with their heads and shoulders in shadow. Hints of the light glinted off the Joker's wildly unkempt green hair and the points of Batman's cowl. The Joker regarded the two of clubs in his hand, holding it aloft for a beat as if for dramatic effect... then he played it.

Fnap. Card against card.

"Hello," Batman said evenly. "I came to talk."

No response.

The Joker played a jack of clubs. *Fnap.* Water dripped intermittently from the faucet, part of the cell's built-in metal sink. The drips weren't regularly spaced, Batman noted. Rather they occurred randomly. A perfect metaphor for the actions of the cell's inhabitant; a rational man would have given up on this agent of chaos long ago.

"I've been thinking lately. About you and me."

Again, no reaction from his arch-nemesis dressed in an inmate's drab gray shirt and pants. Where others had their last names on a patch sewn where a breast pocket would have been, for him it was just his cell number.

"About what's going to happen to us in the end."

It was warm in the cell, yet the man's pale skin was perfectly dry. It was an oddity Batman had observed over the years. For instance, he'd encountered the Joker dressed in wool coats when the temperature was in the nineties, and there had been no perspiration on that pasty face of his. Perhaps it was a weird by-product of whatever it was that had transformed him.

"We're going to kill each other, aren't we?"

Fnap.

The Joker played another card, loudly slapping it on a pile of others. Batman gritted his teeth, his broad shoulders sagging imperceptibly. *Why try?* What could have motivated him to do this? The man had kidnapped children and left them scarred for life, if he didn't snuff them out for a lark. All without the slightest hint of remorse. Had he been born that way, or had some horrible incident made him what he was now? Was he tormented by the death of a loved one, as young Bruce Wayne had been that momentous night?

Even after all his training, all the good he'd done, he could never shake the slow-motion images, snippets of which replayed themselves each time he put on the uniform of his alter ego. It might happen as well when he was exercising, or watching a news show, simply to see what was going on in the world.

Or just the other day, when the sky was overcast and the rain a day away, cold wind buffeting the windows. He'd been sitting in his maple-paneled study, going over a sheaf of Wayne Enterprises paperwork listening to one of Bach's sacred cantatas, "Ach Gott, wie manches Herzeleid." It was melancholy music to match his melancholy mood.

The tragedy that shaped his life had rippled up from his subconscious as he sat there, working through the events when he and Barbara had raided Maxie Zeus's lair. Not unlike the Joker, Zeus was his own form of warped self-image, having styled himself on the Greek god of thunder. *Entirely* unlike the Joker, however, the gangster's motivations, based on grandeur and greed, were readily understandable.

Maybe that was what had brought him here.

After the Zeus mission, he'd felt somehow off-balance—

though he would never admit it. Not to Batgirl, not to Nightwing. It was as if he'd begun to question his perceptions, that the arena in which he operated had shifted. He'd been thrown off, and he knew he had to regain his balance.

His dealings with the likes of Clayface, Poison Ivy, even relatively inconsequential criminals like the Zodiac Master all boiled down to one core objective—to eradicate their kind once and for all. To restore order, at least enough that the normal denizens of the city could go about their lives without worrying that homicidal vines might suddenly erupt through the floor, or a pint-sized wooden puppet might open fire in a public space.

Such a mission demanded absolute focus.

Yet Barbara didn't seem thrown off balance. As Batgirl she approached this burden of the never-ending mission in cavalier fashion, and still got the job done. Who was he to impose his single-minded brand of morality on a colleague? Dick, too, was more likely to accompany action with a sarcastic remark. And like Batgirl, when the situation demanded it he remained focused and disciplined. He was proud too that Dick Grayson had segued from his role as Robin to become Nightwing, leader of the Teen Titans.

•

Focus, Batman reminded himself. *Focus on the task at hand.*

"Perhaps you'll kill me," he said, his voice offering no hint of his internal conflict. "Perhaps I'll kill you. Perhaps sooner. Perhaps later." He paused, but still there was no response. "I just wanted to know that I'd made a genuine attempt to talk things over and avert that outcome. Just once."

The Joker played another card. Thudding his gloved fists on the table, Batman again gritted his teeth, fighting the frustration roiling within him.

"Are you *listening* to me?" he demanded. "It's *life and death* that I'm discussing here. Maybe my death…"

The Joker flipped over another card. Batman's hand shot out and he gripped the Joker by the wrist. He wasn't going to be dismissed.

"Maybe yours." He withdrew his gloved grip, pointing an accusing finger at his opposite. *That* got a reaction. The Joker glared at him from the shadows, holding his hand upright next to his face, gripping it with the other as if offended that Batman had dared to touch him.

"I don't fully understand why ours should be such a fatal relationship," the cowled man continued, "but I don't want your murder on my…

"…hands…"

Batman stared at his palms. Stark against the dark blue of his glove, streaks of white greasepaint stood out.

That's not possible. The Joker's white did not come off.

The defiant gleam left the Joker's eyes.

Batman lunged across the table in one smooth motion. The Joker didn't flinch. He just sat there, seeming almost… unplugged. His eyes went wide.

Fear.

Batman put his hand to the Joker's face.

"Don't," the person who wasn't the Joker said, his monotone voice almost too soft to hear. The voice was wrong. The Joker had a particular lilt to his speech patterns. There was no mistaking it. That voice echoed in his nightmares.

"Don't you touch me!" the man hissed between clenched teeth. "You're not allowed to…" The white came away on Batman's fingertips, leaving streaks of flesh exposed beneath them.

"… touch me."

He pulled the gray-garbed inmate into the cone of light. Stark terror reflected in the man's expression as Batman stared at him with unbridled fury. Cunning, ruthlessness, twisted mirth, those attributes he'd seen in the Joker's eyes. Not confusion. Never. This was an imposter—but it meant his long-time adversary was gone. Gripping the man by the front of his shirt, pulling him close until they were nose-to-nose, he uttered a growl.

"Where *is* he?"

"Aaaaaa! Oh, God, no…" the man pleaded.

"Do you realize?" Batman said, his baritone voice echoing through the tightly confined space. "Do you realize what you've set *free*?" Guttural, almost too low to hear clearly, he repeated, "Where is he?"

"Get him offa me!" the pretender screamed. Then came unintelligible gurgles from his throat. He became stony and frozen, near catatonic.

•

"Dear God, he's gone berserk," Gordon said, hearing the screams from his position outside the cell. He was surprised at how matter-of-fact he sounded. An acknowledgment that deep down he always knew the man who donned the garb of a walking bat didn't have both feet planted solidly in the sane world. "Open that door, man," he commanded Badoya.

His hand shaking slightly, looking as if that was the *last* thing he wanted to do, the officer got the key in the lock and turned. Belying a man of his years, Gordon felt a burst of adrenaline and easily slammed the door open. In the cell the bat loomed over its helpless prey.

"Okay, that's enough!" Gordon barked. "You know the laws regarding mistreatment of inmates as well as I do! If you harm one hair on his head—" He peered at the man the Dark Knight held, and choked off the rest of the words. *Oh, God... not again.* The wall-to-wall media saturation would itself be maddening.

Batman straightened and turned toward the two as if they were interlopers on his private keep of the depraved. In his upraised hand he held a green wig.

"Commissioner," he said to the shocked top cop, "if you're concerned about it, it's yours. Take care of it." His mouth a tight thin line below the cowl, he tossed the wig aside and returned his attention to the pretend Clown of Chaos.

"Now, you whimpering little smear of slime, I'm going to ask you politely just one more time..." He paused to let the words sink in.

"Where is he?"

TEN DAYS BEFORE

3

The golden light of late afternoon settled over the city. Its warm tones shone into the third-floor office of Antonio "Python" Palmares who sat in his plush chair, eyeing the marvelous figure of the woman before him as she mixed his vodka tonic at the wet bar. A metal attaché case rested next to the chair.

The woman making his drink had big hair, wore a wide-belted leopard print jumpsuit as if she was heading out to the disco, and tall heels. On the floor below them, standing and working at long tables were numerous other women, dressed in their underwear and assembling glassine packets of Palmares' newest product, Giggle Sniff. The packets of green twinkling powder had been stamped with a logo showing a black oval with an open white grinning mouth.

The women were dressed that way to make certain nobody was trying to rip Palmares off, and that they didn't take home a tell-tale chemical smell on their clothes. It pervaded that floor even though the lab area was well ventilated.

Thanks to the profit margin on the drug he'd introduced to Gotham City, the up-and-coming gangster paid a decent living wage. He was of the opinion that money made for better loyalty than fear—though he wasn't shy about regulating when the need arose.

With high cheekbones and slicked-back black hair long at the nape of his neck, Palmares wore sharkskin slacks, Italian loafers, no socks, and his pastel dress shirt was untucked, the top three buttons undone. A small ornate hinged heart inlaid with ivory hung around his neck on a silvery chain. The stubble on his chin had been dutifully barbered for just the right three-days'-growth look. Part of his python tattoo was visible. The elaborate skin art done in the style of Japanese prints encircled some of his front torso and all of his back.

There was a soft knock at the office's padded double doors.

"Come in," he said.

In stepped yet another woman. She was bespectacled and professional in a charcoal gray Chanel business suit. Her hair was cut short and her glasses complemented the fine bones in her face, her fashion model lips set in a line.

"Good afternoon," she said.

Big Hair gave her the once-over, but said nothing.

"Here you go, Wanda," Palmares said, rising.

Wanda Washawski took the aluminum attaché case in hand, nodding her head curtly toward the gang boss. There was half-a-million in 100s in the case.

"Very good, Mr. Palmares."

"See you soon."

"I look forward to it." She turned and walked out.

Palmares eagerly watched the prim woman's backside undulate under her clothes as she left his office. She was some kind of fine-ass money laundering accountant, he reflected gleefully.

Big Hair brought his drink over, taking a sip first then handing it to him. She sat on his lap and began massaging his muscular chest with her red-nailed hand. She had a vacant look on her face as Palmares began unbuttoning her blouse.

The doors banged open.

"Frankie, what'd I tell you about knocking first?" Palmares blared. It was Frankie Bones, born Franklyn Marris.

"Couldn't be helped, boss," Bones said. "One of the lab rats ingested some powder and is going apeshit down there. Figured you'd want to hear about it."

Palmares shot up, upsetting the woman. She stuck out her hand in time to break her fall to the floor. Being a pro, she didn't complain. Palmares was helping big time on her rent.

By the time she regained her feet, he had already crossed to the door.

"You got somebody handling this right?" he demanded. "He suck in the straight venom?"

"Naw," Bones said, "it was diluted, but he sneezed when he was mixing a batch and he took in too much."

"Well, get him calmed the hell down or croak him, one or the other," Palmares said. He regained his composure and headed toward the door. "Can't have him running around outside and calling attention to us."

"I hear that," Bones said as the two exited.

"Be back in a few," Palmares called over his shoulder. "Help yourself to whatever, Suzi."

•

Standing under the skylight, its glass grimy with city soot and pigeon droppings, Susan Klosmeyer with the big hair, who went by Suzi Mustang when on stage, buttoned up her shirt. It was chilly in here, even given the sunlight.

Stepping back over to the wet bar, she made herself a drink, and then moved to the window, hoping the direct sun would warm her up. She watched as in the distance a small jet banked in the sky and headed out toward the water.

When Palmares returned, she would have to restore the mood. Had to keep him happy and satisfied if this was going to work. Being arm candy for a gangster was harder work than shaking her ass for catcalls and dollar bills at the Lacy Pony, or the occasional skin mag shoot. She had to have the opportunity to hustle Giggle Sniff. It was all part of her self-improvement plan, she reminded herself.

•

The unique plane Suzi Mustang saw in the sky banked again as it came in over Gotham Bay, on its course to the Springer mountain range. Set on whisper mode, it hardly made a sound. Bearing the same nose ornament as the Batmobile, the jet was piloted by Bruce Wayne's so-called butler, the ex-SAS soldier Alfred Pennyworth.

"Good luck you two," Pennyworth said in his British accent as he worked the controls. "Any last-minute requests?"

"How about some of those delicious three-cheese grilled sandwiches of yours when we get back, Alfie?" Batgirl spoke while fastening her rig. The man who was far more than a butler sighed dramatically.

"And I suppose you'd like some of my Mexican sweetcorn succotash to go with that, Ms. Gordon?"

"That would be yummy."

"Focus," Batman said, tamping down his annoyance.

"Always." Batgirl grinned broadly, enhancing his irritation.

"Bringing her around now," Pennyworth said, veering the aircraft and dipping down into a cotton candy fluff of low-hanging clouds. With the flick of a switch he opened the rear hatch, and the two jumped from the plane. As it sped quickly away, they descended silently on the western side of the range that overlooked Blackgate Prison. The facility was located on its own outcropping, safely away from the city proper—but it wasn't their objective.

Their customized wing gliders were in keeping with the motif of the two costumed crime fighters, so that from a distance they would look like gliding bats. This illusion depended on a fallacy: in truth, bats didn't glide. Their pre-planned trajectory took them in toward a stand of trees and underbrush.

"Now," Batman said, tugging the release mechanism on his harness. Batgirl followed suit and released her wings. The two dropped the remaining forty feet or so to land and roll expertly so as to absorb the impact and avoid injury. Robbed of the weight needed to stabilize the wings, the gliders were caught in an updraft and flitted rapidly away across the island of Gotham.

Moving forward quickly they entered the grove that ringed a part of the former Mount Olympus Casino. They were just outside of the city line, and Gotham's county laws were far less strict when it came to organized vice.

It had long been rumored that shipping magnate Maximillian "Maxie" Zeus brought in more than coffee and apricots on his ships docked in Gotham Harbor. Using his substantial profits, he had built a casino which quickly attracted sports figures, social climbers, and the movers and shakers from the city's financial and political circles. But that wasn't enough for Zeus. Like his namesake, his appetite for more became legendary.

That attracted the attention of the detective. Doing some digging, Batman uncovered that Zeus had been blackmailing the power brokers who made up his clientele, setting them up in the "VIP" rooms of his casino just to tape them in… compromising situations.

Zeus himself had been busted and sent away to prison, only to be released on a technicality. Soon thereafter he had disappeared from any radar. His casino remained shuttered, but due to various lease entanglements the property hadn't been bought, and remained as he left it.

Two nights earlier, Batman had been in the My Alibi bar patronized by underworld types…

•

"I'm telling you, Malone, this is a sweet deal," Jo-Jo Gagan said. "Yeah, he's overdoing it with that 'god of thunder' thing, but hell, look at the type of whacked-out criminal this city breeds." Gagan swung his hand around the My Alibi bar, as if to take in the entire city. "I mean, jeez, Killer Croc, the Penguin, Black Mask…" He shrugged his shoulders.

"But Zeus is cagey, I tell you. He's got some new connection backing him. My buddy who's on his payroll told me about it. No details, but the money's steady and Zeus's got a thing in the works that once he pulls it off, he's gonna expand the ranks, see?

"Hell," he went on, "I got a good thing going with Python, but I might jump ship." He had a faraway look on his face as he sipped his whiskey.

"And he's operating out of his old casino again?" Malone said, a wooden match dangling from a corner of his mouth, beneath the moustache.

"He's got it laid out," Gagan replied. That was all he would say, though—not that he had any more, really. Malone was a nice enough guy, but Jo-Jo didn't *really* know him, so they continued with some small talk. Then after about half an hour Malone headed out.

As soon as he did, two men approached. Gagan had noticed them hanging back, and he was pretty sure he recognized them. One was sallow-faced, the other had a set of big ears. Both were lean and rangy as their former boss, the Scarecrow, who liked his henchmen skinny.

"Hey, Jo-Jo," the big-eared one said, clapping Gagan on the shoulders. "Let me and my friend buy you a drink."

"Yeah, sure Beatts," Gagan said. He was already pretty snooted, but wasn't about to turn away a free drink or two.

•

Leaving My Alibi, Bruce Wayne shed his disguise as Matches Malone. He headed toward the Batcave and its state-of-the-art computer system. As he drove to the outskirts of Gotham, his cell phone buzzed. He hit the hands-free control.

"Lucius."

"Bruce, where are you?" Lucius Fox demanded. "The city financial board will be meeting soon. You and I need to prepare."

Fox was his business manager and ran Wayne Enterprises. He had a head for numbers, and was an ingenious inventor, as well.

"You'll have to handle it without me."

There was a silence on the other end of the call as Wayne continued at a rapid pace. It was late morning, and the streets were crowded with traffic, but he wove in and out of the flow without missing a beat.

"Bruce, you're one of the wealthiest men in Gotham," Fox said, carefully controlling his words. "Your input is essential. You know the risk of letting them make a move without you."

"You understand the data as well as I do," Wayne said. "Most likely better. They know you have the authority to speak for both of us—for all of Wayne Enterprises. Just make certain they don't do anything foolish."

"It's not the—"

Wayne turned the wheel and headed toward the hidden entrance to his underground lair. The car was top-of-the-line, and could steer itself, but he preferred the hands-on approach.

"Lucius, it's fine," he said, interrupting his friend and associate. "Just handle it. Listen, I'm about to enter a dead zone, so the phone's going to kick out." Before Fox could reply he cut the connection.

•

Batgirl was there, in uniform, sitting at a computer terminal.

Logging in to the most secure system in all of Gotham, he quickly confirmed what Gagan had told him. Although the casino was shuttered, satellite imagery confirmed plenty of activity around Mount Olympus, particularly at night.

That bore investigation.

He'd intended to go in alone, but Barbara insisted on accompanying him. She'd been on the trail of a drug kingpin they called Python Palmares, seeking to identify and eliminate his pipeline. When Zeus had been sent up, there'd been a scramble among various parties in the underworld to absorb his assets—among them a truck line and distribution system that had been an offshoot of his fleet of freighters.

Palmares had made a grab for it.

The system included a group of "safe houses," the secret warehouses Zeus used to store and distribute his contraband in and around town. The deeper Batman dug, the more evident it became that her inquiries paralleled his own.

So he relented. Not that he really had a choice.

•

The two moved silently through the underbrush, the confines of the faux Mount Olympus rising before them, all open-air columns and too-white marble and stone.

Batman held up a hand signaling caution. In his other he held a rectangular device that had a small screen on it showing an oscilloscope-like readout. This was for detecting ground sensors. There were none present, and he returned the gadget to his utility belt. From their vantage point they saw Zeus's henchmen, dressed in military garb as befitting the setting, a theatrical affectation to humor their boss. This included polished steel-alloy armor protecting their torsos, tunics, the puttees, the laced-up leg bindings, and absurd plumed Corinthian helmets.

They did not carry swords, though, but modern deadly efficient assault rifles no doubt converted to fully automatic.

"Yeah, no sweat," Batgirl whispered next to him. "I'll go left, you go right." She didn't wait for his response and moved off quickly.

Batman took a breath and crept forward. He came up quietly and quickly behind one of the guards, clamping a gloved hand over his mouth, bending him back, and delivering a swift chop with the edge of his hand to a specific nerve point at the base of the neck. The burly man collapsed before he could make a sound, and Batman caught the gun before it hit the concrete.

Following a path that paralleled Batgirl's, he didn't encounter any more sentries. Most likely Zeus thought he was running entirely under the radar. Coming around a corner, he found his companion, two guards lying prone at her feet. She had her hands on her hips and tossed him a playful look.

"About time," she chided.

"Let's go," he said, slipping past her without another word, cape swirling slightly in the still air.

"A woman's work is never done," she wisecracked, scooping up one of the assault rifles and falling into step.

"Put it down," he ordered without looking back.

"Aw, I'm just going to use it to make them, you know, compliant. A little nick here and there. No permanent damage."

He stopped without turning.

She cocked her head and removed the magazine, tossing it into the bushes. Then she tossed the weapon aside.

Next to a high wall, they proceeded below a bleached white balustrade. Peering upward, Batman pulled a gun-shaped device from the rear of his belt, covered by his cape. Extending his arm he shot a grapnel hook and line. The hook flew upward with negligible sound, powered by the release of compressed air.

"That's a new model," Batgirl said, unlimbering a silken line of woven steel cable. It had a lightweight collapsible grapnel secured to the end. She gave it a practiced spin, twirling it faster until she released it and sent it hurtling upward to catch hold above.

"I try to keep up with the times," he quipped, starting up the wall, hand over hand on the knotted line.

"Old dogs and new tricks." She gave her line a tug, confirming a firm grip, and followed.

Ascending to the gangster's version of Mount Olympus, they cleared the wall and found themselves on a patio near the main structure, a large building styled like an ancient Greek temple for worshipping the gods. This had been the casino where the players had come to pray for luck. The patio boasted fixed marble benches, and the topiary was manicured in the shape of deer, horses, rams, and bulls.

"Jeez," Batgirl said, taking in the scenery. "Kinda swank for a hoodlum's getaway."

"He's not making much effort at hiding," Batman said, nodding toward a number of guards standing in plain sight. "That suggests that whatever Zeus is up to, he feels rather secure about it. Maybe like in legend, he's looking to defeat the Titans."

Batgirl shot him a puzzled look, but he didn't react, maintaining the perfect deadpan. A quick scan showed that the casino's security cameras were inoperative—more overconfidence on Zeus's part. The two darted across the patio and reached the side of the building, searching for an unobtrusive way in.

With a deafening roar, sections of the wall above them disintegrated in a rain of stone and mortar, as a hail of bullets tore into it.

4

"The *hell*," a guard bellowed from the patio. "We got company!"

He rattled off more bullets as the two bats split apart, making themselves harder to hit. Batgirl wrapped her cape around her upper body, the material a weave of Kevlar and other polymers developed by Lucius Fox's research and development division of Wayne Enterprises. Still, the force of the impact drove her back against the wall of the former casino.

Batman dove and spun, pulling a bat-shaped collapsible boomerang from his belt. It was designed with the aerodynamics of a ninja's throwing star, and he threw it even before he landed. His aim was true, and its sharp edge sunk into the guard's shooting hand, causing him to swear and drop the weapon. Even as the gun clattered on the stone flooring, Batman covered the distance between them. A roundhouse kick and two swift punches sent the guard down on his back.

Two more would-be soldiers ran up, the clatter of their boots drowned out as they leveled their assault rifles and opened fire. Not wishing to be knocked off balance again, Batgirl sought relative safety behind a large potted plant in a stone urn some four feet high. The high velocity rounds destroyed the stonework, but were stopped by the urn's swath of earth. Recalling those old WWII movies she'd watch with her father, she plucked two small plastic balls from her utility belt and lobbed them over her head like a soldier in a foxhole throwing a hand grenade.

Colors swirled below the translucent surfaces of the spheres as they landed and rolled across the patio. When one of the guards stepped forward, jagged bolts of electricity erupted from the things and engulfed the man's body. He shook and drooled and, when the discharge ceased, he collapsed, his clothing tattered and charred from the raw voltage.

"No need for subtlety now," Batman said, taking advantage of the distraction and decking the other newcomer.

"You've got that right," Batgirl agreed, rushing forward as yet another guard arrived. The first non-male member of the squad, she hunkered down behind the balustrade. Though more of a generalist than a history expert, Barbara the librarian was pretty certain there had been no female soldiers in the male-centric world of ancient Greece. Not that Maxie Zeus seemed concerned with historical accuracy. Indeed, she recalled, most soldiers preferred the company of other men, thinking they were the only ones capable of higher intellect.

"How modern of old Maxie," she muttered as she threw down an object that released a smoke screen, obscuring her location.

As the guard fired blindly, Batgirl raced around the topiary, coming near her target. The woman spun toward the crime fighter, firing, but Batgirl was a blur, kicking the barrel aside, rounds zinging close, grazing her armored shoulder and severing hairs of the red wig sticking out beneath her cowl. Before the guard could recover, she used a combination of American boxing and kung fu, dislocated her shoulder and, knocking her helmet off, punched her unconscious.

She rejoined Batman as he twisted a knob atop a slim canister and tossed the object toward the massive double doors of the main entrance. Each portal was adorned with a large bas-relief of Maxie Zeus's sneering face. The doors were made of iron, and the magnetic canister stayed where it struck. The resulting blast from the explosive device ripped one of the doors off its top hinge, and it dangled at an awkward angle. The opening this created was large enough to allow them entry.

"Be alert," Batman said, sprinting forward.

"Aren't I always?" she quipped, flowing close behind.

He made a sound in his throat as he peered inside. Abruptly he swung around, wrapped his muscular arms around Batgirl, flinging them from the doorway. Before she could react a lightning bolt sizzled from somewhere inside and struck the spot where she had been standing. The force of it was such that it blew the listing door completely free of its damaged moorings.

It toppled away with a metallic *clang*.

"What the hell caused that?" Batgirl asked.

"Come and get me, you pointy-eared freaks," Maxie Zeus taunted from inside his would-be temple. "Let's see if your Bruce Lee moves can get the best of me, as I now truly harness the power of the gods." His laughter receded as he went further inside his headquarters.

"Brag much?" Batgirl remarked. She pulled out two more of her electro-spheres and Batman another of his mini-bombs and a smoke grenade. He ignited the latter at the broken entrance as guards on the other side riddled the doorway with automatic fire.

While the soldiers concentrated on the smoke-filled doorway, their two targets burst in through a side window. Batgirl collided with one of the soldiers and together they went over. It was like slamming into a brick wall. He was big but not flabby, and when he connected with her jaw, a mortar went off in her head.

If he hit her again, she'd be cooked.

Landing in a roll, Batman sprang to his feet and jabbed an elbow into one guard's throat, while planting his boot dead in the chest of another, sending him into a column.

The brick wall pinned Batgirl beneath him, and she couldn't leverage her knee between them.

"Always dreamed I'd get one of you costumed broads under me," he gasped, a pleased leer on his face.

"Keep dreaming, dude." Envisioning the various nerve paths that ran through the body, she pressed the tip of each index finger against a particular location below the edge of his helmet, close to the collar bone. As he shifted to react, reaching for her shoulders, she jabbed inward with precise force.

His hands came away and curled inward as if he'd been hit with a severe carpal tunnel spasm. The tension left his arms as they twitched uncontrollably.

"What did you do to me, *bitch*?"

Batgirl twisted out from under him and landed a well-aimed kick that sent his helmet flying. Several rapid blows to his face, unopposed, put him out. Turning, she gestured toward three remaining opponents.

"You get Zeus," she said to Batman. "There are only a few more of his goons to deal with."

"Very well," he rasped. But before he left he used his grapple line gun to shoot what at first looked like a wad of plastic at one of the guards. As it flew the material expanded, hitting the guard in the chest. Then ropey extensions of the stuff wrapped around his torso, pinning his arms so that he couldn't raise his weapon.

Before he hit the floor, Batman was gone.

"Show-off," Batgirl said, but she had two more to handle. Her lithe figure went prone and she slid across the polished floor as gunfire followed her. As bric-a-brac exploded into pieces above her, she stopped behind a marble statue of Zeus—the one from history, who fortunately sat on a substantial throne.

•

Batman ran deeper into the complex, his battle senses on alert. Dodging around idle slot machines and gaming tables, he passed lush tapestries and friezes of cavorting creatures such as satyrs and centaurs and luscious maidens.

Angling around a column he felt the air heat up in front of him, and dove to one side. A nanosecond later, a lightning bolt sizzled millimeters past his shoulder, shattering plaster off the column.

"Bow before the power of the heavens, Batman."

Maxie Zeus held a futuristic-looking rifle, gripping it in both his hands. The barrel was smoking. Unlike his guards, the goateed Zeus wore a business suit, but no tie. On his head was perched a gold laurel leaf crown, his one conceit.

He shot another bolt from the weapon, sending it searing into the gloomy hallway as Batman disappeared into the shadows. With a grunt of disapproval, Zeus turned and rushed away.

•

One of the guards moved confidently toward the Zeus statue, laying down a barrage of gunfire.

"Come on, Batgirl, take it like a woman." He laughed as he continued shooting. The other guard stalked forward from another angle, also rattling off rounds from his assault rifle. Their booted feet crunched on the stone shards scattered about the floor. Both stopped several paces from the now pockmarked and nearly unrecognizable statue.

The guards looked at each other, grinning.

"We gonna make our bonuses on your body, Batgirl," the guard on the left said. He had a nasal voice and hairy legs.

"Course it ain't the same as tagging Batman, you just being an imitation and what not," the other one cracked. With that they darted around the ruined sculpture, then froze.

There was no one there.

Jaws set, they scanned left and right.

"Imitation, am I?"

Together they looked up and found her perched on the statue, her back to the polished stone, arms spread wide, her sky-blue cape draped behind her black-clad sinewy form. Before they could bring their weapons up she opened one hand. A mini flash bang grenade was dropped and went off before it struck the floor.

The hairy-legged man hollered, firing his weapon impotently—but Batgirl had already leapt down. A stiff-finger jab to a spot just above his elbow caused him to loosen his grip on his weapon, and a sweep of her leg connected boot to jaw. As he dropped, she spun toward his partner.

"You don't seem to know what to do with this," she said, grabbing the barrel of his rifle while using the edge of her other hand to strike him on the bridge of his nose. It was a blow designed to affect his sight. "Better give it to me." She wrestled it free without encountering any real opposition, as he stumbled back several steps, trying to clear his vision.

This was the guard with the hairy legs. Regaining his senses he lurched forward, seeking to wrap his arms around Batgirl's waist and drive her back into the statue. She planted herself and clubbed him viciously on the back of his head with his own rifle. Even with his helmet on, he was dazed.

The other guard on the floor rose, blinking hard as he swung his weapon around and fired, Batgirl spinning away. The man's body jerked as the bullets slammed into it. His torso was protected by his armor, but his legs were badly wounded and bleeding profusely. He dropped to his knees.

"Man, what does it take for them to stay down?" Batgirl planted her hand on the back of the kneeling guard, vaulting over him as he fell to the floor. The thick sole of her boot again smashed into the other guard's face when she arced upward, knocking him back as she landed on her feet.

It hadn't been a solid strike, and he'd recovered quicker than she liked. The impression of her boot's sole on the side of his face, he clicked dry on his weapon. He cursed and threw the rifle on the floor. He was mad as hell, and that made him sloppy. Easily dodging his wild haymaker, she used his own momentum against him in a crisp judo throw that left him on his back at her feet, with the wind knocked out of him. She gave him a stiff heel stomp to the throat.

That did it. He was out.

"Hello, pretty lady."

5

Batgirl spun to face the source of the new voice. It was a warm, husky female voice, like honey and rusty nails, calling out to her from an arched doorway on the far side of the room.

There stood a tall, elegant woman silhouetted in the light from the other room. She was dressed in an asymmetrical, bias-cut gown of pale gossamer silk with a gold Greek key pattern along the hemline and gold, high-heeled gladiator sandals. Her thick, dark hair was pinned up with a gold, leaf-shaped ornament.

"Who the hell are you?"

"I'm Koinonia," the woman said, stepping into the room, "but you can call me Koi. You'll have to forgive Maxie. He has an inferiority complex. That's why he invents all those silly gadgets. He hates a fair fight."

Now that the woman's face was fully illuminated, Batgirl could see that she wasn't traditionally beautiful. But what she lacked in facial appeal she made up with grace and poise. She moved her long, lean body with the fluid, easy confidence of a dancer or Olympic fencer. Pulling the ornament from her hair, she let her raven waves spill down her back as she thumbed a switch, causing a long telescopic shaft to expand from the bottom of the razor-edged gold leaf until it formed a glittering spear.

Koinonia tipped her chin toward a rack of antique weapons hung on the far wall.

"Shall we?" she purred.

Batgirl smirked and stepped over to the rack. Using a foot to kick at the base of a weathered iron spear, she caused it to flip free and caught it in mid-air. Extending her other hand to perform a terse palm-up gesture with her fingers, she invited her new adversary to bring it.

Needing no further urging, Koi lunged forward with a series of high and low thrusts that were easily parried. Batgirl had the impression that the woman was feeling her out to get an idea of her strength and skill.

This woman was bigger and more muscular, so she was going to have to be strategic and unpredictable. She spun her body away and then bent herself over backward, thrusting her weapon up past her own face and toward Koi's midsection. The woman grunted with surprise as she curved her body inward to avoid the sharp tip. Continuing her spin until she was facing the ground, Batgirl swung the shaft of the spear at Koi's legs.

Koinonia leapt up and over her swing, bringing her spear down in a slashing motion that caught the left side of Batgirl's ribs, slicing through her costume and into the flesh below.

Damn, that hurt.

Adrenaline spurred her on, drowning out the sting as she jumped forward, stepping first on the bent knee and then off the hip of her taller opponent to deliver a smashing blow to the side of Koi's head.

The larger woman staggered backward, through the doorway she'd entered, and Batgirl followed with an aggressive offensive of kicks and strikes with the shaft of the spear as if it were a bō staff. Koi countered and dodged each one with hissing ferocity.

The new room was dimly lit with wavering aquamarine light, and before Batgirl's eyes could adjust to the change, her enemy ducked to one side and kicked her sharply in the back of the knees, causing them to buckle.

As Batgirl fell forward, she rounded her right shoulder and twisted her body, planning to roll when she hit the floor and spring immediately back up to her feet. There was just one problem.

There was no floor.

Instead, she found herself plunging into warm, chlorinated water. *A pool.* Forcing herself to remain calm, she tried to open her stinging eyes and assess her surroundings, but all she could see was swirling silver bubbles. There was no bottom that she could reach with her kicking feet, and her spear had been knocked from her grip by the unexpected rush of water. The weight of its iron tip had caused it to sink.

She had exhaled all the air out of her lungs in preparation for impact with a floor that wasn't there, so she had no choice but to risk breaking the surface. When she did so, she quickly glanced around and found herself roughly at the center of the deep end of the pool.

The only light in the room came from four small glowing disks set in the four sides of the pool, just beneath the surface of the rippling water. Her eyes were still burning from the chlorine, but she could make out a vast, windowless chamber with a low, rococo gold ceiling, thick gilded columns, and clusters of nude mosaic nymphs dancing on the walls.

What she couldn't see was Koinonia.

That's when she noticed a pale, sleek shape headed right for her beneath the surface of the water. She barely had time to suck in a lungful of air when a steely grip grabbed her ankles and pulled her down.

Kicking out against the grip, she felt her boot connect with something. The grip loosened for a fraction of a second before switching to wrap clutching arms around her waist, pulling her deeper and deeper underwater.

Her combatant's long dark hair swirled around in the water. Batgirl grabbed a fistful as the two of them spun into a roll. Her heart was slamming inside her chest, exertion burning up her limited oxygen way too fast, but she could feel Koi's grip weakening, too. They both needed to breathe, and soon.

Pulling her knees up, she planted her boots in the center of what her woozy underwater vision told her was the approximate center of her attacker's body. She gave a powerful push, breaking Koi's grip on her waist, simultaneously shoving her away and propelling her own body in the opposite direction.

She twisted in the water and began swimming at top speed. Her cape worked against her, dragging her back, and she hoped that she was headed in the direction of one of the closer sides of the pool, and not toward the far shallow end. Her luck held out, and seconds later her hand hit an edge.

Batgirl pulled air into her aching lungs as she dragged her dripping body out of the water. She found herself near a doorway by the short side of the deep end, while Koi was over to the left, pulling herself up on one of the long sides about halfway between the deep and shallow ends.

Moving toward the door, Batgirl noticed Koi's ornate golden spear leaning against the wall.

Koinonia was out of the water now, breathing heavily and standing with one palm flat against the face of a mosaic nymph. Her thin white dress had gone completely transparent, and Batgirl couldn't help but notice that one of her large breasts was clearly artificial—a lump of smooth, featureless rubber held in place by a wispy lace bra.

The woman noticed her gaze and smiled.

It was a dangerous smile.

"It's an Amazon thing," she said. "You wouldn't understand."

"You'd be surprised," Batgirl quipped, flashing a challenging smile of her own. She grabbed the spear and pointed with its wicked, leaf-shaped blade. "I read a lot." Myth held that Amazons cut off a breast to better aim their bows and arrows and that looked to be where Koi got the idea for her over-the-top theatrical persona.

Koinonia arched a dark brow.

"I thought this was going to be a fair fight?" she said. "Then again, I suppose a cute little thing like you has to cheat in order to win."

Batgirl frowned.

"Fine," she said, dropping the spear and raising her fists in a ready stance. "Have it your way. Because the bigger they are, the harder they—"

She stopped as Koi grinned and pressed against the mosaic nymph's pearlescent nipple. A small compartment was revealed. The next thing Batgirl knew, she was looking down the barrel of a snub-nose .32 revolver.

"What the hell happened to a fair fight?" Batgirl asked, furious at herself for being so gullible but still not worried about this pea-shooter.

"There are no fair fights." The wolfish grin went even wider. "There are people who will do whatever it takes to win, and people who won't." She shot at Batgirl.

The warning voice of Batman yelling in her head reminded Batgirl that it might not be such a good idea to simply stand there and let the small round bounce off her body armor. She dove aside and the top of a freestanding column and a bust on it boomed into pieces behind her. Hell, she realized, the damned gun was loaded with explosive rounds.

Batgirl's gaze darted this way and that. The spear was of no use against a pistol and she was light on gadgets in her utility belt. There was a large jug of liquid, dark in the dim light, sitting on the floor between her and Koi. A small, inflatable pool lounger sagged partly deflated about two feet to her left. It was a long shot that probably wouldn't work, but...

Ducking and running, she kicked the lounger, sending it sailing. This was merely a distraction allowing her to unlimber her grapple and line from its bracket at the small of her back. She leaped and, twisting in mid-air, sent the grapple straight at Koinonia. The hook raked the back of the other woman's hand just as she squeezed the trigger. The round nicked Batgirl's shoulder blade, causing her to grimace despite her protective clothing, but it went past and struck the wall behind her.

The explosion was deafening in the closed chamber. Koi was smiling, in no hurry to finish her sport. Another report, and there was a resulting explosion of tile fragments where

Batgirl had been standing only a millisecond earlier. But she was already in mid roll, grabbing the spear as she went and stabbing its golden tip into the jug of chemicals.

The harsh searing odor made her gasp and cough as she hoisted the jug on the end of the spear and flung it with all her strength. The container hit Koi in her asymmetrically altered chest, releasing a fountain of caustic blue chemical that splashed up into her face.

"*Shit*," she screamed, staggering back, dropping the gun and covering her face with both hands. Batgirl stepped swiftly forward and delivered a roundhouse kick to the side of her head, knocking her off her feet and into the pool. Then she kicked the gun across the tile and into the pool after its flailing, gasping mistress.

Spinning, she ran back through the doorway to rejoin Batman, and put an end to this little toga party once and for all.

•

Batman paused, assessing his surroundings. He was in a carpeted hallway, a series of ornate wooden doors on either side of him along its length. At the end of the hall was a statue of Cupid, his arrow drawn back.

He'd followed Zeus to the second story, and then to here. Behind him was a blackened, smoking hole in the flocked wallpaper. Zeus had shot at him and Batman again had evaded the zig-zag of lightning. When he turned back, the gang boss had disappeared behind one of those doors.

A glance inside one of the rooms told him that this had once been the VIP section. All types of wanton behavior had gone on behind these doors, but now they implied deadlier possibilities. He took several more steps down the hall, and felt a pressure plate give beneath his boot. As he sprang back a steel barrier dropped into place behind him, a tube hissed out of the wall, and a yellowish gas issued forth.

Chlorine.

Batman locked his oxygen mask in place and continued forward, his eyes burning behind his slits. He quickened his pace. In the mist he saw the twinkle of a trip wire, and stepped over it. On his left, the second door from the end was ajar, and there was an almost imperceptible sound from inside. Most likely this was the path Zeus had used to escape. Creeping to the door, Batman used his elbow to strike it, causing the panel to reverberate.

A lightning bolt shattered it in an instant.

6

Stepping into the room, an unharmed Batman saw Maxie Zeus slipping through a sliding glass door and onto a flat rooftop. Bright sun shone through the door, making it difficult to follow the movement. Nonetheless he continued on.

Sharp claws on concrete brought him up short.

Blocking the doorway were two guards unlike the others. At first glance, they appeared to be a pair of identical bull mastiffs with packed muscular bodies on heavy, powerful legs. A closer look revealed that these were robotic constructs, each the size of a 140-pound beast of flesh and bone—all alloy and hydraulics, steel teeth snapping open on well-oiled gears. Sunlight shimmered across their sleek lethal forms. Red glowed from their eye sockets. There was something rat-like about their faces, and Batman had a feeling he knew their origin.

Zeus turned to face him. "I'm sure I don't need to tell you this," he said, smiling broadly, "but one is named Orthrus, and the other is Cerberus." He gestured toward each of them in turn. "Most fitting, don't you think?"

Gotham's protector didn't waste time talking.

Zeus snarled. "Give Batman the Mount Olympus welcome,

boys." He clapped loudly and the two robot dogs, barking and baring metal teeth, leapt forward. "I have a city of non-believers to address."

Stepping back, Batman kicked a large chrome and black lacquer coffee table at the clockwork attackers. The sudden movement caused them to pause, but only for an instant. They ran around the barrier and were airborne even faster than he'd expected. The first metal beast hit him with the force of an automobile. He got a hand on one side of the large head as the thing snarled and snapped at him. In place of breath, it had a peculiar, nauseating odor emanating from its muzzle, like overheating toy train transformers combined with burning hair.

The second attacker closed in on his left and, with a grimace of sheer effort, he toppled the one onto the other. The clashing of forged hides was drowned out by the whine of large gears. Looking through the sliding door, Batman watched hinged metal panels open in the rooftop like sidewalk elevators. A half-dozen howitzer-sized hulks rose into place, moving smoothly on hydraulic ball joints.

As he processed this Orthrus charged at him again. Cerberus hung back. The metal mastiff leapt. Batman controlled the momentum so that it carried them over, and he landed on his back. Leveraging the massive creature's weight, he released it and sent it sailing, crashing into a wet bar. Bottles of liquor exploded as if blown apart, soaking the artificial creature—to no ill effect.

From his prone position Batman extracted an incendiary capsule from his belt and flung it at the charging machine. The robot ignited at the same moment Cerberus bit into Batman's boot at the calf. Though the material was designed to withstand any blade, those metal fangs glistening with oil still penetrated, but not all the way into his muscle.

Still the metal dog had him pinned, and it wasn't about to let go. Worse yet, Orthrus hadn't stopped. It circled him, looking for an opportunity to strike. Focusing as he had been taught by Chu Chin Li on Mount Qingcheng, Batman gritted his teeth and lifted his leg, getting it about two inches off the floor.

The words of the master echoed in his head.

"No hesitation, just do."

The simulated beast continued the assault, its teeth rending his boot in pursuit of a reward of flesh and bone. Batman bellowed incoherently as he shifted his entire body and whipped his leg around, then brought it down forcefully, careful not to strike the jaws. The creature was jarred for an instant and its grip loosened on the lower leg.

Batman lurched free and got back to his feet. His calf muscle throbbed, but it wasn't bleeding, nor had he sprained anything in lifting the large android. Barking and slavering like the real thing, Cerberus lunged for him, its front claws raking at his trailing cape.

Orthrus echoed the motion from the other side.

Leaping up, Batman did a barrel roll in mid-air, and the two creatures collided with a grinding impact of metal on metal. A glowing electric eye popped out of Cerberus's head. The fire was out on Orthrus, but it had done as he'd hoped. He could see an opening between the alloy joints in the dog's legs. The joint connections were covered in neoprene and the flames had eaten the material away in a few places.

Coming down on his side, Batman reached for a nodule on his utility belt as the machine creatures regained their footing, baring their teeth, and closing in. He scrambled forward on his belly and got hold of a plush chair, which he shoved at Cerberus, pinning him against the wall for a beat or two.

Orthrus charged him again, but he dodged and sprang into a handstand, his heavily muscled frame objecting to the effort. As he flipped his body around to stand, he whipped out a small cylinder and shot out a thin stream of acid. The chemical squirted onto the exposed joint revealed in the burned-out gap in the creature's front leg. The connectors of the lower limb bubbled and sizzled and the leg became separated from the rest of the body.

The robot stumbled, but its internal gyros got it righted. Snarling, it leapt at him on its two rear legs. Batman went low and used the remaining acid to repeat the action on a back leg joint. When the dog landed, the right rear limb snapped away cleanly, and the creature ground to a halt, falling onto its side.

The remaining steel-toothed canine charged, knocking a chair aside with its tackle-block head. As it did so, the cowled vigilante leapt sideways onto the wall feet first, using the momentum to springboard himself onto a sofa and then leap through the gap of the sliding glass doors.

As Cerberus charged after him, Batman grasped the door and slammed it on the android's neck. The door was heavy, most likely bulletproof, and there was a crackle and pop, followed by the distinct smell of burning metal. The machine-made creature's head hung at an angle from the neck. Wiring, connectors, and miniaturized motors were exposed.

Nevertheless the creature rasped out a bark and tried to move, but Batman had damaged its central computer stem. It glared at him with flickering eyes as behind it,

Orthrus attempted to crawl forward, without success.

Spinning, he turned his back on the crippled constructs. It was late, and he was peering directly into the sun, low on the horizon. Lenses dropped into place in his cowl, muting the glare.

"How do you like these, Batman?" Zeus said. He stood near a bank of advanced cannons, his lightning rifle held in one hand and a remote-control switch upraised in the other. It was clear to him that similar technology had been used to design the rifle and mill the cannons. Batman wanted very much to confirm where the crime lord had obtained them.

"What do you want, Zeus?" Behind him he could hear the constructs pounding against the glass doors. Damaged as they were, they couldn't get through the reinforced glass.

"What do I want?" Zeus repeated. "Only my due as the rightful Caesar of Gotham."

"Of course," Batman said, as if it was the most logical thing in the world. He'd run out of patience and didn't want to trade words with a lunatic. So he started to close the distance between them, palming a Batarang out of sight.

"Ah-hupp," Zeus said, pushing a button on the remote control. With a whir of motors the five cannons pivoted in unison, moving to the right. "The next move you make, you'll be responsible for the death of thousands."

Batman froze.

"This isn't like you, Zeus," he said. "You're all about profit— not mayhem for mayhem's sake."

"Like your nutball pal the Joker?" Zeus said, watching carefully for a reaction. When he didn't get one, he continued. "You're right, my friend, this is about wealth, the sort that comes with power. I intend to control all that is Gotham. Along with my... silent partners, shall we say, I will run it like a business, and reap the rewards."

Abruptly there was the crunch of footsteps on the tar and gravel roof, and four soldiers came around a corner. Each was armed with a handgun, and they surrounded Batman. Zeus turned his full attention to the cannons. Once again the motors hummed. The weapons swiveled one way, then another. Finally he seemed satisfied with their positioning.

This is it, Batman thought.

"Those are lightning cannons, like your rifle," he said, stalling for time.

"Indeed they are, and they're pointed at a very specific target," Zeus replied, "the financial center."

"There's an emergency meeting of the city's budget council tonight," Batman said. Lucius Fox would be there, among the bankers, financiers, and local politicians—including the mayor and members of the city council. Fox'd be giving his input on behalf of Wayne Enterprises. If they were to be killed, the local economy would spiral into chaos.

The kind of chaos that could be exploited.

"Very good, Batman," Zeus said wryly. "You'll get to watch as I bring the city to its knees and make way for the rise of a new order—the order of Zeus." He chuckled at his own words. "The irony is that, in the confusion, no one will realize what's actually happening. Not until it's too late."

The costumed thugs shared his laugh, momentarily turning their attention to their boss.

Now!

Batman lashed out in a modified wing chun move, instantly

launching into a flying kick with a tilt to his boot that took out two of the guards. Simultaneously he flicked his Batarang at Zeus's hand, seeking to separate the man's fingers from the control.

Another projectile got there first.

The sharp end of a Batarang sliced into Zeus's thumb. The gangster swore as the remote dropped to the rooftop, landing near the edge. He gripped his rifle in both hands, one of them dripping blood, and leveled it at the newcomer.

"You're fried meat, Batgirl," he bellowed as she sprinted toward him. The costumed heroine was on open ground, with no cover readily available.

Batman scooped up the dented helmet of one of the soldiers, hurling it at Zeus. It connected with the side of his head, staggering him and throwing his aim off. A swath of lighting seared from his rifle, blinding in the fading daylight. The bolt struck off target, its white-hot energy blasting apart a metal duct. Batgirl remained unscathed.

"Thanks a-plenty," she said, changing course and reaching the remote control. Using her boot heel she stomped down once, twice, until it fizzled and crackled as it broke apart. Spinning she kicked out at Zeus and knocked the rifle aside as he tried to shoot her again, then slugged him hard with a right cross.

The two remaining guards opened up with their weapons, both aiming at Batman. Though his Kevlar weave provided protection, he dodged to the side so that the rounds that hit him were glancing at best. Surprising the henchmen, he dove *toward* them, barreling into the two. They wilted under a quick succession of blows, which avoided their body armor and sent them staggering.

One of the thugs who'd been knocked down started to get

up, but a stiff finger jab to a specific nerve cluster sent him to slumberland. Within moments all four of his opponents had been laid out. They wouldn't be getting up again soon.

"It's nice work if you can get it," Batgirl commented. She stood over the downed Maxie Zeus. He lay on his back, the corner of his mouth bloody. His crown had been knocked off and rested on the gravel near his head.

Despite an evening breeze, her cape hung straight down.

"Why are you all wet?" Batman asked. He approached one of the lightning cannons, shaking his head. "Never mind. Just secure the prisoners."

"Sure, boss," she snarked, pulling out some zip ties.

Paying her no heed, Batman examined one of the high-tech weapons, his eyebrow arching beneath his mask. This technology was beyond anything he had seen recently. There was no way a thug like Zeus, albeit a grandiose one, could have developed it.

"What's got your shorts in a bunch?" she said, tying the ankles and wrists of the guards. She glanced over to where he stood.

"These devices are of a sophisticated design," he replied, his concentration on a part he'd uncoupled from one of the weapons. "*Very* sophisticated." He had a bad feeling about this.

"Bad guys always have some of the best gadgets," she observed. "Look at Luthor, over in Metropolis, always giving Superman a run for his money. If he can do that, what's to say he couldn't supply other criminal types?"

"Zeus hasn't had dealings with Luthor," Batman said, turning the piece over in his hand. "It would have shown up in our research. We know what to look for."

She snapped her fingers.

"Hey what about that little gnome guy, Gizmo, who was part of the Fearsome Five. He's a big-league gadgeteer, and this kind of thing would be right up his alley."

"Possibly," he allowed, "but it's not part of his methodology—he doesn't supply tech to others. And this…" He shook his head. "No, this is something else. I have a feeling…"

"There's just no pleasing you, is there?" She cinched the bonds on Zeus, giving them an extra tug, just out of spite.

Batman glanced over at the damaged mechanical dogs on the other side of the sliding door. They had ceased their futile attempts to break out, but their eyes remained lit from within, bright in the falling dusk.

I wonder if they could be transmitting, he mused. Dismissing the idea as irrelevant, he strode in the direction from which the soldiers had come. Those red eyes followed. Batgirl trailed after him, massaging the knuckles on her hand.

Descending to the ground floor, they passed the prone form of Koinonia. Her skin was a scarlet swath that looked painful, but she was breathing, albeit unevenly. Batman grunted.

Batgirl cupped a hand at the side of her covered ear.

"Was that the sound of approval?"

He continued in silence. Locating Zeus's personal office, he stepped behind the large desk and sat in a high-backed banker's chair. The room was decorated in a mix of Greco-Roman themes with columns and tapestries, standing potted plants and gold trim. Ostentatious statuary adorned the shelves and flat surfaces. A large painting hung on the wall opposite the desk.

"You might think about this look for the Batcave."

The suggestion of a smile came and went, quickly subdued.

He picked the lock on the middle drawer and pulled out a remote boasting a number of square buttons and switches.

Batgirl stood before the painting. It depicted Maxie Zeus presiding over a table of twelve of Gotham's most redoubtable super villains including Mr. Freeze, Two-Face, the Joker, and Lady Shiva. It was a warped version of da Vinci's *Last Supper*, down to Zeus in the center smiling beneficently with his hands raised as if bestowing grace.

"Oh, brother," she muttered.

After some quick study, Batman pressed one of the buttons on the control. A small semicircular monitor rose out of the desk. He stabbed another control—there was momentary snow, then the picture cleared. In frame was the upper body of a man with a broad face of flattened planes, wrestler's neck and shoulders, tanned and with a trimmed thick mustache. Looking off to one side, he wore an olive-green suit, black shirt, and tan tie.

Batman knew that face.

"You better be calling to tell me everything is jake, Zeus," the man began, an irritated tone to his voice. "I—" He turned toward the screen, then realized who he was talking to. His eyes went wide, and he snarled. "What the hell are you doing on this fancy blower, Batman?"

"It means what you think it does, Mannheim," the Dark Knight replied. "Your plan is done. Your lightning cannons will be turned over to the authorities. Should you try and use them elsewhere, we'll find you and cut them off at the source." He'd make sure to have Lucius Fox examine the weapons as well, to develop defenses that would render them useless.

Mannheim let loose a roar of indignation, pounding his fist

on an unseen tabletop while reeling off a string of expletives. Then the feed blinked out. Batman turned away from the monitor. Legs crossed, Batgirl had a hip up on the desk.

"What was that?"

"Bruno 'Ugly' Mannheim, regional head of Intergang," he replied, a wary edge in his voice. "It's an outfit that uses off-world tech." He knew more, but didn't elaborate. He'd recognized the template for the robot dogs. They were based on flesh-and-blood dog cavalry of Apokolips. Pursuant to information supplied by Superman, the Justice League had an extensive file on that dark planet and its power-mad dictator, Darkseid.

She waited for him to say more.

He didn't. He kept the irony to himself.

Here was a common criminal who modeled himself after a god of earthly mythology, supplied with weapons designed by gods of an entirely different pantheon. Gods who were *far* from mythological.

"I see," she said, leaning over the desk, her supple fingers toying with the control box. "So these intergangsters were to be his 'silent partners' in a takeover of Gotham's rackets, I suppose."

"It would appear so," he said.

Batgirl knew that distant tone. Whatever was going on in his head, he was *way* ahead of her, and not likely to share. He was already working out what the permutations of this off-world tech meant and what steps he would take to thwart this new threat. As if the usual threat of Killer Croc running around biting people's faces off wasn't enough to worry about.

She huffed.

It was nothing new, but she didn't have to like it.

7

Python Palmares felt good, but he was pissed at the same time.

He'd had a fabulous roll in the sack with Suzi, who'd done a magnificent job of sexing down his body and mind, so there was nothing to complain about in that department. But afterward, when he and Frankie Bones went over the counts again, damn if one of their dealers wasn't skimming.

What the guy turned in was correct, as far as the territory he was responsible for, but Palmares wasn't so far from the streets that he couldn't tell when something was screwy. So he and Frankie called a meet with the skimmer.

•

"You like your bourbon neat, don't you, Jo-Jo?" Palmares asked over his shoulder.

"That'd be great, Python."

Palmares stepped away from the wet bar and brought the drink over, handing it to Jo-Jo Gagan.

"Thanks, boss."

"My pleasure." He took a seat opposite, in one of the other plush chairs. They'd been arranged so that each was at an angle to the other. Frankie Bones stood over by the drapes, the late afternoon sun slanting in between the gapped slivers of fabric.

"You've been out there earning, Jo-Jo," Palmares began, taking a sip of his drink.

"I've always been a hustler, Python," Gagan replied, grinning. "And hell, Giggle Sniff practically sells itself."

"Like free pickled eggs in a bar?" Bones' hand listlessly moved the drape.

"Oh no," Gagan said, turning slightly in his chair, "I ain't talking down the product, Frankie. This stuff is dynamite how it hooks 'em. Them junkies hear about it from another junkie, and you don't even have to give them a free taste, like you do with other junk. They want it bad." He grinned broadly at Palmares. "But like you said, I'm out there earning for you, Python."

"And I can't tell you how much I appreciate that, Jo-Jo. I understand you've been working so hard that you been working deals with other suppliers, to carry my product on the sly along with their regular shit." He sat back in the chair, setting the glass down on the carpet.

Gagan shifted about in the seat, his grin disappearing.

"What're you talking about, Python?"

"I'm talkin' about you lining your pockets with the sweat of my brow."

Gagan held up his hands. "I don't know what you heard, Python, but it's lies." He leaned forward urgently. "All lies. Don't I turn in my cut like all the others, and on time? Fact is, my percentages have gone up steady, you said so yourself."

"The percentages I assigned you, yeah, those are fine." Palmares laced his fingers together, elbows resting on the arm of the chair.

"I don't know nothing 'bout no under-the-table dealing, Mr. Palmares. I swear on the head of my mother."

Frankie Bones *tsk-tsk*ed. He moved in from the drapes.

Gagan made to stand.

"Sit your ass down," Palmares said.

He did.

"Look you guys, this isn't what you think it is," Gagan said. "Okay, see I was trying out this, ah, what do you call it, expansion plan. Yeah, that's it. Taking the initiative, right? I got the money tracked and accounted for, no problem. I wasn't trying anything slick, not on you, Mr. Palmares. Nothing like that."

"Where's that money you owe me, Jo-Jo?"

He laughed nervously. "Got a locker at the bus station." He gestured again with his hands. "I know how that looks, but it's not like that, see? Just wanted to keep the funds in a safe place, you understand?"

"I understand," Python said. "Completely."

Gagan reached down to unlace one of his shoes. "Got the key right here in my sock, for safekeeping. Yes sir, right here." He took his shoe off and pulled his sock partly off his foot. The locker key dropped onto the carpet, and he bent to retrieve it. As he did, Bones stepped behind the chair.

Gagan leaned forward, holding the key out to Palmares.

"See, nothing underhanded at all."

Frankie Bones slipped the thin wire around Gagan's neck, and yanked back hard.

"No, please," Gagan wheezed out as his air was cut off. "I've been loyal, P-Python. I won't... this won't... happen again."

"Damn straight it won't." Palmares pried the key from

Gagan's hand. Then he watched dispassionately as Frankie Bones snuffed out the betrayer's life. The man's eyes bugged out wide, and his tongue stuck out of his mouth as he futilely clawed at the wire that was ending his existence.

After a moment, the lifeless body slumped back in the chair.

"Call Carl Grissom," Palmares said. "He's got that abandoned amusement park out there, just outside a' town, and for a fee he'll take care of burying this rat's body. For sure nobody'll find it out there."

"Got it." Frankie Bones smiled crookedly.

That handled, Palmares left to see his dentist for a special fitting.

8

"I assure you, this is totally unnecessary."

Professor Linus Stephens addressed the man with the straight razor. "I'm not insane, and I'm *certainly* not suicidal." When there was no reaction, he pressed onward. "Don't you see, the knowledge I possess will change the course of human history. If I were to end my own life, everything inside here would be lost forever."

Twisting, he attempted to tap his temple, but was reminded that his wrists were locked in tight leather cuffs.

He let out a heavy sigh.

"If that happens, *they* win."

The man with the razor just nodded.

An unyielding steel collar kept his head and neck locked in place so that he could only look forward. There was one of those boxy, portable televisions with a snowy screen the size of a playing card, sitting on a shelf between the razor strop and a jar full of snaggletoothed combs floating in deep blue Barbicide. Its crooked antenna was wrapped in tinfoil, but that didn't seem to improve the clarity of the picture. Stephens vaguely made out the blonde bouffant silhouette of a news anchor.

Through the static she breathlessly gave details of some sort of violent crackdown on the city's underworld. The criminal in question went by the unlikely moniker of "Maximillian Zeus." That grabbed his attention for a moment, but when it became clear that it was just another thug grasping for media attention, Stephens lost interest. Besides, the poor picture quality gave him a headache.

Other than the television, however, there was little of interest in his unfortunate surroundings. The barber shop in Arkham Asylum was a long, narrow, industrial space attached to the inmate showers. What it lacked in style, it made up for in decay. The walls, floor, and ceiling were covered in moldy, cracked, and maddeningly irregular white tiles. There were rows of rusted metal tubs like industrial sarcophagi, and a grubby, doorless shower stall inside of which Stephens had been hosed down in a most undignified manner.

Dressed in a clean inmate's uniform, he was about to lose the carefully cultivated Vandyke beard he'd worn since grad school.

"I don't understand why you have to—" he began.

"No facial hair allowed," the man with the razor said, gripping Stephens' chin between a large thumb and forefinger. "And no talking while I'm shaving, unless you want to get cut."

Stephens took the man's advice and shut his mouth. If he had to endure this shameful incarceration, then he would do so with dignity.

The barber was around forty years old, tall and lanky with some threads of white in his precise black fade. His dark eyes seemed jovial and friendly, but the long brown arms revealed by his rolled-up scrub sleeves were sinewy and roped with lean, hard-earned muscle. Like all the staff here, he might be called upon to deal with rough, violent offenders of the criminal class. So there wasn't much a genteel and well-bred academic like Stephens could do to stop him.

Besides, he observed, the man's razor could easily double as a weapon. Superior intellect offered no advantage against a well-sharpened blade.

There were no mirrors in the barber room, or anywhere else in the asylum for that matter. He wouldn't be able to follow the progress of the ruthless shearing. That was probably just as well, he supposed. It would just add insult to injury.

Despite the restrictions imposed by his bindings, Stephens noticed movement in his peripheral vision, as another inmate was placed in the chair to his left, and fastened in place. He saw a disturbingly pale hand with strangely discolored nails, fastened in its own leather cuff, and heard the snipping of scissors. Hair trimmings began dropping silently to the tile floor.

Was that hair… *green*?

Surely it had to be the strain of incarceration that was playing tricks on his senses. But he couldn't allow that to happen. He needed to stay focused at all costs. Otherwise, *they* would win.

The barber stepped back to survey his work. The professor had to give the barber credit, he certainly was efficient. The shearing had been completed in under three minutes. Stephens was shaved clean as a freshman, and the man moved on to trim his admittedly somewhat unruly white hair.

"You can talk all you want now, Prof," the barber said with a conciliatory tone. "I'm all ears, and I got no victims scheduled after you."

"Ah, right," Stephens said, happy to be back on topic. His *favorite* topic.

"They had gotten so close this time, you see," he said, picking up the thread of his thoughts. "*Too* close. I never in a million years could have imagined that they would stoop so low as to take over the minds of innocent students. In doing so, they forced my hand. Believe me when I say that it broke my heart, to have to kill such promising young people—but I didn't have a choice, did I? Those young men and women had been compromised. Brainwashed.

"Their skulls were implanted with advanced technology," he continued, "all in order to steal my data. Yet I foiled their nefarious plan. I'd wager they didn't think I had it in me, didn't have the wherewithal to take such decisive action at my admittedly advanced age."

"They who?" the barber asked as he snipped away. "Who wanted your stuff?"

"Why, the Russians, of course," Stephens said. "Who do you think?"

"The Russians?" The barber was behind him, but he could almost feel the disbelieving smirk floating somewhere behind his left ear. "Haven't you been keeping up on current events? *Glasnost* and all that? That new guy Gorbachev's changing everything. The Cold War's gonna be ancient history, Prof."

Stephens sighed heavily. It was never easy communicating with his intellectual inferiors. They simply couldn't grasp the complex and multilayered issues relating to his work, or the profound global implications of cutting-edge research.

"Ah, but don't you see?" he persisted. "That's what they *want* you to believe. The Soviets are playing the long game, because *they* can see into the future. As can I. Not the sort of sideshow trickery designed to amaze the masses. This is the real thing—extrapolating scenarios using computer models, rigorous study of infinitely variable probabilities.

"In as little as ten years," the professor continued, "the fundamental principles of my research will be used to construct a global network of interconnected computers. This network will change day-to-day life as we know it." He lowered his voice, as if afraid he would be heard. "On a more sinister level, it will allow unscrupulous parties unprecedented access to every facet of our lives. Nothing will be exempt from manipulation. Our government, our banks, our private communication, even our very identities will be laid bare. Wars will be fought and won on a virtual battlefield inside a machine.

"You see, the Arpanet will be the key to everything!"

"Whatever you say, Prof," the barber said, continuing his work. More and more hair fell to the floor.

Stephens clenched his teeth. Such scorn, coming from an inferior, was far worse than the physical indignities. He felt his heart beating in his chest, and there was a buzzing in his ears. As was always the case, he felt utterly alone. None of these people were capable of understanding his genius.

"I don't know why I even bother…" he muttered.

"Please, Professor, don't stop *now*."

What the… ? Stephens jumped, startled. It was the inmate sitting in the next chair. The man with the green hair. His voice was high-pitched, reedy and distinctive, with a kind of plummy, almost sing-song intonation that he could have sworn he had heard somewhere before. *On TV maybe?*

"Do go on. I'm *dying* to hear more."

•

Alfred Pennyworth's footfalls echoed as he descended the circular iron steps that took him from the comforts of the mansion down into the Batcave.

There were several sections to the subterranean lair, including a state-of-the-art crime lab and a tricked-out mechanical repair facility designed to accommodate any sort of vehicle—land, sea, or air. Further along lay the open area where the Batmobile was kept at ready. Scattered among the polished steel supports and the naturally hewn rock walls were keepsakes from past cases.

While many were kept in display cabinets, others were enormous—like a twenty-foot-tall penny that had crushed the criminal who made it, a massive animatronic replica of a Tyrannosaurus, and a similarly huge playing card taken from one of the Joker's earliest lairs.

A series of pumps similar to those found in the Gotham City underground transit system controlled the water that flowed naturally through the cavern. Environmental control units kept dampness at bay to avoid damage to the array of often delicate equipment, and to maintain a comfortable temperature in every area.

Finally there was Pennyworth's goal—the computer lab.

"Care for a snack, Master Bruce?" he said as he arrived. He was dressed in dark slacks and shirt, and a gold-colored vest with paisley designs. His tie was loose, sleeves rolled up. The sound made by his leather-soled shoes was barely audible as he moved across the steel plating. Under his shirt, on his right bicep, was a tattoo from his days with the SAS. To say he was the butler was to say the Taj Mahal was just a building.

"I'm fine, Alfred, thank you."

Up a rise reached by a built-in ladder, Bruce Wayne sat before his super computer. It had a huge monitor array, curved like the dual window of a 747, and a wide console. Various windows of various shapes and configurations appeared on the monitor. As his fingers played rapidly over the keyboard, numerous images from microfiche files to closed circuit camera feeds appeared, disappeared, or were moved to the side. Pennyworth was always amazed that Bruce could keep track of the overwhelming stimuli.

"Have you found anything that leads you to Mister Mannheim?"

"So far I've been unable to back track the transmission," Wayne said, irritation plain in his voice. He wore his Batman uniform, the cowl pulled back to sit on his shoulders. He tapped a button on part of the console, and one of the screens to his left enlarged. A red dot slowly moved across a rudimentary topographical map of Metropolis and its environs.

There was movement on a screen next to the map. Letter by letter, a message appeared in glowing green type on the black background. Yet the man seated at the console wasn't typing.

"My word," Pennyworth muttered, as much to himself as to his employer. "Has this infernal machine gained a consciousness of its own?" The thought made him... uneasy.

Having reviewed many of the files, he had found too many instances where such technology—often extraterrestrial in nature—had led to disaster.

"What?" Wayne said. He turned to peer at what Pennyworth was viewing. "Oh, that. That's a reply coming in from a theoretical physicist, a Dr. Hawking. I consult with him when the situation demands his particular expertise."

"Fascinating," Pennyworth responded. "So far from having its own personality, this device is little more than an advance teletype system." That concept eased his concerns.

Wayne let loose an uncharacteristic chuckle. He turned to face his confidant.

"It's quite a bit more than that," he said. "It's called the Arpanet—a term that seems to be giving way to 'the Internet.'"

"And what do these 'nets' accomplish?"

Wayne smiled thinly. "Nearly twenty years ago, computers at Stanford and UCLA communicated with each other, linked over telephone lines. The technology was developed for the Advanced Research Projects Agency, part of the Defense Department."

"Ah," Pennyworth replied. "Hence the 'arpa.' What was the purpose of this communication?"

"The applications are still being explored, and one of them is distinctly military," Wayne replied. "As you know, Alfred, the Cold War heats and cools—though Mr. Gorbachev seems sincere in seeking reforms of the Soviet state. As promising as that may be, our generals wanted a way to maintain computer reliability in case of a nuclear strike. Thus enabling the various branches of the military to maintain their defense activities without allowing them to be compromised."

"And this is part of that network?" Pennyworth pointed at the screen. A small green rectangle blinked at the end of the transmission.

"Electronic mail it's called," Wayne said. "E-mail for short."

"Not to be confused with V-mail from World War II, eh?"

"No, though the idea has its similarities."

During the war, letters to and from soldiers stationed overseas were photographed for microfilm. In that way many letters could be carried on a single roll of film. "Victory mail" freed up space that was needed for ferrying supplies.

Pennyworth considered the implications. "Am I correct to assume you're not using this... advancement, just to trade quips and recipes with this Hawking fellow?"

"You know me well, Alfred," Wayne said. "As science fiction writers have long predicted, linked computers will be capable of all sorts of tasks. For instance, if I want to access GCPD files without interference, I first need to bypass their security, then I need to dig through boxes of files, most of them abysmally organized." He had done this at various times, disguised as a janitor so as to sneak into the archives at Gotham Central.

"Imagine if those files were on the Arpanet," he continued, "and could be accessed by computer."

"Surely a network such as this one will have its own form of security."

"Anything they can build, I can crack."

"Yes, well," Pennyworth sniffed. "There's one thing they *can't* duplicate." He hoped. "The human brain can never be replaced."

"Not yet," Wayne agreed. "The brain is the most efficient data processor of all, and as yet it can't be cracked." He turned away again and began tapping at the keys. "No, for now computers are just sophisticated tools."

"Sophisticated tools that can be wielded for good or for ill, depending on the whims of human nature." He shook his head, clearing his thoughts. "Tonight, however, my primary concern is that I'm not late for an engagement."

"Who's the lucky lady?" Wayne asked as he replied to Hawking.

"Dr. Thompkins and we shall be attending *Don Giovanni*."

"Hmmm, that seems a bit racy for you, Alfred." *Tap, tap, tap.*

"I've had my nap," Pennyworth said dryly. "I'll be taking the Jaguar."

"The XJ?"

"Not likely, Master Bruce. The classic of course."

"Of course." There was a pause in the rapid-fire tapping. "Shall I wait up?"

Pennyworth snickered as he straightened his tie and buttoned his collar.

9

Stephens was ecstatic to finally have a companion capable of carrying on an intellectual discussion, particularly in this dingy cesspool full of damaged and inferior minds. Truth be told, he found the company of his new green-haired friend both amusing and intellectually stimulating.

The two of them had retreated to the far corner of the recreation room. A soft foam set of tic-tac-toe blocks sat on the rickety metal card table between them. It had been the Joker's idea that they pretend to be playing the game, so that the aides would leave them alone.

"It'll be easy for intelligent people like us to pull the wool over the eyes of the brawny but intellectually inferior orderlies." That was how his new friend had phrased it, and the professor couldn't have agreed more. He would have preferred a game of Go, or chess, or just about *anything* else, but they'd had to make do with what was available.

There was a noise behind him, and he watched warily as Kurt Lenk, a long-time Arkham resident, took a chair in the corner. The shambling inmate showed no affectation on his blank face, so Stephens turned his attention back to the Joker.

The green-haired man had made some strange modifications to the uniform he wore. He'd added thick purple stripes that looked to have been drawn on with a cheap, waxy crayon. Below the unfinished crew-neck he'd sketched in a set of faux lapels, adding a strange ragged carnation that seemed to be made of brightly colored Monopoly money. The odd boutonniere proved advantageous as they talked. Stephens would focus on it when looking too long into his companion's mad eyes became unsettling.

For the moment, however, he was energized by their discussions. In the Joker he saw the same fire, the deep-rooted intellectual yearning he'd encountered far too rarely. It reminded him of his one loyal assistant. A student he hadn't— thank goodness—been forced to kill in order to save him.

"Zach Tazic is an exceptional young man," Stephens said, picking up where he'd left off. "Only two of my students possessed the genetic fortitude and sheer intelligence necessary to resist the Russian brainwashing. Zach was one of them, and that's because he has a place in history. A greater destiny, if you will—I'm certain of it. You see, he's the one who developed the chip."

"A computer chip?" The Joker lifted a soft X block and twirled it between his long spidery fingers before placing it, seemingly at random, on the board between them.

"That's right," Stephens replied. "And it's the key to the future. It promises functionality and widespread practicality that will be needed to expand our fledgling network. Right now, it's simply an academic curiosity. A bulky, slow, and expensive way to pass rudimentary notes between well-funded universities." He clutched one of his own corresponding O blocks, using it to gesture emphatically without placing it on the board.

"But with Zach's new chip comes the promise of portability," he explained. "Imagine if you will a day in the near future in which, instead of requiring a huge, climate-controlled room full of hulking computer equipment, you could carry the equivalent of your own portable television broadcasting station in your suit pocket. A machine capable of delivering your own content to every single computer in Gotham City!"

He was becoming overexcited again, his heart lurching like a kicked dog in his chest. *Oh, how much longer must I rot in this hell hole, away from my crucial work?* He set the O block down on the right side of the board, and then passed a shaking hand over his eyes. In what seemed like inhuman torture his captors wouldn't even allow him to keep a handkerchief to blot the anxious sweat from his brow. His eyes stung from the salt, and he wiped the sweat away as best he could with his clumsy fingers.

The Joker placed another X block on the board, achieving the win with a diagonal Stephens hadn't even noticed.

"Fascinating," the green-haired man said, drawing out the word in his tinny voice. "What did you say this kid's name was?"

"Tazic," Stephens said. "Zach Tazic."

Why do I even bother? He felt grouchy, with a touch of vertigo, and couldn't organize his thoughts. *It's this wretched place. It bleeds away the intellect.*

His companion seemed distracted, as well, though by external stimuli. His mad and merry gaze had shifted across the room. The professor turned to look, and recognized a slender, mousy blonde with a sloppy topknot and round glasses. She entered the room dressed in an oversized doctor's coat over a tight plaid pencil skirt. Her blushing cheeks and bright eyes implied strange, almost frenetic excitement that seemed utterly out of place among staff members whose only visible emotions were mild annoyance, boredom, or contempt.

A laminated staff badge hung on a ball-chain around her neck. It featured a blurry, unflattering photo of her angular face and the improbable name QUINZEL.

"Well, Professor, it's been a pleasure chatting with you," the Joker said with exaggerated formality as he stood, straightened his ratty boutonniere, and gave a perfunctory bow. "If you'll excuse me, it's time for my... physical therapy session."

"Indeed," Stephens said. "Indeed."

He struggled to rise, but by the time he succeeded, the Joker and his questionable therapist were already gone.

•

Leaving the computer lab, Pennyworth followed a tunnel lined with recessed lighting. More man-made than natural, this route took him under part of Wayne Manor and to an elevator that lifted him into the mansion's more conventional garage.

Stepping past several cars that were housed there, including a pedestrian Dodge Diplomat and a sleek Porsche 911, Pennyworth came to a silver, low-slung Jaguar XKE. He got inside, turned the key in the ignition, and the car came to life instantly.

Pennyworth guided the vehicle up a ramp, where automatic doors slid back, and out onto a road that ran alongside the property. There wasn't too much in the way of traffic at this time of the evening, and soon the Dark Knight's aide-de-camp was negotiating a new sort of caverns—the streets of Gotham.

His route took him into a neighborhood that at one time had

been frequented by the upper crust of city society. Now the streets were lined with files of garbage, and many of the buildings were dark, with broken-out windows that resembled sightless eyes.

Here, not that many years ago when the area was still referred to as Park Row, Thomas and Martha Wayne had taken their son to a theater, and after the performance they had chosen a shortcut as they headed for home. It was the last thing they would do among the living, and their murders would haunt the boy for the rest of his life.

The place where Batman was born had come to be known as Crime Alley. Each year, on the anniversary of their deaths at the hands of small-time criminal Joe Chill, Bruce Wayne returned to the place where they were slain, lay a rose on the filthy concrete, and rededicated himself to his cause.

The Thomas Wayne Memorial Clinic was an oasis of healthcare among the ruins. One of the people who had comforted young Bruce in that dark time was Leslie Thompkins, a resident of the neighborhood. Today as *Dr.* Leslie Thompkins she was a clear-eyed, dedicated physician who served as the clinic's director, and persisted in her crusade to make a difference.

The facility serviced the working poor, the indigent— indeed, any who needed help. Though the streets appeared to be all but deserted at this time of night, in fact the area was dense with people living under the worst conditions in crackerjack apartments. For many, the clinic was their only relief.

Older cars and vans parked damn near bumper-to-bumper, Pennyworth had to park several blocks away. After setting the alarm on the Jag, he began the brisk walk to his destination. As he passed a twenty-four-hour laundromat, he heard footsteps behind him. The two he'd clocked following him from a block or so back were about to make their move.

"Well, look what we got here," a voice said as its owner came even with Pennyworth. "You get lost, old man? Your car break down or something? Maybe me and my friend can help you out." He was over six-foot-two, heavy in the arms and legs, with scraggily blond hair. His jeans jacket was cut off at the sleeves, revealing a stippled tattoo that most likely he had received while in prison.

His companion came close to Pennyworth's back, trying to be quiet about it. However, the man didn't seem to have been acquainted with a shower in quite some time, so his presence didn't go undetected.

"That's a nice suit you got," the robber behind him said, sniffing loudly. Pennyworth didn't think it was because he had a cold. "But we ain't into fine threads, you dig?"

"I'm afraid I do," Pennyworth said.

"Wallet," the one beside him said. He stepped just ahead, a knife appeared in his hand, and he flicked the tip of the blade against a brass button on Pennyworth's vest. "Make it quick, pops."

"I will endeavor to do just that," Pennyworth replied. "A gentleman doesn't keep a lady waiting."

"Yeah," the other one said. "M-make it quick." He stepped closer, and his voice was shaking as if he had been plugged into a wall socket. "D-damn patrol blimp is gonna be circling back this way any s-second, so hand it over."

Pennyworth's arm shot out as he leaned in to get his hand behind the elbow of the man in front of him. At the same moment he used his other hand to grab the wrist of the second man's knife hand.

"Hey man," the startled ex-con said.

From behind his partner put an arm around Pennyworth's neck, seeking to throw him to the ground. Most likely he expected an easy target, and was surprised when he encountered corded muscle. As he grunted with unanticipated effort, Pennyworth kicked backward so the heel of his shoe struck the man twice in quick succession.

The grunt turned into a howl of pain.

While the assailant in back crumpled to the ground, Pennyworth calmly dislocated the other one's elbow.

"Ke-*rist*," the tattooed man bellowed.

Somehow he managed to hang onto the knife, though. He switched it to his other hand and came at Pennyworth. A flurry of blows landed faster than he could see them. Losing his grip on the blade, he went toppling backward to land on his ass. A quick kick to his forehead sent him onto his back.

Holding the knife, Pennyworth turned to find the second mugger rising to his feet. The thug was about his height, and surprisingly much older than his partner. This man had a lined face and, even accounting for the ravages of drugs, a great many more years behind him.

Why, he must be near my *age*, Pennyworth observed.

"What on earth, man?" he declared. "One would think you would know better."

"The fuck," the older robber replied, his tone a mixture of anger and indignation. "What do you know, what with your suit sounding all David Niven? You don't know nothing." He wiped his runny nose with a grimy sleeve, and spat at the ground between them. "You got nerve looking down your nose at me.

Who are you to judge? You don't know what I've been through."

"Yes, but…" Pennyworth began, then he squelched a sarcastic retort. Holding the jackknife at his side, he stepped back a few paces until he could keep the two of them in his line of sight.

"Off with you then," he said.

"Hey, look, fancy pants," the older man said, holding out a gnarled hand. "How about a little something? You know, just to tide us over." As Pennyworth considered it, the man added, "Giggle Sniff don't grow on trees, you know."

A cold anger rose in Pennyworth, and it took him a moment to understand why. When he did, he was able to tamp it down.

"I'm not going to give you money," he said evenly, "but I know a place where you can get help." The one he'd kicked in the head groaned and began to come around. The man lifted himself into a crouch, and he peered with hatred at the man who had beaten him.

"If you do anything but sit there, I'll bury this in you," Pennyworth said, brandishing the blade. "Do you follow?"

"Fuck you," the man said, but he didn't move.

"Well?" Pennyworth said to the one who was standing.

"Well what, padre?" the older mugger growled. "You gonna take us to a clinic? Get us clean? Be a hero? You think I haven't tried to kick before? I have, more than once. Even stayed clean for almost a year. But it gets real out here." He spat again. "You wouldn't know anything about that."

"You'd be surprised at what I know," Pennyworth said quietly.

"Okay, fine, you ain't even gonna fork over a couple of bucks, just for pity's sake. Fine. Take your lecture, stuff it up your ass, and leave us alone."

The hand holding the knife trembled, and Pennyworth brought it up in front of his face. The knife's edge reflected the neon glow of an overhead sign.

EMPIRE LIQUORS
CHECKS CASHED HERE

"Leave you to prey on someone else you mean," he said. "Leave you to address your addiction by assaulting some other passerby, or worse."

"What about it, hand-wringer?" the crouching man growled. "What's it to you?" He rose to his feet and thumped his chest. "I got a right to do what's necessary for living, just like anybody else."

The hot rage returned. Before the man had finished speaking, Pennyworth drove a fist into his mouth, staggering him. He hit him again, and before the man could react he snaked an arm around his throat and pressed the knife to his neck.

Pennyworth's eyes were wide, and he was breathing rapidly. He pressed the tip in until blood trickled down, leaving a trail.

"Go ahead," the man said, his voice a coarse whisper. "You'd be doing me a favor."

"I should…" Pennyworth said, but he didn't finish.

"Hey, man, *hey*," the ex-con yelled. He had both of his hands up now, palms forward. "Just be cool, okay?" he said, lowering his voice.

As if he were outside his body, Pennyworth watched as the trail of blood ebbed downward. The man put up no resistance— it was as if the life had already left him.

Then from the dark came a thrum of turbines. A light speared down and swept across the upper floors of the dilapidated brick buildings then swung downward, illuminating ground floor stores such as a shoe retailer, a nail salon, and the liquor store. Finally it pinned the men where they stood.

"Here, look, we give up," the scraggly haired man shouted. He stared up into the light, his hands raised. "Come on, arrest us, huh? Take us to the precinct. Just get that crazy old bastard off of us."

"Don't move," an amplified voice said, coming from the bottom of the blimp. "A patrol car is on its way. I repeat, do not move."

The older man turned, gaping. His partner was on his knees again, his head down. He was still breathing, but other than that he didn't even twitch.

They were alone.

•

From the shadowed gap between buildings next to the shoe store, Pennyworth watched as the men waited to be arrested. After a moment he heard sirens in the distance.

Carefully he placed the knife on the ground to be found by the police. It was incriminating evidence and while he did not have a nylon line or clever gadget to subdue the two brigands as Master Bruce would have, he could do his duty to testify against the thieves, if it came to that.

10

Arriving at Dr. Thompkins' clinic, he walked up the steps to the front door. While its cinderblock exterior wasn't much on style, he knew the building housed the most modern equipment money could buy. Much of it had been supplied by the Wayne Foundation, while the rest had been paid for through tireless fundraising efforts.

He knocked on the shatterproof glass of the locked front door, and saw movement behind the drawn blinds. A latch was turned, and the door opened.

"Hello, Alfred," Leslie Thompkins said. A tall, trim woman with close-cropped white hair and an alert face, she wore a white lab coat.

"Hello yourself, Leslie." He stepped inside.

"I was just finishing up my records for the day," she said, leading the way back toward her office. As they continued down a hallway, they passed the rooms that housed the clinic. During the day various staff members went about the business of caring for patients young and old. But now it was after hours.

"Would you like some coffee? It's reasonably fresh." She gestured toward a kitchen nook.

"Yes, that's fine." She walked on, and he poured himself a cup from the steaming carafe. On the refrigerator door, stuck in place by magnets, were several pictures that had been drawn by the neighborhood children. He blew on his coffee, stepped back into the hallway, and followed her into her office, where she was sitting behind a desk.

In a corner was a human male skeleton held upright in a stand. It had been painted in various colors, and a stethoscope was draped around its boney shoulders.

"I'll just be a few," she said, making notations in a file. He sat opposite her and gathered his thoughts, doing his best to push the mugging to the back of his mind. Watching her work, he remembered the conversation with Bruce.

Pennyworth wondered if one day she'd be making those notations in a file floating on a computer screen. He'd been to the newsroom of the *Gotham Examiner*, and watched the writers use desktop computers to prepare their stories. That was a far cry from the complexity required for medical work, but what if she had something more like the equipment in the cave?

For the moment, equipment like that was prohibitively expensive, and took up far too much space to be practical on a daily basis—but would that always be the case? Though it wasn't the same sort of thing, the Dark Knight's mission required precise calculations and an attention to detail not unlike the medical profession.

Batman's mission…

He set his coffee cup on her desk.

"Not to put a damper on our evening," he said, "but have you heard of a drug called Giggle Sniff?"

She stopped writing, looking up at him over the rim of her thin glasses. Then she put the pen aside.

"Sadly, I have, why?"

"I just... it came up today, in conversation," he replied. "What is it, exactly?"

She sighed wearily. "It is our version of the West Coast's crack, I suppose, that's recently made the scene on Gotham's streets."

"Crack is a rock-like crystal, isn't it?" he said. "Derived from boiling down powdered cocaine."

"Yes, and in that concentrated form, the high it provides is intensified. It's pernicious as it triggers certain receptors in the brain. The effects don't last long, yet because of its effects on the physiology, the addict craves more and more as time passes. A growth industry for the criminal world."

"And this Giggle Sniff is similar?"

She made a face. "To some extent. Like crack, on Giggle Sniff your performance and dexterity increase. You're aware of its effects, yet... floating along. Giggle Sniff makes you happy, damn near *giddy*, as befits its origins."

"Where did it come from?"

She seemed surprised by the question. "Why, right here, Alfred. It's a homegrown product, derived from Joker Venom." She paused, then added, "And yes, it's green."

"Oh, my."

"Oh my indeed. Now I don't exactly know who was the enterprising back alley chemist to figure this out, but the stuff's been on the streets for about six months now. And like all American dream stories, all of the crabs in our underworld barrel are clawing to control the Giggle Sniff trade. Men like Antonio 'Python' Palmares."

"Competition is that fierce?"

"Oh, yes. There's no shortage of opportunists."

"Fascinating." He would make sure to mention this to Bruce. Not that it was likely to come as a surprise.

She returned to her notes and Pennyworth sat in silence, sipping his coffee, sorting out the business on the street. What had it been about that man that had unhinged him so? He'd witnessed the atrocities of war during his time with the Special Air Service. He'd seen innocents frozen by Mr. Freeze, their limbs shattered, and morgue photos of bodies where Killer Croc had bitten off body parts. Yet this petty thief had somehow gotten to him.

What was it about using violence to address problems of a systemic nature? Night after night Bruce would go out as Batman, attempting to stem the tide, staring in the face of madmen like the Joker or Two-Face, who operated on a twisted pretzel logic that only the insane could devise, and sought to define life through one heinous act after another.

"Done, at least for tonight." Thompkins closed her last file folder. Pennyworth surfaced from his reverie.

"Then *Don Giovanni* awaits."

•

As they stepped outside into the cool night air, and Dr. Thompkins locked up the clinic after setting the alarm, she put her arm in the crook of Pennyworth's elbow as he escorted her to the Jaguar.

"That smear of blood on your cuff," she said with

remarkable calm. "I hope there wasn't a mishap on your way to the clinic's doorstep?"

"Oh that," he said lightly. "Rushed my shave, you see. Too excited to see how this new baritone Vitalli handles his chores in the title role."

"Mmm-hmmm," she murmured.

Pennyworth patted her hand and watched the shadows. He didn't expect another incident—one was quite enough for the evening. Then he glanced down at his cuff, and decided there was no such thing as being too careful.

Still, he knew that even among the lowest of the low here in Crime Alley, the word was you didn't mess with Dr. Thompkins or the staff of her clinic. The place was considered off limits—they serviced whoever came through the door, no matter angel or devil. So that even those who would readily steal their mother's wedding ring to pawn for a fix had at least *one* damn thing they could cherish.

As Pennyworth was well aware, Gotham was too often bereft in the upstanding department.

•

Sparks spewed from the motorcycle as it skidded into the gutter. Using her newly acquired grapnel gun, Batgirl latched onto a truck with the logo of Tri-State Freight on the side. She swung up and onto its boxy cargo area and went flat as one of the goons in the car behind them took another shot at her.

This replaced one dilemma with another. Since they were on one of the city's wider thoroughfares, she'd ditched the motorcycle to avoid having any innocent motorists caught in the crossfire. Now she would need to stay toward the back of the truck, lest a stray bullet strike the driver. At least the cargo unit afforded her some protection.

Her target, an AMX muscle car with a built-in hood scoop and a throaty big barrel V8 under the hood, sped to go around the truck and leave her in the dust. Running along the top of the bobtail, she launched herself into space and landed on the car's roof, gripping the front edge and securing a line—along with a surprise package.

As she knew would happen, they shot through the roof trying to tag her, but she rolled off and let herself fall onto the trunk. The line held and she was up like a jet skier daunting a wild wave. A thug twisted around and leveled his pistol to shoot at her through the windshield, when the present she'd left on the roof ignited. It was a magnetized device that pierced the top of the vehicle and shot smoke inside. Instantly the occupants of the car were engulfed, but the gunman managed to get off a shot, shattering the back window.

Even as the glass exploded outward, much of the choking cloud remained inside the vehicle.

"Watch it!" one of the occupants shouted.

"Can't see for shit," the driver bellowed as the car skidded, tore across the lanes, then vaulted over a concrete-and-grass divider.

In this area of town there were bars and restaurants catering to the college and young adult crowd. People stood in doorways or bunched behind plate glass windows, enthralled by the excitement. An elevated subway train rumbled overhead. It was just a matter of time before someone got hurt.

•

Seeking a line on Giggle Sniff, Batgirl had taken her cue from Batman and made the rounds of her own network of informants. The tip had come from a campus contact, a part-time instructor who Barbara Gordon knew from her job at the library. This man had gone out a few times with one of her coworkers, Cassie Lane. She knew too he smoked pot, so that put him in tune with some of the drug crowd.

From him she'd learned about a trio of thugs who'd been hitting the campuses, looking to recruit customers and pushers. He'd described the three men and the flashy car they drove. Sure enough, after some time on solo patrol, she had spotted them.

•

As the car careened out of control, she timed her move just right, jumped free, somersaulted in the air, then rebounded off another car top. The dizzying series of moves landed her on top of a mailbox. The AMX slammed into an iron girder, part of the metal and concrete holding up the elevated tracks for the crosstown subway. The top of the driver's head hit the windshield, leaving a spider's web of cracks, and he was out.

His two companions were still mobile.

The one in the front passenger seat was out and running, limping a little but looking to put as much distance between them as he could. For good measure, he shot over his shoulder without looking back.

The one in the rear seat was trying to extricate himself, but the crash had driven the driver's bucket seat back off its rails. He was pinned, and had to use both hands to shove the broken seat off his legs. Finally he pulled himself loose and fell out of the car, clambering to his feet. The entire time he glanced around, frantic that his pursuer might be close.

"Boo."

He spun around, waving a gun this way and that. She jumped on him from above. Three quick chops to his neck had him dazed, and a left to his face had him bloodied and reeling. One more punch put him out.

Not far away there was a gunshot, and she took off at a sprint. Her quarry was running along beneath the train tracks, shooting at phantoms. He approached a stairway just as a wave of commuters descended from the platform. With a toss of her line and grapnel Batgirl was airborne, swinging over his head and dropping down in front of him.

Instantly she cursed herself for being over-confident. The thug grabbed a woman and pressed his gun to her temple.

"One more step, and her head disappears in a red haze."

"All right, just be cool," Batgirl said, hands forward so he could see they were empty.

"Now you're gonna let me walk, and me and this chick here are gonna find someplace else to be."

"Who're you callin' a chick?" the woman said as she drove her heel into the man's foot, pushing the gun upward and away.

The guy bellowed and she elbowed him to open space between them. Batgirl threw a dart retrieved from her utility belt, embedding it in his chest. He jerked violently as the gizmo sent an electric charge through him. She covered the distance between them in a bound and grabbed his wrist, twisting the gun loose and clubbing him with it.

He sank to the pavement groaning.

"Way to go, Batgirl," one of the commuters enthused.

"You showed him," another said.

Forearm at a ninety-degree angle to her waist, she bowed slightly. Using a zip tie to secure the thug, she was off, eager to reach her motorcycle before it could be impounded.

Sirens got closer in the distance.

As she neared the wrecked car, Batgirl paused. The trunk was loose, and she kicked the ruined lock with the heel of her boot. The lid sprang open, and she found the mat normally used to cover the spare tire. Lifting it she spied numerous packets of Giggle Sniff, loaded into a cut-down cardboard box.

Well, well…

She smirked. One of the geniuses must have figured it would be clever to offer the drug at a frat party or some such, using the cardboard like it was a serving tray. Turning the cardboard over, she noted the stylized double Ns in a circle. As she hurried to retrieve her motorcycle, she wondered if maybe those clowns had just found that box they cut down in the trash. Yet the Novick Novelty company had been closed for some time. What other trash would that have been in?

11

"It wasn't a real baby."

Dr. Joan Leland crossed her legs and leaned in closer to her patient, notepad balanced on her knee.

This was an extremely interesting case. His name was Kurt Lenk, average in every way except for his IQ—which was low, but not abnormally so. Pale, thinning hair beating a swift retreat from his large, freckled forehead. Small, dark eyes darting around in constant motion. Sharp nose and chin in a long, horsey face.

He'd worked for a local slumlord as a general handyman, dealing with minor maintenance issues in several tenements on the south side of town. Lived rent-free in a one-room basement apartment that had been provided by his boss. No family, no romantic connections, aside from the occasional professional. No prior record. Nothing to set him apart from the rest of humanity.

Until the day the Collins baby disappeared.

Dr. Leland had been patiently working her gentle, safecracker's touch on the combination lock of Lenk's mind for nearly five years. For the first three he'd refused to speak at all, to her or anyone else. Then came monosyllables. Then slowly, cautiously, he began to open up. They had discussed his poor and lonely childhood and his well-meaning but emotionally unavailable single mother. His profound anxiety at dealing with his own emotions, which he preferred to subjugate or deny. His obsessive junk collecting and peculiar habit of anthropomorphizing inanimate objects, often endowing them with the emotions he himself could not express. Up until that point, however, any attempt to discuss the Collins baby evoked an immediate retreat into his safe stony silence.

"If it wasn't a real baby," Dr. Leland said, keeping her voice even, and non-threatening, "then what was it, Kurt?"

His whole body was tense, and he was vibrating like a plucked guitar string. He balled his fists in his lap, staring down at them.

"It was…" he began.

The door to Leland's office swung wide open and the Joker sauntered in, plopping himself down on the couch beside Lenk and slinging a chummy arm around his hunched shoulders.

"Boy, did that hit the spot," he said. "I feel like a new man. You know what I'm talkin' about, don't you Kurt?"

Damn him!

Leland pulled in a long slow breath through her nose, fighting to blunt the edges of her fury, and remain calm and professional. It was impossible to guess how much this would set Lenk's progress back. But she didn't want her other, more gregarious patient to feel as if he'd scored points by making her blow her cool.

Instead of addressing the intruder, she turned to face the door.

"Ms. Quinzel," she called. Her young intern appeared in the doorway, looking sheepish. Her hair was down, she was sweaty and disheveled, and the buttons on her white coat didn't line up.

"Yes, Dr. Leland?"

"Why is this Class A patient in the therapy wing, unaccompanied by his legally required security escort?"

The Joker tipped his chin toward the girl in the doorway, waggling his eyebrows and pulling Lenk close.

"Too old for you, huh?" he whispered loudly. "Sure, I know how it is, but beggars can't be choosers, am I right?"

Dr. Leland got to her feet and pushed a button on her desk.

"I'm so sorry, Kurt," she said, taking Lenk by the wrist and helping him to his feet, bodily inserting herself between him and the Joker. "We'll have to continue this discussion next week. Would that be okay?"

Lenk remained silent, eyes to the floor and his body shaking all over as two muscular orderlies arrived in her office. One of them gripped Lenk's upper arm while the other cocked a thumb at the Joker.

"Want us to take this one, too?"

"No, leave him," Leland said, pinning the Joker with a withering stare. "And Ms. Quinzel?"

"Yes, doctor?"

"Report back to my office at the end of your shift," Leland said. "This is your second strike. One more incident like this, and you'll be transferred to the geriatric dementia ward."

The young intern pouted, abandoning any pretense of contrition. She flounced away in an elaborate show of sulky drama. Leland frowned after her. Although the girl seemed to have a genuine rapport with some of their most troubled patients, she was turning out to be far more trouble than she was worth.

"That would be a terrible shame, Dr. Leland," the Joker said in that irritating voice of his. "I assure you that Ms. Quinzel's unique skills would be utterly wasted on the senior set."

Leland refused to rise to the Joker's bait. She'd been working at Arkham Asylum since before Lenk even knew where babies came from. She'd heard it all and much, much worse. She picked up her notepad and sat back down in her seat at the head of the couch.

"Is that what you'd like to discuss in our session today?" she asked. "Sex? Why don't we start with your compulsive need for conquest as a cover for deep-seated feelings of insecurity relating to your physical appearance?"

"Come on now, Doctor," the Joker said. "Appearance is only skin deep. You know as well as I do that what women really want is a man who can make them…" He leaned in, a merry glint in his eye. "…laugh."

"I see," Dr. Leland said, taking notes. "So *that's* the real source of your insecurity. It's not about sex at all, is it? It's the fear that you'll bomb. That no one will laugh at your jokes. Why don't we talk about that?"

The Joker's smile wilted at the edges. His gaze hardened.

"That's not funny," he said. "Or true."

"It's not?" Dr. Leland replied. "My mistake. Why don't you set the record straight?"

"You want to know the truth?" He smiled that Joker smile, cocking his head.

•

"You *stink*."

Someone booed. Another patron hissed.

"Go back to your day job, you ain't funny."

Standing in the wings, the portly owner of the Laughing Fool made a cutting gesture across his throat. The stub of a cheap cigar dangled from a corner of his mouth. It was unlit. Every night it was unlit.

The long-faced would-be comedian looked from the owner back out at the sparse but nonetheless cruel assortment of customers. Most were drunk or high, and it seemed to the man on stage—in his dark suit and bowtie—that the only reason they stayed for the last showcase was to torment the performers. As he turned to walk off stage, someone in the gloom started to clap.

For just a moment, he hesitated.

"Good riddance, you sorry joker," the man in back shouted. He guffawed as he slapped his hands. Slowly. Cruelly. "I want a free drink for having to put up with you. The whole house wants a free drink. *Haw, haw.*"

The owner, Gaynor, gave the defeated comic a reassuring pat on the shoulder. He wore a lavender suit and matching tie, which should have looked ridiculous, but somehow on his fat man's frame he carried it off. It made him look like a circus pitchman dressed for a night on the town.

Walking onto the stage, Gaynor raised his arms and spoke. "As always I want to thank you all for coming out, and remember to tip your servers." A canned rim shot sounded. Off to one side the sole waitress in the place gave a little bow. She had dark circles under her eyes and her earrings twinkled, despite the low lighting. The owner left the stage and the curtain closed.

He found the long-faced comedian in the threadbare dressing room, leaning on the back of a chair as he stared into the makeup mirror ringed with round light bulbs. Several had burnt out.

"Look, you got some chuckles out there," Gaynor said to the long-faced man. "Comedy is tough, especially for a guy who's just starting out. But it's like riding a horse—you get thrown off, you gotta get back on." He clasped the taller man on the shoulder again.

"You'd have me back?" the man said without turning. He seemed to be examining his future in the reflection. The club owner pulled the cigar stub out of his mouth, holding it in his pudgy fingers and waving it about.

"Lemme... lemme think about how that'll work," he replied. "But hell, you soldiered on in the face of a hostile crowd, and that's half the battle. I'll give ya a call... maybe." He stuck the stub back in place and handed over two limp twenties.

The comedian looked at him, confused.

"Sorry, but that's all we cleared," Gaynor said. "It was a lean night."

Long Face straightened, picking up his hat. Thanks to the dark suit, his lanky frame was indistinct in the gloomy space. He looked like a shadowy specter, looming above the earthbound club owner. For a moment the fat man wondered if there was going to be trouble.

"I'm not proud. I'll take what I can get."

"S-sure, kid." The voice that had come from the figure had unsettled him, so different than the guy's usual upbeat tone. "Look, ah, have a drink on me before you go. Okay?"

The tall man moved to the doorway, and spoke without glancing back.

"I don't drink. It dulls the mind."

•

Stepping out onto the street, he put on the shapeless fedora with a jaunty feather sticking out of the band. The night was chilly, and a light rain had begun to fall, but it wasn't that long of a walk and anyway, he didn't want to waste money on a cab.

It was an old part of town. Nearing his place, he passed a working girl stationed in the alcove of a doorway that provided shelter from the rain. She was dressed in a micro-mini skirt, sheer top, no bra, fake lamb's wool collar waistcoat, and thigh-high boots. She might have been twenty or forty.

"Want a date?" she said, giving him the up and down while smacking her gum. Plastered on one side of the alcove was a handbill announcing a new show at the Bonus Brothers Amusement Park.

He couldn't even work up a weary smile for a response. On he went, past bars where people were laughing, drinking, and lining up action for the night. He reached his apartment building and stood outside, as if somehow held fast to the sidewalk.

What a dump, he lamented yet again. What kind of provider was he? One of the building's many cats padded near him on the iron railing that bordered the concrete steps. It looked at him with baleful eyes.

"I'm not crazy about you either," he said.

The cat jumped down and moved on. A sash cracked open slightly in the corner window above him, and he heard a radio playing. It was *always* playing, he thought. Mr. Ramirez, a widower, lived in there. He stayed up long into the night, and again early in the morning, sitting in his kitchenette listening to whatever it was insomniacs listened to in those lonely hours.

Just now it was a news bulletin.

"…the mysterious masked vigilante, known to many as the Bat Man, has been busy again. Earlier tonight he prevented an armed robbery in the fashion district. Witnesses said…"

The door closed behind him as he entered, pausing in the vestibule. There was a shuffle of feet behind a door to his left, and he was certain the landlady, Mrs. Burkiss, had heard him come in and watched him through her peep hole. With her long, tangled hair tied in ribbons, her hook nose, and her flowery house dress, she too was a late nighter. From her ground-floor apartment she could see who came and went. She watched them all on the sly.

Climbing the two stories to his apartment, he stopped at the top of the stairs and took a deep breath, forcing himself not to slump. He unlocked the door and went in. Their sparsely furnished place was warm thanks to a space heater next to the small kitchenette table, and hand-washed laundry hung from a line strung next to the window. Through the window he could see the brick wall of the adjoining building, close and claustrophobic. Water dripped from the roof above.

"Hey, Jeannie," he said brightly, seeking to mask his frustrations.

His very pregnant wife sat at the table in a hard-backed chair. She wore a slip and slippers, her robe open for comfort. There was a bowl before her, and she'd been shucking crawfish tails in preparation for making some of her gumbo. There was a bowl of okra on the sink, and she'd be firing that up later. He liked her gumbo a lot.

"Well, how did it go?" she asked. "Did they like your act?"

He chuckled mirthlessly as he walked over to the sink, picked up a raw piece of okra, and took a bite.

"Well, they, uh… They said they might call me," he said, chewing. "I dunno. I, I got nervous and messed up a punchline."

"You stink!"

The shame came rushing back.

"Oh," his wife said.

Storming back to the table, he leaned in on her.

"What do you mean, 'oh'?"

"I… I didn't mean *anything*…"

The hell she didn't. "Yes you did," he growled. "The way you said it. 'Oh.' Like *that*."

"Jesus, all I said was—"

"You said 'oh.' As in 'Oh, so you didn't get a job?' As in 'Oh, how are we going to feed the baby?'" He stared at her angrily, but she didn't give ground.

"You think I'm not worried about that?" he continued, stepping away from the table and clenching his fists in sheer frustration. "You think, you think I don't care, that it's all a big joke to me or something…"

Then his anger was gone, replaced by despair. He fell to his knees at her feet, his arms tenderly around her, his head in her ample lap.

"Oh, God," he said. "Oh God, I'm sorry…"

"Oh, baby." She laid a hand on his back. With the other hand she smoothed down his unruly thicket of hair, which she'd always found so appealing on him. They'd wondered what those curls would look like on their child.

"I don't mean to take it out on you," he said, sobbing. "You're suh-suffering enough, being married to a loser."

"Honey, that's not—"

"It's *true*. I can't support you." He gulped in air. "Oh, Jeannie. What are we going to do?"

"It'll be okay," she answered, her voice soft and sure. "Junior won't be here for another three months, and I think Mrs. Burkiss will let the rent go a little longer. She feels sorry for me."

"She hates me," he said, a hint of anger returning. Climbing to his feet, he leaned against the window. "She comes out into the hallway to scowl at me every time I go upstairs. This house stinks of cat litter and old people." Outside the rain had increased, and rivulets of water ran down the bricks.

"I just want enough money to get set up in a decent neighborhood," he said, staring into the night. "There are girls on the street who earn that in a weekend without having to tell a single joke."

To his surprise, he heard a chuckle. Turning, he saw that she was *laughing*. There was no malice in it, though.

"Honey, don't worry," she said, reaching out for him. "Not about any of it. I still love you, y'know? Job or no job, you're good in the sack…"

He had to smile at that. Even six months pregnant, there was a grace and sureness of movement about her. What a lucky bastard he was. He just had to do right by her.

"…and you know how to make me *laugh*."

12

The three of them were sitting at a round table in the Boondoggle. The tavern was crowded, though it wasn't even that late in the day. The place was bustling and humid as hell. They had a bowl of boiled crawfish appetizers sitting between them.

He was drinking.

When did that start?

He'd never liked the taste of alcohol. Especially when he'd worked at the chemical process plant. He'd taken precautions, but he was pretty sure some of those chemicals had leeched their way under his skin.

Yet here he was downing his second beer, and it wasn't even late afternoon.

"Y'see... Y'see, I have to prove myself. As a husband, and, and as a father," he heard himself say. Why in the world would he admit that to these two... hoodlums. Thugs? Why would he be so forthright? *Must be the booze. That's why I shouldn't drink*, he noted, taking another belt. "I mean, I, well, I wouldn't be doing this thing, if it wasn't something important."

"I hear you," the heavier guy, Joe, said. He was in a suit and bowler hat and, despite the heat, wasn't sweating. His mustache was heavier, bushier than his skinny partner's. "You want to provide, and we're gonna make sure you can do just that, pally."

"It's like, I began as a lab assistant, right?" he continued. "Was a good job. *Real* good job. So what I did, I quit to become a comedian." Biggest mistake of his life. "I was so sure. So *sure* I had talent." He got the notion watching those guys on TV. They had the audience in the palm of their hand when they were on a roll. *I mean, I always made Jeannie laugh, so I figured I had a talent for that sort of thing.*

"But, *ha*, well, look at me. I guess my talents didn't lie in that direction," he said. "So you see, if I just do this one big crime—"

"Hey, jeez, man," the skinny guy said. He was rakishly built, with pointy shoulders in his suit, and he wore a slouch-type hat. His mustache was old-fashioned like a matinee idol might have worn in the 1930s. He rolled a cigarette around between his reedy lips. People smoked in the Boondoggle, even though they weren't supposed to.

"I'm sorry. I'm sorry," the long-faced man said. "It's just, if you're sure we can get away with this thing and that nobody will know I was involved…" He shut up, worried that he was saying too much again.

"Don't worry, friend," Joe in the bowler said. "We'll take care of you." He picked up a crawfish, plucked off its head, and stuffed it in their guest's mouth, leaving the tail hanging out. "We need your help getting through that chemical plant where you worked," the man continued, "to the playing card company next door. We really appreciate your expertise."

"So, like, to absolutely guarantee nobody connects you with the robbery…" The skinny guy pulled a fancy, old-fashioned carpet bag out from under the table. It looked like something from the 1800s. He opened it and held it up. "…you'll be wearing this."

What the hell?

Inside the bag was a bright red, tube-like thing, round on the top. It looked like the sort of domed covering he'd seen on the clock on his grandmother's mantle. But this was larger, and opaque, and it looked like it would fit over his entire head down to the shoulder blades. The jangled comedian took the dangling crawfish out of his mouth, spitting out pieces of the creature.

"Wearing…?" he said, confused. The thing looked vaguely familiar. "B-but there are no eye slits. I won't even be able to see." This had to be a joke. *Maybe they're testing me, to see if I'll go along with them.* To his right side Bowler Hat busied himself tearing apart another crawfish, pulling its spindly legs off one by one.

"There's these lenses o' red two-way mirror glass set into it," the skinny guy said. "Pretty smart stuff, right?" He smiled a thin smile.

"I dunno. That mask…" the long-faced man said. "Isn't it the one that Red Hood guy wears, who raided that ice company last month?"

"Smarten up." Skinny closed the bag again and put it on the floor. "There ain't no 'Red Hood.' There's just a buncha guys, anna mask."

His heavy associate downed the crawdad and nodded. "Right! It doesn't matter who's under the hood. We just sort of let the most valued member of the mob wear it for, uh, additional anonymity." He made it sound like the most logical thing in the world. Behind him a pro was chatting up a sailor.

"Sure," the skinny guy said. "The most valued member.

That's you, man." He picked up a crawfish and started to shuck it. His partner followed suit.

Somewhere in the bar, someone threw up.

The would-be comedian wanted to believe them. This could solve all of his problems, give them a new start.

"Ah, look," he said, "really, I don't know… that chemical plant's so grim and ugly. That's partly why I quit." That and what they were making there. Stuff for the military, *"worse than Agent Orange,"* he told Jeannie. And there were things he *couldn't* tell her. Psychoactive drugs. Compounds tested on people without their knowledge. There had been a slip-up, and he'd gotten a dose.

God, he hoped it didn't affect the baby…

"But you said there's minimal security, man," Skinny said.

"Listen, do you *want* to raise your kid in poverty?" Joe added. They continued to tear the limbs off of crawfish.

He buried his head in his hands.

"No, no, of course not. You're right," he said. "I mean, it's just this once, then I can switch neighborhoods and start a proper life." With a real home, and a proper school for his son. He'd give Jeannie the sort of existence she deserved.

"That's the attitude," Joe said, patting him on the shoulder. Why were people always patting him on the shoulder? "So… next Friday night, at eleven?"

The man who would be funny nodded tentatively, laughing a little as the stress lifted from him. "Sure," he said. "Sure, why not? Friday it is. And then, starting from Saturday morning, I'll be rich." He liked the sound of that. "I can't imagine it. My life's going to be completely changed! Nothing's going to be the same…

"…not ever again."

13

Friday arrived, and the three would-be thieves met at the Boondoggle again, to go over last-minute details. It made sense to meet back there, since the customers and the staff were used to looking the other way.

It was that kind of place—not a bar to which you took your date.

It was where you went when she dumped you.

•

What a dump.

Miller, the plainclothes cop in his trench coat and snap brim, reflected on the establishment as he and a uniform stood looking in on the bar through the dingy glass in each of the swinging double doors. He glanced briefly at his beefy fellow policeman, McCorkell, and then pushed one of the doors inward.

Mrs. Burkiss, the landlady who smelled like kitty litter, had told them they might find him here. Not that she advocated drinking before the sun went down, she'd added, but she and the deceased used to talk. The poor dear, the landlady had gone on, had been lonely, what with her husband out all hours.

Comedians who worked in strip clubs frequented the Boondoggle, or so she'd been told.

•

"So, everything's settled for tonight?" the robber with the matinee mustache said, leaning back in his chair. Today there were no boiled crawdads out in bowls.

"Uh, well, of course!" the grasping jokester said. "I'd be crazy to back out now." He leaned on the table, trying to sound confident. "I mean, the worst part, lying to Jeannie, that's over. She, she thinks I have a club engagement tonight..."

"No reason why she shouldn't keep right on thinking that," the heavier thief said, adjusting his bowler.

"Right, man," the skinny thug agreed. "No reason at all."

"Listen, tonight," Joe said, "wear a suit and bowtie. It's a kinda trademark with this Red Hood business."

"Of course," Long Face replied. "That's what Jeannie will expect me to wear, for the nightclub. It's perfect."

"Uh, Joe..." The rakish one looked over at the bar, and put a hand on his partner's shoulder. From where he sat, the comedian saw two men talking with the bartender. One of them was a cop.

They made a beeline for the table.

The guy in the trench coat had to be a detective. While the two robbers did their best not to let their faces be seen, the plainclothes cop dropped a photo on the table, and spoke to the long-faced would-be comic.

The photo was him and Jeannie.

"Excuse me, sir," the detective said. "We're police officers.

Could we speak to you outside for a moment?" It didn't really sound like a question.

"It'll only take a moment, sir…" the uniformed cop said. Something in his voice sounded sad.

"Me? B-but… why?" Confused, the long-faced man looked at their set faces. "I haven't… I mean, uh…" He tried his best to look innocent. *How could they know?* Giving up, he stood and followed them out to the street.

"Uh, listen, what," he said to the detective. "What's the problem here? I—"

"Sir, I'm sorry," the cop said, interrupting him.

Sorry?

"But your wife had an accident this morning," the cop continued, not making eye contact. "Apparently testing a baby-bottle heater. There was an electrical short, and, uh…" He looked really uncomfortable, and at that moment the comedian knew.

"Well, she died, sir. I'm sorry."

Still avoiding the long-faced man's gaze, he put a cigarette into his mouth, and lit it with a match.

"What?"

What else could he say?

"Listen, I hate to break it to you like this," the detective continued, finally looking at him. He sounded sincere. "It was a million-to-one accident. They have full details waiting for you at the hospital." He laid a comforting hand on the comedian's shoulders. "There's no hurry."

"If I was you," the beefy uniform said, "I'd have another drink."

With that they left.

•

The long-faced man just stood there, watching them walk away. There wasn't anything he could say, or do. Like a sleepwalker, the comic went back inside and sat down. There didn't seem any other place for him to go. Jeannie and the baby...

"Hey, pal, you okay?" the skinny guy said, draining his beer.

"My wife," he responded. "She's dead. My wife..." He heard himself say it as if from a pronounced distance.

"Gee," Joe the heavy one said. "That's terrible. We're really sorry."

"Yeah. Hey, listen, man," the skinny one said, standing and leaning over the table. "You probably wanna be left alone right now, huh? We'll see you here tonight, okay?"

What's he talking about? the comic thought, his eyes going wide. "Tonight?" he said. "But... but I can't do *anything* tonight. Th-there's no reason anymore. Jeannie... Jeannie..." He choked, then continued. "Jeannie's dead. You don't understand—"

Joe didn't let him finish.

"No, no, no," he said. "No, I'm sorry about your wife, but it's *you* that doesn't understand." He rose, as well, and they stood on either side of him. "What's happening tonight, it's no little thing. Nobody backing out now remains healthy." He let that sink in, then added, "No exceptions."

"But..."

"No buts," the skinny guy said, giving him a grotesque grin, a cigarette clenched in his teeth. "Tomorrow, you bury your old lady in luxury. Tonight, you're with us. Get the picture?"

He knew they'd kill him if he didn't comply. He had to be alive, if only to take care of his wife's remains. The remains of their child.

"Yes," he said. "Yes, I get the picture."

They left without another word. Pausing in the doorway, the skinny thug looked back over his shoulder. His message was clear.

The long-faced man watched them go through teary eyes. He lowered his head, crossing his hands over the top of his hat as they trembled, and he cried. He couldn't shake the feeling that the patrons in the bar were watching him, and laughing at his pain. But what kind of people would they be to do that?

Who would be that monstrous?

14

He stood on the edge of the concrete channel, studying his dark-eyed reflection in the slow-moving filthy water. A light rain creating ripples that distorted his appearance. He was dressed in a black suit, white shirt, and bowtie—the suit Jeannie had taken in for him last week—and looked ready for the stage.

His companions wore trench coats. How come he hadn't?

The narrow waterway ran along the side of the Ace Chemical Processing Company. Streams of oily fluid dribbled out of round, three-foot-wide drainage pipes that snaked from the plant. Up a slight embankment stood a chain-link fence topped with loops of concertina wire.

"Hey, c'mon! Quit daydreamin'. Are we doing this thing or ain't we?"

The comic hardly heard. Didn't even know which of the men had spoken.

"Uh, yes, yes, of course," the comic said. "I was, I was just remembering… I used to walk along here on the way to work each morning…"

"Yeah, yeah," the skinny one said. His hat was pulled low against the weather, and he was struggling to pull the red tube mask out of the carpet bag. "Now put this sucker on, man. An' shut up."

"What, right now?" he said as the guy lowered the thing over his head. "I mean… I mean, are you sure it's okay? Will I be able to breathe?"

"Hey, man, everything's cool," the guy said. "Jeez, y'know, you got a funny-shaped head." After a moment it was resting on his shoulders. "There… you still see okay, man?"

"Wuh, well, yeah. I guess," he said. "Except everything's red… It's kinda stuffy too, and it smells funny." Like old sweat and desperation. "Does my voice sound echoey to you?" Seen through the bizarre red lenses, the skinny thug looked strange, with dark eyes and a grotesque grin.

"You sound great," Bowler Hat said impatiently, leading him over to a crumbling set of steep concrete steps. "Now… how about guidin' us through this stinkin' factory to the joint next door?"

The skinny guy went ahead of them, backing up the stairs and steadying the comedian to keep him from falling.

"Watch out, man. Steps."

"Sure. Sure thing." The red-hooded comic had his hands out to balance himself. "Y'know… this feels kinda weird. Like a dream. I keep remembering Jeannie…"

They cut through the fencing and made their way into a huge open area—a labyrinth of concrete walkways between pools of stagnating liquids from which vapors rose. There were towering steel vats, rows of pipes and gauges, and steel catwalks. Just as it had been in the day, security was concentrated at the entrances. The plant's owners were cheap-shit, so there weren't any patrols until after darkness fell. Or so the comedian had informed the two.

"Okay, we go through here," he said, leading the way unsteadily. "Past the filter tanks and then Monarch Playing Cards is just beyond a partition." Though he heard the throb of machinery and churn of pumps, it was after hours, so there weren't any personnel. "Y'know, this place… it looks even worse in red. It looks like—"

"Hey, you! *Freeze!*"

The shout seemed to come from above.

"C'mon, c'mon, get 'em up!"

Twisting to the right, he had to shift his entire upper body to see the uniformed security guard on the catwalk. The man had his legs spread wide, his feet planted, and a pistol leveled at them.

"You *asshole!*" the skinny thief screeched. "You said there was no security!"

"They… they must have altered things since I left…"

"Altered things? I'm gonna alter your stupid horse face, man." The thug pulled out a pistol and opened fire upward. The sound was deafening.

"That noise!" He desperately wanted to cover his ears, but could only grip the curved surface of the red hood. "It's so loud in here!"

Someone shoved him. It was the guy with the bowler.

"For God's sake, *run!*" he shouted. "This is all screwed up!" As they took off between the open-air vats, they heard the guard again.

"Murph, get some men over to the rear bays. We got the Red Hood mob in here."

Oh, shit, he's calling for backup, the comic thought frantically. Then it sunk in. *Red Hood mob. Oh crap! He means me!*

"Oh, Jesus!" Joe hollered, wheezing with the effort. "Which way is it? How do we get out?" With no place else to go, they ran past parallel rows of tall domed holding tanks. Chemicals could be heard sloshing through a convolution of pipes. The rain continued to fall.

"I… I don't know! This mask… can't see where I'm going."

"I'm gonna *kill* you, you useless son of a bitch," his skinny cohort gritted. "When we get outta here, I'm gonna—"

Thunder overwhelmed his every sense.

Just in front of him, the two criminals burst out from the narrow rows of pipes, then twisted grotesquely as bullets ripped into them. Through the red filter of the hood, the blood looked black as it spurted wherever the bullets penetrated. A thick mist sprayed everywhere. He couldn't tell if it came from the pipes or the bodies, but it seeped into the cloth of his suit, made him itch, and he felt as if his skin was bubbling from underneath. He stumbled against a fifty-gallon barrel stenciled with the black ace of spades.

The skinny one got off a last shot, but a bullet went straight through his skull, knocking off his hat.

The two crumpled to the concrete.

But pudgy Joe wasn't dead. "Aw hell… aw hell…" he said, groaning in pain. "You guys… you guys don't want me." His voice rose. "You want *him*. He's the ringleader. He's the Red Hood!"

"What?" the comic said, and then he realized he was covered in something sticky. "What is it? What is it?" He lifted his hands. "It's all over me…"

Above them, someone shouted, "Watch out! He's pulling a gun!" A shot rang out, just missing him. Another hit the pudgy guy in the chest, and blood spurted out of his back.

"Oh no," the hooded man screeched. "No no no no..." Desperate to get away, he scrambled up a metal ladder.

•

"Up on the catwalk!" A guard sighted down his barrel. "I've got his ass good and dead."

"No more shooting."

The sibilant voice came from behind the security personnel. As one they turned—and gaped.

"The human bat," one of them gasped.

"I'm here now," the Bat Man said. "I'll take care of it my way." The ears on his mask were as long as his head, and his black cape draped over his shoulders like wings. His spiked gloves made it look as if he had claws for hands.

From a standing position, he effortlessly leapt over the men, balanced for an instant on the rail of the catwalk, then ran along it like a tightrope walker. Leaping into the air he did a perfect somersault over vats of chemicals, moving gracefully and fluidly, his cape flapping behind him as if it had a life of its own.

•

Hearing the sound of close pursuit, the helmeted man looked back over his shoulder, then stopped. He held his hands out to ward off the newcomer.

"So, Red Hood, we meet again," the Bat Man said. His cape settled around him like a shroud, and his eyes were slits in the mask. Through the hood, everything was blood red. Perhaps it was the chemicals, absorbed through his skin, affecting the hooded comedian's perceptions. What he faced was a stygian beast, come to drag him down to the pits. To pay for the sin of failing his wife and unborn child.

"No, no no *no*," he cried out. "This isn't happening. Oh dear God, what have you sent to punish me?" If his pursuer heard, he gave no indication. "Don't come closer! Don't come any closer, or I'll..."

The bat figure reached out with a claw.

"... I'll jump!"

Spinning, he went up and over the rail, plunging down into the sickly green pool of unknown chemicals. The current moved quickly here, and for a moment he considered letting it envelop him as his clothes became saturated, dragging him along. The burning intensified, then eased as a carousel of colors and shapes swam before his eyes.

Reflex took over and he swam upward, gasping inside the hood as he broke the surface of the toxic brew. The stream had carried him outside, not far from the plant, to a drainage channel like the one in which he had seen his reflection. He coughed violently and vomited inside the helmet. With frantic strokes he moved to the crumbling moss-covered cement edge of the canal.

Suddenly the burning was back.

"I'm stinging," he cried out, the sound echoing in the hood. "*Itching*, my face, my hands... Something in the water? Oh, Jesus, it *burns*..." He clutched at the damned thing covering his head. "Get this stupid hood off. Get it off so I can..."

Finally he wrenched it off and peered down into a puddle of rainwater.

"...see."

What looked back was unrecognizable.

He dropped to his knees and covered his face in his hands. When he looked again, though, nothing had changed. His eyes were pools of darkness in an impossibly white face. And his hair...

I need to get out of here.

Lurching to his feet, he stumbled away from the Ace Chemical Processing plant, leaving the hood behind. His mind whirled, the burning abated, and one syllable escaped his lips.

"Ha."

Suddenly it was clear.

"Ha ha ha."

It was all a *joke*.

Once he started laughing, it became impossible to stop, to hold it in. He had found what he had always sought... laughter.

Unrestrained, inescapable *laughter*!

The joke was on him, for now—but soon *he'd* be the one dispensing the laughs.

His jokes would be killer.

15

Dr. Leland was silent for a moment, waiting to see if the Joker would continue. This was by far the longest and most elaborate story he had told her about the events that had led to his current condition. It was the most emotionally raw, and believable, but that didn't make it true. Next week, he might have a completely different version.

Yet somehow she had touched a nerve.

Leland liked to think that she had a finely tuned bullshit detector. It went with the job and—much to the dismay of the men she dated—tended to spill over into her private life, as well. Something about the Joker, however, messed with her ability on the deepest level, like a magnet throwing off a compass needle.

She'd dealt with more than her share of compulsive liars, narcissists, and psychotics so alienated from reality that they were unable to distinguish truth from fiction. But the Joker was different.

Her testimony in court had led to the judgment that he was not guilty by reason of insanity, and he had been remanded to her care at Arkham. Yet, in her darkest, most sleepless hours she wondered if maybe he wasn't insane after all. Not in the clinical sense, at least. Perhaps it was all just an elaborate act. A complex joke with an unfathomable punchline they might never see coming. If it ever came at all.

The Joker sprawled on the couch with his head tipped back and a hand over his eyes. He seemed physically spent, though she didn't know if it was from his emotional trip down memory lane, or his dalliance with her intern. Finally he broke the silence.

"I'd like to go back to my cell now," he said without uncovering his eyes.

"Very well." Dr. Leland pushed the security button and stood up. "We made some very good progress today," she said, extending a hand.

He stood up, as well, eyeing her hand warily before finally committing to shake it.

"Me, too, Doc," he said with a wink as the orderlies entered the room and flanked him, each grasping an elbow. "I feel on the verge of a real breakthrough!" He giggled softly to himself as the orderlies led him away. Dr. Leland clicked her pen and wrote on her notepad.

> Security risk remains extremely high.
> Transfer to outpatient treatment
> NOT RECOMMENDED.

As if they'd ever consider it.

She circled the last two words several times and then flipped the cover over, closing the pad.

16

The hulking GCPD prowl car drove slowly along the darkened street. The officer on the passenger side had his searchlight on, moving a lever on the inside of the car to aim the beam left to right, up to down. The beam probed the stone and glass exteriors of various buildings, then the car stopped at a specific structure.

Where the windows used to be, barren cavities stared out. The light shone inside the ground floor of what had been the old Meskin Oil and Gas company headquarters. The beam moved around, revealing stained cardboard boxes, shopping carts filled with stuffed black plastic shopping bags, and homeless people sleeping under ratty blankets.

The light remained stationary for a moment, the sound of the big car's engine idling, drifting upward toward chipped and weathered gargoyle outcroppings. Then the cop extinguished the light, and the car continued on, turning at the far corner. The engine's growl faded into the distance.

Inside the ruin several floors had been gutted—walls knocked down and new aluminum skeletons erected, supporting wiring and conduits. A half-dozen real estate developers had tried to make a go of it, converting the building to apartments or condos with retail shops on the ground floor. Eventually they gave up.

A few of the homeless and assorted street people had made their way to the second floor, and a smattering to the third. Above that there were only pigeons, ambitious rats, and the evidence that a roving graffiti artist had found a virgin wall to tag could be found in the gloomy hallways and rooms.

That's why when the three burly men undid a sealed side door on the ground floor and used their flashlights, they weren't too concerned that their shoes echoed on the metal stairs as they ascended to those darkened upper reaches of the abandoned building.

Each carried a nylon equipment bag, and all three could be said to be "men of a certain age." They all had criminal records, having been henchmen of some third-tier masked villain.

They weren't dressed in the ridiculous ways they once had been outfitted, mimicking the attire their bosses had worn. They wore khaki chinos and windbreakers or leather coats.

Having served their prison sentences, they found the pickings slim. This led them to My Alibi, a watering hole along the Gotham docks in the East End where those of the henchman profession could buy beers, talk smack about the old days, and not have to worry about the law or Batman rousting them.

•

"How was anyone supposed to take serious a dude named Mr. Camera?" one of the men said, waving his glass around. "Let alone running around with a helmet shaped like some kind of big-ass Nikon? Sure, he was able to hypnotize people with that thing, but still." Harry Simms had once been the quirky villain Mr. Camera.

He paused and took a swallow of cheap bourbon, setting the glass down heavily and causing the ice cubes to rattle. "But hey, I signed on." Idly he scratched at an earlobe that was no longer there. He'd lost it in a shootout with a rival gang, over a bunch of raw cut diamonds.

"I hear you," his companion said. They sat among others of their ilk. He too downed some of his drink, a domestic beer in a bottle, and used the back of a hand to wipe his gray mustache. "Now when I did my last bid at Blackgate, there was a guy who worked the antique cons. He said that Simms had a kick-ass camera collection. That being his thing and all."

"Yeah, supposedly he had stuff like the camera that belonged to some Nazi officer who took the last photo of Adolf Hitler, and one that belonged to Ray Charles, and—"

"Ray Charles is blind," his drinking buddy pointed out.

"Yeah, whatever," the guy with the missing lobe said. "Maybe he's got people to tell him what's in front of him so, you know." He scratched again. "The point is, the cameras are supposed to be worth a lot of money—money that could get a guy started in a... lucrative pharmaceuticals business, for example."

His companion mused on this. "What happened to them?"

"Who the hell knows."

"I heard he sold it when he was trying to raise money for his lawyers," a guy said from a couple of stools over. He had a serious gut, and held up a beer that showed where it came from. They shot him a dirty look, but he kept going. "Some private collector who paid him handsomely—*real* handsomely. Only Simms got the bright idea to try and pull one last job before his trial. The Huntress put him and his partner away."

The two stared at the third man.

"I used to run with Julian Day, the Calendar Man," he explained. "He was the partner. Got shot by the cops and lived. Simms got away, but Day made a deal and ratted him out.

"Thing is," he added, "Simms was supposed to have left that nest egg hidden away somewhere."

That got their attention.

•

One thing led to another, and the three began making inquiries. Each on his own might have been able to run the information down, but facing the prospect of a major payday, none of them was about to let the others strike out on their own.

They found out Simms had a sister who was middle management at Meskin Oil and Gas. At one point, when the gas company had pretty much moved to an upgraded headquarters, she was one of the few who still worked in the old building. What better place, they'd reasoned, to hide the swag? To further cement this theory, the last time Simms went down, the Huntress had busted him near there.

The sister wasn't around any longer. She'd keeled over from a heart attack one afternoon while attending to her azaleas, and no treasure had been unearthed at her modest house.

That brought them to the sealed door and the metal stairs.

"Hey, slow down," the man with the gray mustache said. They reached the sixth floor, and he was sweating despite the cool of the evening.

"Too many cheeseburgers and brews," the man with the missing lobe chided. He too was feeling winded, but wanted to macho it out. "C'mon, we've just got a couple more floors to go." He pointed his flashlight up the stairs, and thought he saw something move.

"He's got a point," the third man said. "If the swag's up there, it ain't going anywhere in the next few minutes." He leaned against a rail and sucked in air.

"Okay," the man with the missing lobe said, setting his bag down. "Take five, then we hit it so we can quit it."

17

Not all that far from the trio of former henchmen, Harvey Bullock idly scratched his whiskered cheek. As usual, he was dressed in a rumpled suit several years out-of-date, the lapels stained with his recent meal of chili dogs and nacho fries. The suit looked like something he slept in.

In his other hand he held a flask, and he took a sip of bourbon. He stood in the small back room behind the counter of the Aparo Motel. Venetian blinds offered a view of the parking lot, and beyond that cars and trucks zoomed past on the expressway. The Gotham City skyline loomed even further away, past the park that held the statue of Judge Solomon Zebediah Wayne, a nineteenth century Bible-thumping abolitionist who had helped turn a fishing village into a modern-day center of commerce.

A cheap cracked mirror sat on a wobbly table near two hard-backed chairs. There was also a threadbare couch, and a smaller table upon which sat an ancient black-and-white television. On the screen the Gotham Knights played the Star City Rockets baseball team, the volume down low. On the mirror resided the remains of some green powder, next to a razor blade and cut-off straw from a fast food joint. Thea

Montclair used the blade to chop and line up the narcotic.

"Damn," she said, admiringly, "that's some primo giggles."

Bullock took another swig from his flask, leaning against the back of a chair. His shoulder rig was draped over the chair, holding a department-issue three-inch-barrel revolver. His badge in its leather holder was clipped to the holster. He leaned forward as he talked to Montclair.

She sat in another chair, her foot tapping a beat on the floor. She was dressed casually in jeans and a flannel shirt, a bit of cleavage showing that Bullock tried not to zero in on too much. Montclair was the night manager of the motel. Once upon a time, however, she'd been a Calendar Girl.

Not the sort who wore a skimpy bikini and held up a beer bottle. She'd been a henchwoman among a plethora of henchmen. The Calendar Man had come up with the bright idea to recruit females for his gang, as he tried to differentiate himself from the other low-level villains. Julian Day also came to believe that the women on his payroll dug him, and he couldn't keep his creepy hands off of them.

One by one they departed.

Despite years of hard living and hard drugging, Montclair's body was toned and athletic. She'd begun working out when she was a member of Day's crew, and she'd kept it up ever since. Her face, though, was a lined testament to the things she'd endured after running away from an abusive foster home at age fourteen.

Bullock admired her dedication. He still did dumbbell curls on occasion, so there was some muscle tone in his arms and chest. His beer gut, however, sagged over the edge of his elastic waistband.

"You clear-headed enough to go over this again?" he said, "or does the allure of that shit have you in a rapture state?"

Without a word she rose and, in the tiny adjoining bathroom, theatrically upended her compact, watching doe-eyed as the green powder fell like alien snow into the toilet bowl. She flushed the commode and came back to sit in the chair. There was still some powder on the table, but she'd made her point.

"Sharper than a skeeter's peter, Harv," she said. "Lay it out, baby."

Shifting his gaze from the TV screen back to Montclair, Bullock scratched at his tangle of salt-and-pepper whiskers again.

"The main thing is what your girl Suzi told us," he replied. "That she knows for certain Python Palmares has his operation set up in the old Novick Novelties factory."

"She's sure of it." Montclair nodded firmly. "She went through there about a month ago. Palmares brought up a buncha girls for a big party he was throwing. Booze, drugs, chicks flashing their ta-tas, the whole shebang. It was on the top floor, in his office outfitted to be all swank."

"You sure she wasn't so high that she got it all twisted around in her head?"

"No, Harvey, she wasn't," Montclair replied. "Palmares was puttin' on the dog to impress this Intergang guy, Mannheim. You know, lookin' to get more financing to expand up and down the eastern seaboard. His crew met Suzi and the girls on the ground floor by the stairs, 'cause the elevator wasn't working. When they passed the floor below Python's office, it was all closed off and there were guards in chairs, stationed in front of some metal doors. She said she could hear fans going, only she was cool, and didn't let on she knew anything."

Montclair and her friend Susan Klosmeyer, two girls from the hard-bitten Narrows who'd met in the foster care system when girls—had been high on Giggle Sniff when Suzi had gossiped about Palmares and his base of operations. Klosmeyer was really high back then, and that was the night Montclair knew she had to clean up her own act.

Susan had gone on about how Palmares liked to throw his money around, and was using Giggle Sniff as a stepping stone to bigger things. He'd talked about taking over all the rackets in Gotham.

Bullock nodded. The fans were used to disperse the smell of the chemicals, so as not to call attention to what was supposed to be an empty factory.

"Okay, good," he said, moving his holster to the table and sitting down.

"Are you sure you can pull this off, Harvey?" she asked, glancing over at the remaining emerald-colored powder, licking her bottom lip.

"I'm taking a page from that bat-eared freak's playbook." Bullock chuckled mirthlessly. "First I dug up the blueprint of the factory, from the building department. Then I figured out how to cause the distraction I'll need to take him down."

Montclair stood up again, bending over the table slightly and using the edge of her hand to sweep the Giggle Sniff onto a paper napkin. She balled the paper up and wiped the residue off her hands, sending it falling onto the beige shag carpet. He pictured a cockroach sucking up the drug and getting his mind blown, skittering all over the place.

"But won't he be keeping his money in a safe or something?" she asked, moving to the bathroom.

"Yes, he probably does, sugar tits," he replied, "but I'm going to make him move that money, and that's when the snatch will happen."

"Yeah?" she said brightly. She went into the bathroom again and flushed the balled-up napkin. When she returned she sat on the couch and sank into its listless cushions.

"Oh yeah," he responded.

She smiled crookedly. "Aren't you the smart one?"

He let his gaze linger again on that wonderful cleavage. "Don't smart boys deserve, you know, a reward?"

"I'm flattered, but I'm not that high, big boy." She grinned, a greenish tinge to her gums. "Let's keep this strictly business."

Bullock sighed and took another pull on his flask, watching the baseball game. The Knights were ahead by a run.

18

At the one-time Meskin Oil and Gas headquarters, the three former henchmen took out crowbars, battery-powered drills, and two sledge hammers as they set about searching.

Up here in what had been the Accounts Payable department, taking up a large portion of the eighth floor, there were still intact walls and surprisingly a few desks, chairs, and file cabinets. As this was an old building the walls were plaster and lath, not sheetrock. Sweat and muscle was required to destroy the walls to see if there was something underneath. Broken plaster crunched under their boots, raising a floor-level cloud of white dust that swirled in the intense beams of the halogen flashlights.

"Shit," the man with the missing lobe said, breathing deeply and clutching a heavy sledge hammer in his hands. "There's gotta be a better way to do this."

"Money don't breathe," the guy with the gray mustache responded. "We can't exactly put our ear to the wall and listen for it."

"Breathing's about the only thing it doesn't do," the third said. He was sitting on an abandoned swivel chair, and spun it around once. It squealed and wobbled, threatening to collapse under his excess weight. He bounced out onto his feet and picked up the second sledge hammer. "I'm'a show you rookies how it's done."

"Maybe you can show them later." The guttural voice came out of the shadows that lay beyond the beams. "When you get back from Blackgate."

They gaped at the dark figure, near invisible in the darkness. "Aw, hell," Gray Mustache said.

"You got nothing on us, man," the guy with the missing lobe said, his voice rising. "We ain't broke no laws, so you can just fly off or whatever it is you do, and go roust Black Mask or somebody like that."

"Black Mask isn't looking to buy into the Giggle Sniff trade."

"What are you, a mind reader?"

"Shut up," the third goon hissed.

"Men like you aren't important to me," Batman said, shifting his weight to one side. "I want a line on Palmares and his factory. Talk."

"I've heard what happens to guys that talk to you, freak," Missing Lobe said, tensing. Then he swung the sledge hammer sideways at the man in the black cape. Only his target was no longer there. The ten-pound head of the hammer swished empty air and threw him off balance. Before he could recover, something sunk into his shoulder.

It was shaped like a bat.

He bellowed, his arm spasming so that he had to let go of the hammer. The tool's clattering across the floor echoed in the near-empty space.

Gray Mustache snatched up a crowbar and came at Batman,

desperation giving him a quickness he hadn't had as a younger man. He struck the Dark Knight on his arm, but it didn't seem to have any effect. Batman rolled with the blow, and a side sweep of his foot collided with his assailant's head.

He went down hard.

The former Calendar Man henchman knew when they were licked. He looked to get in the wind because he could see that Missing Lobe wasn't done yet. Plucking the Batarang out of his shoulder, the man was bleeding profusely but he was still standing. Hopefully he'd keep Batman busy just long enough.

"You ain't taking this payday away from us, Batman," Missing Lobe growled. Using his good hand he picked up the crowbar, coming at Batman again. He swung it underhand like a baseball player, trying to crack the Bat's rib cage—but in a blur his wrist was grabbed and snapped even before his brain could fully process what was happening.

"Fuck!" he spat. "You lousy, sanctimonious pointy-eared bastard." He pulled back with his other fist, drenched in blood, then stopped. He didn't want both wrists broken.

"Where is the lab?" Batman said.

"How the hell would I know?" The sonofabitch didn't even have the courtesy to be out of breath.

Batman leaned in, looming like a sentry sent from hell.

"The lab," he repeated.

"Calendar Man," he blurted. "The Calendar Man's man." He felt as if he was going to throw up. "Ask him. He said he had a connection." He cringed under the Bat's stare and looked away, waiting for the next blow. "You heard me?" he said after a pause.

No answer.

He looked up.

Batman was gone.

"He must be feeling magnanimous tonight," he mumbled.

•

Down below, the third man scurried down the stairs, keeping silent as best he could. Darting through the side door he reached the van, and then realized he didn't have the keys.

The problem was too much fast food and cheap booze. Add a bum knee to the mix, and his running was little better than a brisk walk. He glanced over his shoulder, then all around into the shadows. Nothing there, but he knew better. As he turned a corner, there was a barely audible swish in the air.

"Oh shit."

Suddenly his lower legs were entangled in a thin cable. He went airborne, upside down, and his head slammed against a wall, the side of his face colliding with rough bricks. Lights exploded behind his eyes and he screwed them shut as he fought to stay conscious. After a moment he opened them again.

He was hanging upside down from a fire escape.

Batman stood before him.

"Where is the lab?"

"I don't know, man," he gasped. His mouth was impossibly dry, and he had to work saliva around with his tongue. "I've never been there. Just heard about it through one of his people."

"Who?"

"I don't know, man," he repeated.

"The name."

"See, well, that's just it," he said, bile working its way down his throat. "I met him once, kind of on accident, but I figured I could hunt him down again once we had the bankroll. He, uh, he didn't give me a name."

The Bat glared at him.

"Jo-Jo, okay?" He swallowed. "That's his name, the name he goes by anyway."

"Jo-Jo Gagan?"

"Yeah, that's him."

"He's low level," the Bat said. "Not a high roller."

"No, no, he's supposed to be up there in the food chain," he replied. "Dealing big time for the Python. Really! He's the guy you want."

Again the masked vigilante went quiet, his eye slits pulled into tight lines.

"We'll see."

"Yeah, I'm telling you straight. Gagan is the man."

Batman turned and began walking away. Relief flooded over the thug, then he remembered...

"Hey, what about me?" he called, his voice cracking. "You just going to leave me like this?" He wasn't sure, but he thought he heard a chuckle whisper out of the gloom.

19

The six-four Carl Grissom walked out from underneath the sign.

BONUS BROTHERS CARNIVAL
AND AMUSEMENT PARK

His footfalls were silent on the hard-packed dirt. Some of the sign's hand-painted letters were faded. It tilted precariously in place, and the pockmarked surface showed that it had been used for target practice.

Grissom had acquired the dilapidated property from the two so-called "Bonus Brothers" when they were deep into him for their markers. Irv and Stan Bonassa came from the circus world and, when they were younger, had been very hands-on with the amusement park, performing as ringmasters, barkers, chief cooks and bottle washers. They had owned the land, and back in the day people would come from Metropolis, Star City, and beyond to see the two-headed baby, the bearded woman, the half man-half alligator, and other assorted freakish attractions.

But times and tastes changed.

There were still those who came—teenagers who'd heard

about the place from their folks, and groups like the Shriners who might book the place for a special night—but the Bonassas' vices got out of hand. Irv liked the cards and he'd hit a streak now and then, winning big. This led to over-confidence and the chance to lose it all chasing an inside straight or full house that never materialized.

For Stan, the lonely widower, it was about the women.

Past the Ferris Wheel, dark and skeletal on the cold rainy night, and the House of Fun with its creepy clown mouth for an entrance, he stopped at the carousel, one hand in his pocket. Grissom smiled ruefully, looking at the hand-carved horses, elephants, and carriages, brightly painted not that long ago.

A product of the East End with a half-crazy alcoholic mom for a parent, he'd grown up hard. Because he was naturally good with his fists and had a quick wit, he thrived while others from the old neighborhood ended up in the graveyard or doing a bid in Blackgate. He'd been one of the top enforcers for the Galante family and, unlike the other knuckleheads he'd rolled with, he didn't blow his money on booze and broads—well not all of it, anyway.

His chance came when he dated a chick who stripped at a club called the Lacy Pony.

The dude who owned the joint had his nose too much in the Colombian marching powder he dealt on the side. He was behind on the mortgage and Grissom had lent him the money with the appropriate vig attached. Needless to say, the man's business habits hadn't improved, and one day the prospect of another beating from his lender loomed large. He signed the club over to the muscle-turned-entrepreneur, and Carl Grissom became a business owner.

That didn't mean that Grissom had cut the strings from Junior Galante. The crime boss gave him the green light to branch out. In that way Galante was able to launder money and have the girls in the club push drugs on their customers, back in the private VIP rooms.

Grissom got his cut of the action. He figured Galante would one day force him out, but when the day came he'd socked his money away. He then took on the mantle of loan shark, and did the occasional hit, if the price was right.

Stan Bonassa frequented the Lacy Pony, and Grissom got to know him. Stan had a real bad infatuation for one of the broads who worked there, went by the name of Suzi Mustang. Grissom did some checking, and found out about the brother and their holdings. He encouraged Bonassa to spend money on her in one of the back rooms, and was more than happy to get Irv into a few of the underground games around town.

So here he was, owner of a run-down amusement park, or—more correctly—part owner. Wouldn't you know it, but an ex-cop named Gavin Kovaks had already owned a piece of the place. He'd been on the pad to Carmine "The Roman" Falcone back in the day. He'd been busted and did a jolt at Gotham State Penitentiary. When Grissom first met him on the carnival grounds, he'd taken Kovaks for some sort of broke down alkie caretaker. Well the alkie part had been right.

"Yeah, crazy how these things work out, isn't it?" Kovaks said. He smelled like liniment and lost dreams, sitting in his little shack at the back end of the amusement park. A couple of dog-eared skin mags sat on a wobbly table, peeking out from under a dingy dishtowel. There was a poster tacked to one of the walls—Ronald Reagan, but not in the Oval Office. It was a black-and-white of him in his acting days, smiling and squint-eyed on a horse, a cowboy hat atop his head. "But as you can see, Mr. Grissom, right here in this copy of the deed, I got a five percent interest."

"Lemme guess, the original is tucked away someplace safe."

Goddamn Stan Bonassa didn't tell me about this shit.

"Oh yes, sir," Kovaks said cheerily, his goofy fur-lined winter cap cocked on his head, ear flaps down. "Got to protect that which is precious, don't you know? Prison taught me that." He gave an innocent grin.

"Yeah, smart," Grissom drawled, but he knew how it was going to go. Once he found that original deed, Kovaks would be saying *sayonara* to his crappy little shack, permanently. He'd bury him out there near the marsh with those few others, including the newly arrived corpse delivered by Frankie Bones.

He didn't want people to think of this as the disposal graveyard, but a buck was a buck, and Palmares offered top dollar.

"So how is it you own a piece?" Grissom said as casually as he could muster. Kovaks grinned again, and it wasn't a pleasant look for him.

"Back when I was in harness, I got around a lot before that prick Gordon tripped me up." He leaned closer across the small table, increasing the smell. "Stan had a thing for the ladies. He didn't always look like a gnome, like he does now, and back then he had green lining his pockets, yeah?"

Grissom waited, resisting the urge to strangle the man.

"He got to going 'round with this contortionist who worked for him. I seen her do her stuff, and believe me she could put herself in all kinds of positions." The grin turned into a leer.

Grissom remained stone-faced.

Kovaks shrugged. "Anywho, as you might imagine, she caught the eye of more than one guy and this leather vest, chopper type shows up at the office here one time, telling Stan in no uncertain terms he had to keep his mitts off her. The guy slapped him around some to emphasize the point. Wouldn't you know it but ol' Big Tiny the strongman sees this, and as he's the protective type, so he slaps the biker around some."

Now this was interesting.

"Knocked him around too good, and motorcycle boy cracked his head open on the corner of a table." He sat back, spreading his hands. "Good thing the boys had come to me a time or two before, like say when the knife thrower had nicked a dutiful taxpaying citizen, and they needed the trouble to go away."

"For a fee," Grissom guessed.

"Um-hmm." Kovaks paused, a self-satisfied smirk settling on his face. "But getting rid of a body, even that of a reprobate like the biker, isn't as easy as you might think, even in Gotham."

Grissom appreciated initiative. "So for this service, you requested a larger-than-usual payout?"

Kovaks spread his arms wide, like a priest about to give a blessing.

"It was sweet for a while," he said. "Getting my little quarterly percentage." He shook his head. "It was amazing, too, how much they made on popcorn and cotton candy alone. But those days are gone."

"I see the power is still on," Grissom said. He'd flicked on a light in what had been the main office.

"There was some money left in the operations fund, and I figured I might as well keep up with the light bill as long as possible. It's only on in a few specific places, because you can do that with a commercial property. I'm betting we can sell the park. People always want to laugh. The right owner comes along, and who knows?" He beamed.

"You think so?" What Grissom figured was to hold onto the land long enough, and sell to a developer who would raze all this clown crap and build an outlet mall or something. Of course, if by then he had a few bodies to unearth, chop up, and burn, it'd be no big thing.

He checked his watch. He had a plane to catch to Miami.

"Oh yes, it could be a hell of a carnival again," Kovaks said. "Wouldn't take much to make a real go of it, I'm figuring. I've got a few feelers out now, you know, looking for investors."

"Uh-huh," Grissom said. He wasn't convinced, but decided it wasn't worth wasting the breath to argue. Rising, he took a last look around. "You never know, Kovaks, you never know."

20

Police Commissioner James Gordon's office at Gotham Central was as orderly and unadorned as the man himself. There was an old-fashioned wood desk upon which sat a gooseneck lamp, a combination phone and intercom, and a stack of manila file folders of varying thicknesses. In front of the desk were two chairs and behind it a swivel chair that needed a new ball bearing.

The folders represented a wide variety of concerns, all of which he needed to address at some point. There were open cases from the Major Crimes and Homicide units, disciplinary matters, budgetary concerns, and more. *Plenty* more.

His office door boasted a frosted glass window with his title stenciled on it. Just outside stood a water cooler and a bank of three battered metal file cabinets.

It was daytime, and the Venetian blinds kept the sunlight at bay. Outside the window there was a ledge that, at times, seemed to have more traffic than the office door. Especially at night.

Because it was daytime, however, Gordon preferred not to be holed up in his office if he didn't have to be. He shut the file concerning an officer-involved shooting. A perp had tried, unsuccessfully, to rob Empire Liquors in Crime Alley. It was a simple administrative matter, and now that it was past tense, he stood to take his customary stroll through headquarters.

"Heading out, Commissioner?" his administrative assistant asked. Helen Flynn wore a crisp, starched white shirt buttoned at the wrist and a dark blue skirt that rose a scintilla above the knees. Her desk was located just outside of his frosted glass door. From that vantage point she could see his comings and goings, and look out over the entire open area where detectives and civil service employees went about their business.

"Eventually," he said absentmindedly. Something about the shooting incident stuck in the back of his mind, and he considered having his detail take him over to Empire Liquors, to see the scene in person. Photographs only revealed so much. Maybe he wasn't out on the streets anymore, but he wasn't going to let his brain go soft. Not like he'd done with his middle. He'd never been built like Batman—not even when he was a cop on the beat—but he used to keep in fairly decent shape, doing push-ups, weights, and shadow boxing.

Where had those days gone?

"I'll let you know when I leave the building," Gordon said, pulling on his jacket and promising himself to get back into a health regimen.

"Sounds good," she said.

Gordon walked through the rows of metal desks, nodding to this or that plainclothes officer or dispatcher. Most were concentrating on their work, but a few nodded back. He spotted Harvey Bullock as he entered the room.

"Harvey, have a minute?"

"Sure, Commissioner." Bullock paused, and Gordon joined him. Together they strolled in the general direction of the detective's desk.

"Where do we stand with Python Palmares and his lab?" the Commissioner asked. "Have any of your CIs been forthcoming? This damnable Giggle Sniff epidemic is just getting worse, and we've got to get a handle on it."

Damn the Joker, he thought. *Is that madman going to be the bane of Gotham forever?*

"I've been leaning on a couple of them," Bullock replied. "Had to get pretty firm with a couple of them."

"You didn't work any of them over with a phone book, did you, Harvey?" the Commissioner said dubiously. "That bought us a world of trouble the last time." The two found themselves standing off to one side in the operations section. Personnel sat at a bank of consoles with screens that made it look like an air traffic control tower. Incidents of lesser and greater degrees of severity were being called in. Each person wore a headset, and a few sat in front of bulky computer monitors.

"No, no," Bullock said. "Hands off, and strictly by the book. I mean, *adhering* to the book, not using it like a club."

Gordon regarded the disheveled detective. The incident had led to a two-weeks' suspension without pay, and Bullock was lucky it hadn't been worse. On the plus side, Harvey's extreme methods had revealed where an eleven-year-old had been buried alive, and enabled them to rescue her before she suffocated.

The detective continued. "Palmares might be using the old Apex cement plant—or what's left of it—for his operation. I'm told he's got a couple of the old chemists from Ace Chemicals on his payroll. I'm going to check out the location this afternoon, strictly on the sly."

Gordon considered this.

"Keep me in the loop."

"Of course, Commish. I mean, sir."

"And Harvey, how about a shave," Gordon added. "I allow a lot of latitude with the detectives, but there are limits."

"You got it," Bullock said, scratching at his chin. "Is that all, boss?"

"Yes, Harvey, that's all for now."

Bullock gave a slight nod, then turned and left. Absently Gordon adjusted his glasses as he watched the man go. *God help him*, Gordon reflected. More than once he should have busted Bullock back down to patrol, but the sonofabitch got results. Like Batman his unconventionality helped him keep the madness at bay, and wasn't that the bigger goal?

Loath to admit it, Gordon needed those like Bullock—the Id he could release when it was needed to maintain the order.

As long as he doesn't stray too far over the line.

As he moved away from the operations area, Gordon remembered another cop, someone a lot like Bullock, in a way. Gavin Kovaks had been a captain and, like Harvey, he'd employed whatever methods were needed to get the job done. Unlike Harvey, though, Kovaks always dressed sharp—too sharp for a plainclothesman. The latest cut to his suit, maybe a stickpin in his tie, and his shoes always polished to a fresh out-of-the-box shine.

In hindsight, Gordon realized such had screamed *"Hey, I'm on the take."* Kovaks had danced too close to the line, but solved a lot of thorny cases. Once he'd *crossed* the line, there had been no going back.

Ego aside, Gordon knew what the difference was—what kept Bullock more or less in line.

Batman.

Bullock knew that if he truly crossed the line, the masked vigilante would be relentless in bringing him to justice. Sometimes Gordon thought it had led to a competition of sorts. As if Harvey felt like he needed to prove himself. Prove that he was better than the Bat.

Eschewing the elevator he started up the two flights of stairs that led to the rooftop. Once again he swore that he would get back to the gym. The roof was where aero squad was located—the patrol blimps that patrolled the skies above the city.

Reaching the top he stopped and took a few deep breaths.

Maybe he'd take up jogging, like his daughter Barbara.

"Aw, who am I kidding," he muttered as he pushed the crash bar on the door, stepping out onto the roof. Instantly a stiff wind caught his hair and whipped at his jacket. Jogging was boring, but maybe he'd take up yoga, just to stay limber. That might be just the thing.

Kung fu and yoga classes…

Yeah, he chuckled inwardly. *That'll be the day.*

21

Hands on his hips, Python Palmares stared into the impound yard and regarded the wrecked AMX. He and Frankie Bones stood at the chain-link fence, looking over the collection of cars, pickups, and even a giant yellow duck once used by the Penguin. It sat rusting in a far corner.

"They got our college shipment," he muttered.

"That damn slip Batgirl is getting to be as bothersome as the Big Bat," Bones said.

Palmares made a sucking sound, running his tongue over newly installed teeth. "You ain't kidding."

"Maybe we should move along, Python. No sense moping around here, and some curious cop comes over to ask us why."

Palmares tapped the keepsake he kept around his neck, the clasped silver heart inlaid with ivory.

"You know what's in here, right?"

"Sure boss, some of the ashes of your older brother, Gino."

Palmares held up an index finger. "A true stand-up guy. Hardcore member of the original Red Hood gang, yeah?"

"Yeah," Bones agreed.

"And did he get his due?"

"He did not," Bones said.

"Damn right he didn't," Palmares said softly, his voice breaking slightly. This was what pushed him to claw his way to the top. He owed it to Gino, and his legacy.

Palmares looked past the hulks of vehicles to the gray stone of the building beyond. This was central lockup, where three of his crew were languishing. He wasn't worried about them talking—they knew he'd see to getting them a mouthpiece. But replacing personnel took time and money, and he was in expansion mode. That meant watching every cent.

He needed to show those slicksters at Intergang he could handle the freight. The Bats were making him look bad. Maybe it'd been kind of stupid to have Frankie Bones drive him over here, but part of him wanted to show the law he wasn't scared of them. Another part of him had hoped his product might still be hidden in the car, but even from here he could tell the cops had been over it like cockroaches on a biscuit with syrup.

"Okay, let's blow."

The two walked back to a black Lincoln. Bones got behind the wheel, and Palmares sat on the tuck-and-roll leather in the back. The car had suicide doors, and its back window was padded with a diamond shape cut out in the center. Bones fired up the gas-gobbling V8, and the two drove away.

Palmares picked up the radio-telephone and asked the mobile operator for a number. After a couple of rings, there was a click on the other end.

"Suzi," he said, "This is Python. Seems there's an opening in my organization. Let's talk about that idea of yours over dinner tonight." He listened to her enthusiastic response, then said,

"Good. The Ocelot, yeah, that's a better class of joint. Make it 7:30, okay? Right, see you then."

He hung up the handset.

"You think the broad can handle the weight?" Bones asked from the front seat.

"She's got what you call ambition, Frankie," he replied. "Plus, men drool at her rack and think she ain't got a brain upstairs. But she does. I know she does."

"You notice it when you got your hands on the rack, you mean," Bones quipped.

Palmares chuckled. He settled back in his seat and stared out of the side window, watching the sights of Gotham roll by. Bats or no, he was going to make this city his.

22

Susan "Suzi Mustang" Klosmeyer sat in the cramped dressing room of the Lacy Pony, balanced on a rickety chair reading a paperback about the habits of successful people. All she wore was a short robe, bikini bottom, and fishnets. The air in the tiny space was hot and close.

Canned music thumped through the walls, rattling the plastic hydrogen peroxide bottles and makeup tubes on the twin vanities. The traditional bump and grind music, favoring the sax and bombastic drums, had been replaced on the sound system with synthesizer electronics like the soundtrack to a science fiction flick, and beats that seemed to repeat endlessly. Worse was that mess they called rap that occasionally got thrown into the mix, and made her grit her teeth.

The music died down and the catcalls and whoops rose from the assembled mouth breathers. Mustang sighed and set aside her book, using an old tassel as a bookmark. She rose as Diane Jalivarez—who went by Lilly St. Regis—breezed in from the stage. She held a decent amount of wrinkly cash, clutching it to her substantial sweaty breasts. Most of it was of the one-dollar variety, Suzi observed smugly as St. Regis plopped the bills onto one of the tabletops. A few drifted to the floor.

At the other vanity sat a girl who only went by the name Dakota. She sat with her back to the mirror, legs crossed and filing her nails.

"Oh, how I love me my frat boys," Jalivarez gushed. She dropped to her knees to get the bills off the floor, and made it a production as she counted her take from that position. It was some kind of goofball good luck thing she did after each set. Dakota and Mustang exchanged a look.

Then it was Mustang's turn as the strip joint's disc jockey Tricky Ricky announced her. She pulled together her outfit, including leather gloves with sleeves that went up her forearms, and had brass studs along the seams.

"And now the one you've been salivating for," Ricky said theatrically. "The one who can bring life to the dead, and make the blind see when she wiggles those God-given magnificent melons. The one, the only… Suziiii Mustaaang."

The music cranked up again to an eardrum-pulsing level, drowning out the clapping and hooting. Mustang steeled herself as she stepped through the gap in the sequined curtain. Overhead, twirling light balls splayed reflected bright white all over the stage, the backdrop, and Tricky Ricky at his control board off to the side. Mini spotlights, operating on synchromesh rotors, jittered her form in circles of red, orange, and yellow.

"Oh, baby, I'm in love," a heavyset man yelled. He wore glasses too small for his round head.

"I'm in lust!" another shouted, gulping down a bottle of overpriced beer. He had on a sweatshirt for Gotham University's rowing team.

"Come on boys," Mustang said, launching into her spiel as she began dancing. "Don't be shy, 'cause I sure won't be."

That got them going. She'd taken a cue from the old pros, updating the opera gloves with the leather. Over her bikini bottom she wore a leopard-spotted loin cloth like a pin-up version of a cave girl, and a matching top that barely covered her ample bosom.

Then she started to dance, focusing on the moves. Long ago she'd learned that she could do it on autopilot, but that would show on her face and how she moved her body. The droolers might throw some bills her way, but that would be on autopilot, too. To get them into the moment, make them feel as if they were *sharing* this time of intimacy, Mustang had to *act*. Had to make it seem as if the music was flowing through her, and give it all she had.

She had to keep the men drinking, too, since that made the house happy.

"Yeah, baby, that's what Mama likes," she said, slipping a leg over one guy's shoulder and pumping her hips lasciviously. All the men roared save for one. He sat back from the others, big arms folded over his barrel chest, his baseball cap pulled low over his forehead. She saw him back there in the dimness, and they shared a brief smile. Then she turned around, bent over and jiggled her rear. That got the pipeline flowing, and the bills cascaded onto the stage—not singles but twenties.

When her top came off another roar went up. Mustang threw her arms in the air and put a smile on her face, letting her head loll back as she basked in the adoration.

She knew the audience was putting on an act, too, for they were in the moment, but she didn't care. If any of them passed her on the street, and she was dressed in normal clothes, they wouldn't recognize her. It wasn't as if any of them even knew what her face looked like. To them she was only an object of sexual desire, and there was a comforting degree of anonymity in that. Here Mustang wielded the power.

But it would be Susan Klosmeyer who reaped the benefits.

The music wound down, and the colored spotlights went dark. Her set over, she blew a kiss to the lonely and the lurking. Gathering up her money, she exited to the dressing room, where another dancer had arrived for her shift. Breathing heavily, Mustang grabbed up a towel to blot at her face and upper body. That done, she put her money in the damp towel, and folded the cloth over.

"Aren't you going to impress us with your stack?" St. Regis said acidly.

"I wouldn't want to make you jealous," she replied. She began to change into street clothes. This had been her last set, and she wanted to get out of here.

"Uh-huh. Like you're all that."

The Lacy Pony's owner encouraged the girls to work so-called "after hours" sets, which meant giving lap dances. If a customer was particularly generous in his donation, that dance could include various extras, and the boss only took twenty percent off the top.

St. Regis was all about those extras.

Mustang knew she should ignore the snark, but small-timers like St. Regis had to be reminded there were people not to mess with. Tucking her bundled towel in a backpack, she walked over to where St. Regis sat on the rickety chair, smoking a cigarette.

"Don't be shy, Diane," she said flatly. "You got something to say, say it."

St. Regis stabbed the cigarette at her.

"Look, skank, maybe you think your—"

Mustang kicked the legs out from under the chair. They broke and went skittering over the dirty rug as the seat dropped to the floor with a bang. The recently arrived stripper let out a gasp and gaped. Dakota just watched.

"Bitch, you're going to regret that." St. Regis was on her butt, trying to get off the floor. Before she could, Mustang sent the backpack upside her head knocking her sideways. Then she loomed over her, pointing down at the dazed dancer.

"I won't tell you how to shake that saggy rump of yours," she said, "and you *damn* sure better keep your trap shut when it comes to my business. Nod if you understand, or I'm happy to make your head go up and down."

St. Regis glared venomously, but did as commanded.

"Glad we could have this little chat, and clear the air and shit." She threw the backpack over her shoulder—it held the money, her costume, platform boots, and a flashlight with two D batteries. As she moved to leave, Tricky Ricky stepped to the doorway.

"Boss would like a word with you, Suzi," he said. "Says it's in your best interests."

"Tell him I got a date tonight, Ricky."

"He won't like that as an answer."

"Is that right?" she said, slipping past him. "I guess you've gotta break the bad news to him then." Pushing through the side exit, she stepped out into the chill air.

As usual, there were a couple of men who, augured by booze and delusional lust, looked to spark it up, impress her with a wad of dough and the promise of fancy dinners and jewelry if only they could have a date—a *real* date.

It wasn't about sex, *oh no*.

Tonight was no different. One of the regulars—Chuck something, she recalled—was standing at the base of the metal steps, a raft of roses in his hand. Over the door was a cowled light bulb. She almost felt pity for the poor bastard. As she descended, she could see the lighter band of skin on his left hand, where normally his wedding ring would be.

"These are for you, Suzi."

No kidding. "That's sweet, but club rules state we can't fraternize with the customers."

"B-but I'm more than a c-customer," he stammered, "I'm an admirer."

"Look, Chuck—it's Chuck, right?"

"Dave."

"Dave. I'm flattered but the rules are the rules." She tried to move past, but using the cellophane-wrapped bouquet like a truncheon, he levered them toward her face. Instinctively she pushed them away.

"Hey!" she said loudly.

"Please, you mustn't rush," he said. "Everybody's in a rush in this town."

Something dropped out of the flowers, and pinged when it hit the pavement. It was a diamond ring. Or at least an imitation one. Dave was wearing corduroys and sneakers, and didn't look like he was made of money.

Looking down, then up, he said, "Th-that was supposed to be a surprise."

"It was," someone said off to her left.

Mustang turned to see the beefy man with the cap standing there. The logo on the cap was a piece of machinery, with the company name in a semicircle above the picture.

"Get on home, Dave," the newcomer said. "I'll take it from here."

"Now see here," Dave began, "who are you to order me around?" While the other man was taller and more muscular, Dave obviously spent too much time sitting behind a desk. Nevertheless, the allure of Suzi Mustang had fired a courage originating in his libido.

"Hi, Brad," she said.

"Hey, baby."

Dave looked as if he'd been punched in the gut, but he got the message. Pocketing the ring, he dropped the flowers on the bottom rung of the steps, and retreated quickly, if not gracefully.

"Who needs Batman, when I have you?" Mustang said, beaming. She put her arm in the crook of his, they moved out of the alley, and walked along the nearly deserted street.

"Sorry I wasn't waiting for you," he said. "When I got in past dawn today, I sacked out, and then after I got up and had a bite to eat, I rushed right over here. But the cab was kind of messy from the road, and I wanted to straighten it up for my lady."

"Nothing to worry about, honey."

He grinned down at her, patting her hand. They got to his bobtail truck. The same logo was printed on the side, along with a name.

Tri-State Freight

Brad Ashford was the owner-operator of a fleet of one truck. Tonight, however, he was looking to expand his enterprise—an expansion not without its share of risk. Yet Ashford was willing to roll those dice when it came to the woman who walked beside him.

Unlocking the passenger side door, he placed a hand under her elbow, and she stepped up into the truck. She wrinkled her nose at the fruity smell. Overkill, but that was Brad. Once he was in, he was all the way in. Once she'd talked him into becoming a criminal, he was determined to give it his best.

Ashford got behind the wheel, turning the key. The engine roared to life and they rumbled away from the Lacy Pony.

"You nervous?"

"A little," she admitted, "but Palmares set this up, so these guys shouldn't be trying any funny business." She always made sure to refer to the drug lord by his last name when she was with Ashford. She didn't want him to know what was going on between her and the boss.

Or that this was all about the money.

He turned on the radio-cassette deck, tapped a button, and tape could be heard whirring. The volume set to low. Rather than the usual country-and-western tune coming out of the cab's speakers, a crooner sang a love ballad.

What a sap.

Mustang stared out the windshield, her mouth set in a grim line. This was it. After tonight, her life would be completely different or more likely she'd be dead. She reviewed everything as they drove along. Given that Giggle Sniff was a local product, Palmares didn't have to worry about sneaking the stuff in by the ports or rails, and having to pay off any of the mob families. He maintained several distribution centers in the greater Gotham area, and was determined to keep them hidden.

One of Palmares' distributors, Jo-Jo Gagan, had up and suddenly disappeared. That had to mean he was worm food, she concluded. But the hole he left in the organization, his campus men getting busted, had been the opportunity for which she'd been waiting. Sure enough, she'd tried to sound properly pleased when Palmares had called her.

Following her directions, Ashford brought them into the Robbinsville area along a highway overpass, exited, and moved down into a cement roadway lined with one- and two-story buildings. This was Airplane Alley, known as such because it had been a manufacturing area specializing in single-engine aircraft and related parts production. The name had stuck, even though the aviation industry had long ago moved away. Today the facilities turned out everything from wooden window blinds to pre-fab bookcases. It wasn't unusual to see a truck like Ashford's coming and going, not even at night.

"There's the place," she said, pointing. She glanced down the street, but didn't see anyone else. *Good*, she thought.

"Right." He pulled to a stop at a nondescript stucco building with a large rollaway door. There was a faded, block-letter sign above the entrance.

SIKORSKY CAMSHAFTS

The engine idling, the truck's headlights shone dull white on the corrugated surface of the door. A metallic grinding sound came from inside the building as a chain and pulley was worked, and the rollaway slid up. Ashford eased his vehicle inside the dimly lit loading dock and shut off the engine. They got out, squinting into the shadows.

The door remained open.

Mustang's eyebrows went up as a man in a dark windbreaker stepped from the rear of the establishment. At first glance she thought this was Two-Face, but quickly realized it was only the skin on one of the man's cheeks. Deformed not from acid, like the former district attorney, but by acne scars. It had a pock-marked, waxy look to it. She had to remind herself not to stare.

He was flanked by two men carrying assault rifles.

Behind him in the half-light, bolted to what had been the shop floor, were the drill presses, lathes, and other types of machinery once used to turn out the camshafts. Though solid and seemingly intact, their disuse was evident from the cobwebs and a thick layer of dust. Here and there were gloves, goggles, even coffee mugs and empty bottles.

The man spoke. "You know how this works," he said. There was a large empty table off to one side, and he moved over to it.

"What about the goods?" Ashford said.

The man smiled crookedly. "Of course." He didn't seem to make any sort of gesture but a third hood, wearing a handgun in a shoulder holster, stepped into view. He carried two stuffed gym bags, and set these on the table with a dull *thud*. Then he unzipped one and stepped back, hands clasped before him.

"Go ahead, check it out," said the pock-marked man.

Stepping away from Ashford, Mustang went over to the

unzipped bag. It was stuffed with glassine packets stamped with a black round oval with a distorted wide white laughing mouth. She wondered if this was how the Joker saw himself, when he looked in a mirror, and smiled grimly at the thought. Casually she opened one of the packets. Touching the tip of her little finger to her tongue, she sampled some of the drug.

"Oh, yes," she said, snorting and squinting. She zipped up the bag and reached for them both. The pock-marked man put a hand on her wrist. Ashford tensed but a sharp look from Mustang cooled him down.

"Python's taking a hell of a chance on you." His gaze was steady on her.

"I'm a big girl, I know what I'm doing."

"You better."

Mustang nodded at Ashford. He went to the truck's cab. One of the hoods went with him, rifle held at the ready. The trucker took out a paper grocery bag, rolled shut, and handed it to the hood who took it back to the scarred man. He put the bag on the table and opened it up to look inside at the rubber-banded stacks of money.

"Looks like you're a Giggle Sniff investor." He refolded the top of the paper bag.

"Aren't you gonna count it?" Ashford said. The way he understood it from Suzi was they were putting up a certain amount of money, the bulk of the funds. Aside from what he'd put in the kitty, he was still not clear how she'd obtained such. Sure her having a bodacious bod had all those hooting drunks raining twenties on her in the club, but there seemed to be way more than that in the bag.

Still, the idea was that in the other gym bag was an amount that Palmares was advancing them, twice what they'd brought. The money and the Giggle Sniff were their calling cards, so to speak, to expand Palmares' operation in other cities. In particular the money was to be used to grease the wheels, bribing this or that cop or judge in the other municipalities.

The scarred man frowned and fixed his gaze on the truck driver, then shot a glance to his men.

"You looking to short us?" That earned a chuckle from the muscle with the shoulder holster.

"No, it's just that—" Ashford began.

"It's okay, Brad," Mustang said, touching his arm. To the head man she said, "We're good."

One of the hoods carried one of the gym bags and the paper sack, the three of them walking over to the truck. Abruptly there was a squealing sound out on the street, and through the maw of the rollaway door she saw two vehicles come screaming around the corner. One was a tricked-out Camaro, lowered in front and raised in the rear on dual fat drag-racing tires. The windows were smoked, and a supercharger stuck out of the hood.

In its wake came a van with mag wheels, keeping pace with its companion as they passed under a street light. Airbrushed on the side of the van were two absurdly muscled barbarians, one a female with balloon-like tits. Each brandished a gleaming sword.

"The hell?" The guy with the shoulder holster went for his weapon. He shot them an angry glare.

Mustang raised her hands like she was being held up,

shaking her head side to side. Inwardly she tried her best to hold off panic.

Where the fuck…?

The Camaro fishtailed, skidding to a stop on the street, with the passenger side facing them. The power window came down and a figure in a scarecrow's mask opened fire with a machine gun.

23

"Get cover," somebody yelled as bullets flew everywhere.

One of the hoodlums holding a rifle unleashed a clutch of rounds. His body was held upright as he jerked spasmodically, then he collapsed, seemingly swallowed up in his heaped clothes.

The machine-gunner in the scarecrow mask opened the door and stepped out of the car, his gun rattling and the barrel smoking. The van pulled to a stop, blocking the loading dock entrance, and the side door slid open. Two more guys, also wearing scarecrow masks, jumped out. One brandished a shotgun, and the other had a .45 in each fist.

Mustang and Ashford took cover behind his truck.

The scarred man ducked behind an upright drill press. The machine gun's rounds pinged off the industrial machine's thick iron body. Without showing the slightest hint of alarm, he reached inside his windbreaker and produced a grenade. Pulling the pin he tossed it underhanded at his targets.

"Oh *shi*—"

Before the scarecrow could finish the device exploded directly to his right, where the Camaro was. The car's gas-filled tank sparked and it went up in a loud blast of fire and flame. The guy was thrown through the air and his head struck an exposed steel beam in the doorway. He was dead before his body fell to the grease-stained concrete floor.

The passenger door of the Camaro went flying end over end through the air and careened off of the wall.

"Babe, we need to get out of here fast," Ashford said. She looked through the loading dock doorway. The hulk of the Camaro was still on fire, and fuel burned and smoked in puddles on the ground near the remains. More scarecrows exited the van, also focused on the drug dealers. She noticed the driver's door was open.

"I'll get the van," Mustang said. "You've got to get the other two bags." In the confusion, the hood who'd been carrying the two bags of money had tossed them aside to shoot at the invaders.

He paused, frowning.

"Both of them, Brad," she emphasized.

"Okay," he said quickly. "Be careful."

"You too." She gave him a peck on the cheek and ran, thankful her boots had short heels. She held one of the gym bags full of Giggle Sniff. As the firefight continued, punctuated by cursing and a moan of pain, she reached the van.

The interior was like something out of one of those beach blanket movies she used to watch as a kid. There was shag carpeting, a bed in back with heart-shaped red pillow, and the seats up front covered in Naugahyde. Fuzzy dice hung from the rearview mirror, completing the cliché.

The engine was running and she slammed the van into gear. An errant round pierced the windshield, but missed her entirely. She backed the van up, tires squealing, clearing the exit and the burning vehicle. From overhead a beam of light pierced the darkness.

Oh, crap!

A loud, amplified voice filled the air from the GCPD patrol blimp.

"You down there, patrol cars and the fire department are on their way," it boomed from the sky. "They will be heavily armed. Cease all hostilities and place your firearms on the ground where we can see them. Otherwise we cannot guarantee your safety."

As Mustang hit the brakes, she glanced into the side rearview mirror. Smoke from the burning car had drifted across the building's opening. She couldn't see anything that was happening. Ashford hadn't emerged and the gunfire continued and she began to fear the worst.

She glanced at the seat beside her, and the bag full of dope the addicts couldn't get enough of in Gotham. How much was that worth on the street? The damn law wasn't here yet, and she still could make a clean break. The blimp would stay where the action was, and as long as another one didn't show up, she could slip away. It wasn't the plan, but if she was going to change her life...

Well, shit, a girl's gotta improvise.

She gunned the gas. She'd been playing Brad for a chump anyway, so this was how it was going to end for him, sooner or later. He got stuck in there—okay, too bad, he didn't deserve that—but the dope game wasn't for the faint-hearted. She was almost to the end of the street when she saw what she was looking for and stomped on the brakes.

A lone figure ran over and opened the passenger door.

"Where the fuck were you?" she demanded, then didn't give the newcomer a chance to answer "I gotta go back for him." The figure stopped halfway in the van.

"I'll go with you." It was a woman.

"No, if this goes bad, you'll just get yourself killed," she said. "No sense in that. Besides, if I don't get shot, I may need you to bail me out." She smiled grimly.

"Okay, then take these," the other one said, placing two black canisters on the seat. They had pull pins and fit easily in the palm of a hand.

"Wish me luck," Mustang said.

The other woman leaned over and kissed her on the lips.

"Good luck, baby."

Wearing a shit-eating grin Mustang wheeled the van around, rear tires smoking and screeching on the asphalt as she did a donut.

Now who's a sap? She chuckled.

She raced back toward the building. As she came closer, damned if Ashford didn't come stumbling out of the haze. He was bleeding from the side of his head and limping, and there was a dark stain on his slacks, but he had the bloody grocery bag under his arm and the other gym bag at his side. One of the scarecrows also emerged from the pall. He was bleeding from his torso and took aim with his shotgun, pointing it at Ashford's back.

Mustang rammed the masked robber with the van. With a sickening *thump* he flew several feet and caromed off a street light.

"Let's go!" she shouted, leaning over and pushing open the passenger side door.

"You don't have to tell me twice." He was halfway in, leaning the bulk of his body on the seat as she backed up again, spinning the wheels. Sirens bleated through the air. Ashford grunted and hauled himself all the way into the van.

Two more scarecrows emerged from the smoke.

"Use those," Mustang said, indicating the canisters. "Pull the pins and toss them."

He did as instructed. The grenades arced through the air, then went off with bangs and intense flashes of light. The hoods dropped their guns and clawed at their eyes.

"Go that way," Ashford said, closing the door and pointing toward a narrow street. It wasn't the way they'd come.

"That looks like a dead end," she said.

"I know this area from deliveries I've done around here," he said. "The cops'll be coming in the same way we did. Douse those lights," he added, pointing at the dashboard.

"I hear you." Mustang turned off the headlights and drove along, straining to see. She banged into some trash cans, scattering them and the garbage they contained.

"Crap!" She over-compensated, steering the opposite way and heading alarmingly toward a brick wall, but then centered the van again along the roadway.

"It's okay," he said, patting her arm. "We're cool." The sirens were louder than ever. "Steady now, just go slow."

Reassurance, fear, and irritation mingled in her as she peered through the gloom, trying to discern their path. Ahead to her left she had the impression there was a gap in the wall, but she wasn't sure.

"Here," Ashford said, "turn right here."

She tapped the brake. "What is this?"

"Just do it, Suzi."

"Yes, master," she cracked, making the turn. The space was tight, and the rear end of the van bumped the wall on the passenger side, but they made it through. She then had the sensation of going downhill. "Brad, I can't see a damned thing." She wasn't about to admit how scared she was.

"Yeah, okay, turn on the parking lights," he suggested. "That should do the trick."

She fumbled with the unfamiliar controls, but found the knob on the dashboard and gave it a twist. The way ahead of them was bathed in dim amber light, but compared to the blackness it was plenty. Their van was on a concrete ramp that descended into an underground parking garage.

A few cars were present in the mostly empty space. Square columns served as supports. Several sections of concrete were missing from columns where a vehicle's bumper had chipped away at them.

"Hold up," Ashford said.

Mustang stopped the van a little faster than she meant to, shifting into neutral but keeping the engine on. She strained her ears but didn't hear anything other than the idling of the motor. After the frenetic activity they'd left behind them, time seemed to move in slow motion. They sat there for what seemed to be forever.

"This way," Ashford said, pointing. She jumped a little at the sound of his voice.

"How'd you know this was down here?" she asked as they started forward again, moving slowly now. "Your truck wouldn't fit on that ramp."

"This garage is used by the workers around here," he explained. "Since it's kind of tucked away, drivers like me get invited for beers and cards sometimes, especially at the end of the day."

She gave him a sideways glance. "What else goes on down here?"

He smiled and pointed. "There's the other ramp."

"You sure about this?"

"Trust me."

Following his lead, she drove up a ramp on the other side of the parking garage. It took them onto a street further away from the turmoil. The sirens had stopped, and in the van's rearview the GCPD blimp hung in the sky, its twin spotlights beaming down steadily on the police mop-up operation.

•

It didn't seem like a good idea to go to either of their homes, at least not yet, Mustang warned. At her suggestion, they drove to a place called the Aparo Motel. The guy at the front desk didn't even glance twice at them, or at the cash they used to pay for the room—in advance.

It wasn't a bad place. Spartan, with a few stains on the carpet and some mildew in the bathroom, but nothing particularly disgusting. There was a TV in the room, secured to a platform up in a corner of the ceiling near a dried water stain.

As they stepped into the room, Mustang made sure the door didn't close completely. Ashford didn't notice. They dumped the duffle and the paper grocery bag on one of the two beds, along with some fast food and beer they'd picked up along the way. Mustang walked over beneath the television set, stretched up on tiptoes, and twisted the dial that turned it.

The first thing that came on was an in-house commercial for "adult" movies. She changed the channel to WGNN. Sure enough, there was an Action News bulletin.

"...authorities believe the shootout occurred between a group of drug dealers and associates of Jonathan Crane, better known as the Scarecrow," the news anchor said. Behind him there was footage of the area they'd just vacated, with the police blimp still hovering in the sky. "His current whereabouts are unknown, and the Commissioner's office has issued a statement saying that they do not know if Crane himself was behind the heist."

She turned the volume down while an image of a wounded hoodlum, handcuffed to a gurney, played on the television. They unwrapped the fast food and beer.

"How am I going to explain my truck being there?" Ashford sat in the room's one chair, his elbow leaning on a small round table. His open can of beer sat next to a thick glass ashtray.

"I don't know," Mustang said, shrugging, then she brightened. "They stole it." She sat on the bed, legs crossed. A hamburger sat on an open wrapper, and she'd squeezed out some catsup next to it. Several French fries dangled from her fingers as she dipped them into the condiment. She gobbled them down wolfishly.

"None of those hardheads will back that story up," he protested.

"No, they won't, but what does that matter? You're a solid, upright, tax-paying citizen. Who're the cops going to believe—you or a bunch of crooks and drug dealers?" She took a bite out of the burger. Narrowly escaping death and arrest had made her ravenous.

"The cops are gonna press." He wiped his hand over his face, pulling it down, distorting his features. "Why didn't I report it stolen?"

She shook a bunch of fries at him. "You were with me and you… lost track of time. Yeah, that's it." She grinned at that. "In fact, call the police in about an hour, to say you just saw your truck was missing."

"I don't know…"

"Don't think so hard." She got off the bed, walked over, and sat on his lap. "Baby, we got away with the cash. We're going to be set."

He shook his head. "Maybe I'm not cut out for this kind of thing. I mean, I guess I got carried away, being with you… living the high life." He shook his head again. "And what about the Giggle Sniff?"

"It was never about the dope." She got off his lap, standing and waiting.

"What do you mean?"

"She means it was always about the money."

Ashford jumped up like a startled rabbit and gaped at the newcomer. It was a woman, conservatively dressed all in form-fitting black and wearing glasses.

"Hey, girl," Mustang said. "It's about time."

"Who the hell are you?" the truck driver demanded as the other woman stepped into the room, closing the door behind her.

"I'm your silent partner," she said.

"Brad, this is Wanda," Mustang said. "Wanda Washawski. She's got the connections that're going to turn our money into gold." He frowned, and she added, "Wanda used to do the books for the Lacy Pony. That's how we got to know each other."

"Huh?" Ashford said. He pointed a finger at Mustang. "Wait a minute. You had this worked out already, didn't you?" He didn't seem happy.

He looked hurt, angry, and confused. She thought it was sort of cute, in a stupid kind of way.

"Yeah, the two of us did," she responded. "It's our way of getting out from under Python, Galante—all of those scumbags. Scoring a payday that'll let us tell them where they can shove it."

It was dawning on him what the score was. "You always figured to rip off Palmares' dough?"

"That's right," Mustang confirmed.

Washawski sat down. "We never intended to sell dope, we wouldn't sink that low," she explained. "The idea was for me to lob a couple of stun grenades into the warehouse, along with a smoke device, grab the money and the drugs, and take off in the chaos. I had in place a false trail so that Palmares would blame a rival gang, and we'd be in the clear."

"But he still might suspect it was an inside job," Ashford said.

"That's true," Washawski replied, "but we'd stick around, no big cars or diamonds. This money from tonight and what I've been skimming from Python's money laundering, that sum is by my calculations the right amount to reap long-term rewards in this new venture."

"This new venture isn't drugs?" Ashford said.

"But then the Scarecrows conveniently showed up," she continued as if not hearing him. "You and Suzi improvised masterfully, I must say. They'll never suspect us, and with luck they'll think the money was absconded with given a couple of them got away."

Ashford tried to absorb all this.

"What now?" he asked, his voice edgy. "If we're not going to sell the drugs."

"Now we go forward," she said, looking pleased with herself.

"It's called the Arpanet and if the pocket protector wearing guys who started this sweet little company on the West Coast are right, one day there's going to be a computer on everyone's desk, home and office."

"Why?" he said.

"If what Wanda has researched pans out," Mustang began, "you can use them to write letters and other stuff, replacing the typewriter. Use them to send messages back and forth and send pictures over the..." She searched for the word. "Airwaves I guess they call 'em."

Ashford stared blankly. If you weren't an engineer or some kind of egghead scientist, what the hell would you need a computer for? Washawski claimed that a tsunami in communication was in the offing.

And they were going to be riding the wave.

•

That night the three stood on a small hill of patchy land behind the motel. They watched fascinated as green-tinged flame rose from the burning gym bag of Giggle Sniff. Possibly they glimpsed their future in the flickering light.

24

Harvey Bullock steered his dented Mercury Marquis along the boulevard. The lit stump of a cigar was lodged in the corner of his mouth and a mournful Chet Baker tune played low on the car's tape deck.

In the trunk were the items he'd assembled for the takedown, including ones confiscated from the special evidence lockup. As he drove, he gave Thea Montclair a squeeze on her knee. She sat next to him, wearing jeans and tennis shoes. Her features were drawn tight.

"Relax, we got this," he said. "Right?"

"It's just… what if something goes wrong, Harvey?"

"Then we make it up as we go." He took the cigar from his mouth and blew a stream of smoke out the partially rolled-down driver's side window. "You can do it."

"I got too much riding on this."

"I know," he said. "We both do." He smiled reassuringly at her.

"I need a hit," she said. "I gotta calm my nerves."

"No, you don't." He glanced at her.

She looked back. "You're right, I don't."

He pulled the Mercury to a stop amid a row of low-slung

buildings, none more than two stories high. Except one.

The Novick Novelty works stood out in the near distance at three stories high. Putting the car into park, Bullock killed the engine, took the key out of the ignition, got out, and unlatched the trunk. He pulled out a thick duffle bag and closed the trunk lid. There was a growl nearby as a worker guided a noisy diesel-powered forklift.

"Okay, countdown to success," he said, handing her the keys through the passenger side window. She slid over behind the steering wheel.

"Good luck," she said.

"Good luck to us both," Bullock amended, hefting the duffle bag over his shoulder.

Montclair started the car and drove away. The man with the forklift removed a pallet of plastic-wrapped cartons from a semi. He paid no attention to Bullock, dressed in a wrinkled cotton shirt and khakis. Given his build, the detective could easily be mistaken for a worker delivering machine parts.

He got to the corner and looked down the block. The "empty" novelty company faced out onto Andru Street and took up most of the short block. The first two stories of windows were blocked out with a reflective material that kept him from seeing inside, but Bullock was pretty sure anyone inside could see out. Closer to where he stood was a single-story warehouse with a large rollaway door in front—storage for frozen produce, busy at the beginning of the day with trucks arriving steadily for pick-ups by local restaurants and grocers. Since it was early afternoon, however, most of the day's business already was done.

Just past the warehouse he turned and followed a narrow

passageway that led between the buildings. About midway to the next block he reached his objective, on the side of but toward the rear of the Novick building. He bent down and unzipped his duffle, which he'd set on the ground. Bullock extracted five mechanical items that resembled reptiles. These were geckos created by Winslow Shott, also known as the Toyman. His usual stomping grounds were in Metropolis, but for a price he helped finance his own endeavors by supplying gadgets to other criminals.

The gizmos had been made for a crew of arsonists who employed controlled fires to pull off their heists. Confiscated when the gang was caught in the act, the mechanical lizards could climb walls and were designed to explode into fireballs.

"All right, you little bastards," Bullock said, "it's time to do your thing." He flipped a switch on each of the robots, and slit irises glowed red in their artificial eye sockets. He'd listened and taken notes on the taped interrogation of one of the arsonists, describing how to program them. Bullock sent the mechanical reptiles scurrying up the outside wall of the novelty works. Each went toward a different destination, identified via the building schematics kept in the public records.

Wearing a lopsided grin on his face, Bullock removed two more objects from his bag—a semi-auto Mossberg shotgun and a Batman mask. The mask was the cheap sort, picked up in the kids' section of a chain drug store. He appreciated the irony as he pulled the stretchy material over his blockish head. Checking the weapon, he returned it to the duffle, then secured the bag onto his back.

"Time to rock and roll," he muttered as he psyched himself up. From previous reconnoitering, he knew there were piles of old crates and pallets strewn all about the building. He heaped some of them up under a set of built-in rungs that scaled upward to the Novick building's rooftop. While he wasn't in the best of shape, Bullock managed to haul himself up onto one of the crates. Standing and balancing as best he could, he reached for the first rung. The crate creaked and shifted under his weight.

"Shit." He'd purposely laid off the chili fries and extra cheese lately, but who was he kidding—he was far removed from the days when he'd been an offensive tackle, back in high school.

"Come on, goddammit," he grumbled. Sweat ran out from under the rubbery cowl on Bullock's unshaven face, and he considered pulling the itchy thing off, but he didn't dare take that kind of chance. The crate began to splinter beneath him, but stretching as far as he could, he got a hold on the lowest rung.

Feet propped against the wall to support his weight, he sucked in air for several moments. Then he started climbing upward, passing between windows of the second floor without incident. As he got toward the third floor there was a flutter behind a curtain at a window off to one side.

He froze.

There stood Python Palmares, staring out over the rooftops of the shorter buildings. He hadn't seen Bullock, yet. Heart beating in his mouth, the detective remained stock still. The curtain partially blocked him from view, but if Palmares turned even the slightest amount, he'd be screwed.

Time stopped.

Bullock's dry tongue touched his dry lips.

He couldn't even produce enough saliva to swallow.

Finally Palmares moved away from the window. Sucking in air, Bullock clambered up to the roof faster than he thought he could move and went over the low parapet.

Taking a knee with a *thump*, he wiped away as much sweat as he could. Adjusting the eye holes in his Halloween mask, he checked his watch. By now his robot geckos would be in place. Lurching to his feet he walked to the square structure that held the roof access door. It was locked, but he pulled out a small container, also "liberated" from GCPD storage. It was a vial of the acid the Joker liked to use on random victims, and just a few drops dissolved the padlock.

He reached to open the door, but then stopped. Examining the hinges, he confirmed that they were covered in rust. Bullock damn sure didn't want to alert Palmares and his boys downstairs—his plan relied on catching them off guard. In another page from the Batman playbook, he took out a small can and placed the nozzle against the hinges, squeezing out a generous amount of oil on each one.

That done, he slowly worked the door back and forth, loosening up several years of decay. The result wasn't entirely silent, but it was quiet enough that he slipped inside without raising an alarm. He descended the stairwell to the third floor, then the second. Regarding his watch again, he began a countdown in his head.

"Showtime," he muttered gleefully.

•

One of the women packing the Giggle Sniff happened to look up. She was originally from a small village in the Mexican highlands, and had seen plenty of lizards in her lifetime, though she hadn't noticed any in Gotham. Shrugging, she lowered her head and returned to her repetitive task. The swing door leading to the lab opened near her as a fresh batch was wheeled out.

Without warning, where there had been a gecko, a fireball appeared with a deafening *bang*. The explosion shattered numerous windows in the large room. A second blast erupted toward the unoccupied end of the room where the crates and supplies were stacked, while a third burst forth from the laboratory, knocking the swing doors off their hinges. The concussive force sent packets of Giggle Sniff flying everywhere.

She screamed and dove under the long table. Other women raced for the exits, some of them with frightful-looking burns on their bare, unprotected skin. By some miracle, no one seemed to have been killed. As they clustered at the doors, the crush made it impossible for them to get any further. There was more screaming as some of them were trampled in the crush, but all still managed to get back on their feet.

Two of the drug cookers wearing rubber aprons raced out of the lab, screaming, engulfed in flames. The women assemblers scattered in every direction to avoid them.

"Hold up!" a guard bellowed, raising his assault rifle. No one paid him any attention, and he was quickly knocked to the ground by the force of the mob.

A second guard, leaning his rifle against a wall, tried to help the first one when the door to the stairwell was blown open by a shotgun blast. The guard grabbed for his weapon as an overweight man in a weird Halloween mask rushed into view. Before he could reach it, the intruder hit him in the head with the stock of his shotgun. The guard collapsed instantly.

The fire was spreading.

•

This wasn't going down quite like Bullock had planned, but there you had it. As the chump he slugged hit the ground, Bullock pointed the business end of the Mossberg at the one already on the floor.

"Where's the money?" he demanded.

If the guard was scared, he didn't show it.

"You don't know the kind of trouble you're in, asshole," he said defiantly. Clearly he needed some more encouragement. There wasn't much time, Bullock realized.

He pressed the barrel against the guy's shoulder.

"You wanna be called Lefty?"

The man thought about it, then jerked his chin toward the burning lab.

"Go ahead, tough guy," he growled. "Your ass is—"

Bullock kicked him in the face. Grabbing up the assault rifle, he held it in his free hand and ran toward the smoke-filled room.

A bullet zinged off an upturned assembly table. He spun and saw that two more hoods were there, standing in the doorway and shooting at him with their handguns. Instantly Bullock was on a knee and returning fire with the AR-15, temporarily forcing the other two to seek cover. Twisting around he flopped down on the floor. With the oily smoke rising and drifting over him, he belly crawled into the lab, and found the fire climbing a wall like runaway kudzu. There was no telling how long he had before the place went up in a huge blast or burned to the ground around him.

Clambering to his feet he searched the metal cabinets in

the room, and knew the guard had lied to him. There was no money here—it had to be upstairs in Palmares' office.

"Shit," he growled. Since the scratch would be the first thing the gangster would grab he had to double time it. The masked plainclothesman began to pick his way back out of the lab when one of the light fixtures dropped from the ceiling, grazing his arm. The fluorescent tubes popped, wires dangling from the fixtures, crackling with electricity as Bullock pushed past.

Back in the assembly room the women had all made it out, and as he had hoped, there were no bodies. Visibility was compromised by the fire and smoke, and as he crept closer to the exit, he heard a cough. Glancing around he spotted a tennis shoe that was on fire—somebody had bolted out of here *that* fast.

Scooping it up and holding it away from him, he moved over a patch of sagging floor, the beams underneath creaking beneath his weight. The guard swung into view from the hallway, and Bullock hurled the shoe at him. Instinctively the man ducked aside, and the rumpled cop peppered his lower legs with buckshot.

"Shit!" the guy bellowed as he dropped to the floor. He still held onto his weapon, though, and rattled off a few rounds. But Bullock moved like he was chasing a naked woman carrying a plate of barbequed ribs. He used the Mossberg like a baseball bat and connected solidly with the side of the guard's jaw, sending him over and out.

Off in the distance, there was the sound of sirens.

Crap!

Abandoning the assault rifle, he hit the stairs moving as fast as his bulk allowed.

•

"Sounds like the fire department, and the cops won't be far behind," Palmares said to Frankie Bones. "Let's get the hell outta here." He gestured to another man, too—a thick-necked individual who went by "Scale." The bruiser brandished an Ingram MAC-10. "Bad enough I gotta deal with the goddamn Scarecrows, now this," he said. "If they're behind it, there's gonna be blood."

"Told you we should have kept the sprinklers working," Bones said, lifting a duffle bag stuffed with cash, settling the strap on his shoulder. "All these damn chemicals."

"Yeah, yeah, next time," Palmares said. "This was supposed to be a *deserted* warehouse," he added, looking up. Through the skylight fifteen feet above, they could see black smoke rising into the sky.

"If there is a next time."

The three thugs spun to find a guy standing in the doorway, wearing a cheap Batman mask. The newcomer didn't wait for a reply, and shot Scale in the kneecap, cartilage and blood exploding from his tattered cotton pants. Moving fast for a fat guy, he crossed the room and kicked the Ingram away. It came to a stop against the wet bar.

"*Fuck*," Scale shouted, landing on his side, both hands gripping what remained of his bloody kneecap. "I'm gonna fix you, dickwad."

•

"Uh-huh," Bullock said, but he wasn't paying attention to the wounded gangster. He eyed the three full duffle bags, two of them lying on the floor.

"The hell you supposed to be, beer belly?" Palmares said. "Batman's hillbilly relation?"

"Your mama's a hillbilly, punk," Bullock replied, trying to figure out how to carry all three bags. Briefly he considered forcing one of the thugs to carry them for him, but common sense interceded.

One bag would have to do.

"Back the hell up," he said to Palmares and his sidekick. He recognized Frankie Bones.

"You ain't gonna get away with this, scumbag," Bones said.

"You want to join big boy on the floor?" Bullock shook the shotgun he held in both hands. Bones and Palmares took a few steps back. "I didn't think so. Now drop the bag." Bones let his duffle drop to his side, leaning it against him as it stood on end.

The sirens were getting closer.

Abruptly there was a *whoosh* of turbines, and fire-retardant foam began sliding down the windows. Like the GCPD, the Gotham Fire Department had been experimenting with the use of blimps. One of their aircraft had to be hovering near the building, spraying it to keep the flames contained.

One hand still on the trigger of his Mossberg, Bullock bent down to take hold of a duffle bag of cash.

"I thank you for your contribution," he said, straightening up with the prize.

Bones barely twitched his upper body as he threw his bag at Bullock.

"What the fu—" the masked cop blared, leveling a blast at the bag. Hundreds, fifties, and twenties erupted into the air as the shotgun pellets tore through the canvas. Green-tinged confetti rained down as Bullock reared back. Before he could recover, both hoods were on him.

Bones socked him in his flabby middle, doubling him over. Palmares grabbed what was left of the tattered duffle bag to slam it down on Bullock's head. He staggered, bent over like a drunk sailor with osteoporosis. Bones swung at him again, but Bullock fended off the blow and countered with a punch to the man's chin, sending him backward.

Bullock turned, dropping into an amateur's version of a boxing stance, figuring to defend himself as Palmares came at him again. The drug lord grabbed a desk lamp and cracked it against Bullock's skull. Stunned, pinwheels cascading behind his eyes, he sagged and Frankie Bones got his arms pinned behind him.

Palmares unloaded a salvo of blows to his face and gut.

"Teach you to mess with me," the tattooed gang chief raged. Bones let him go. Blood and saliva dripping from his gaping mouth, Bullock sagged to the carpet. A grinning Palmares took a knee, grabbing the cop by the shirt and pulling him into a sitting position.

"I've been itching to try these out."

What the fuck? Bullock's eyes went wide, and he blanched at the sight of snake-like steel fangs shining in the crime boss's mouth. *Only in Gotham*, he thought, realizing he was about to die.

"Let's see if you still got something funny to say after I take a bite out of your face."

"Aw, sweet Lord," the detective muttered, damn near wetting himself as the fangs bore down.

There was a crash above them, and glass rained down as the skylight burst. The thugs looked up, and Bullock figured the building must be collapsing around them.

"Looks like a party," a female voice said brightly. "Did you forget to send me my invitation?"

Batgirl swung down on her grapple line. Bones dove to the side, his arms over his head to protect him from the falling shards of glass. Palmares got to his feet, and was rewarded with a Batarang to the side of his head.

"Ke-*rist*," the gangster swore.

Not wishing to waste an opportunity, Bullock lurched upward and jammed the heel of his hand under the man's jaw, shoving him off as he scrambled to get back on his feet.

•

Frankie Bones pulled his pistol and shot at the costumed newcomer. She whipped her Kevlar cape around for added protection of her upper body, the shots ricocheting wildly. As she went into motion, she glanced at the heavyset figure grappling with Palmares.

Is that Harvey Bullock in that cheap Batman mask? Sure enough, she recognized a body nurtured by fried food and rotgut. *What the heck is he doing here?*

Frankie Bones took another shot at her, and she reminded herself to focus. Pulling a tear gas capsule from her belt, she hurled it at Bones. The thing exploded directly at his feet and he was consumed with a coughing fit. Unlike regular tear gas, this compound was designed to cling to body heat even as the target tried to fan the fumes away.

She heard movement behind her, spun, and blocked a knife thrust as Palmares tried to gut her. He grinned as he did so, and she was momentarily startled by his grotesque silver incisor implants glinting in the light. Recovering quickly, she used a standing sideswipe kick to knock the drug lord aside. He dodged, however, and it was only a glancing blow.

"Ain't no slip of a broad gonna best the Python," he gritted, coming at her again. Going low, avoiding a slash of the blade, Batgirl kicked Palmares in the nads and he doubled over, howling.

"You... bitch," he wheezed. "Gonna kill you... for that."

He peered at her with raw hate, and lurched in her direction, but for all of his determination, he was still off balance. Batgirl launched a series of strikes to his head and shoulders. Most of them were for punishment, but one struck a specific nerve, and Palmares collapsed on his expensive rug.

Behind her she heard a loud *thump*, someone let out a grunt, and a shot glanced off her shoulder's body armor. Spinning, she saw Bullock, still wearing that ridiculous mask, holding a heavy duffle. Frankie Bones staggered to the side, his gun held up.

The gangster took a shot at the detective, who moved quicker than his bulk suggested. He dove behind the wet bar as rounds from the pistol shattered decanters filled with top shelf whiskies and bourbons.

While the gunman was distracted, she closed the distance between them and landed a solid blow to the side of his neck. Even that didn't stop him, and when he turned she landed a right hook to the jaw.

That put him down.

There was a clatter in the doorway. Bullock was running.

She pulled a bolo line and used it to snare his legs. He fell face-first to the floor and the bag he was carrying flew out of his hands. It broke open, and bundles of cash flew out, scattering around him.

What the...? Checking to make sure the gangsters were, indeed, out for the count, she stepped over to the fallen cop. "Why, Detective Bullock, what have we here?" she asked, hands on her hips. "Can you give me a good reason not to turn you in?"

He just looked at her, his eyes pleading behind the eye openings in the knockoff rubber mask.

25

Dr. Leland headed back to her office carrying a fresh cup of tea and an apple to tide her over for a few extra hours. She'd promised herself she wouldn't work overtime again that night, but the stack of court documents on her desk wasn't getting any smaller.

Was it any wonder she had no life? Not as if it mattered, anyway. There was no one at home but her cat—the only male she'd ever met who didn't mind her reviewing crime scene photos over dinner.

She was about to turn down the hall that led to the therapy wing when she spotted her intern moving furtively toward security, and the exit beyond.

"Ms. Quinzel?" she called. "Harleen?"

The young intern's blonde hair was messy and loose, hanging in her eyes and hiding her face, but her shoulders hunched a little in response to Dr. Leland's voice. She didn't stop, however, or even slow down as she swiped her badge through the security lock and waved coyly at the armed guards as she pushed the outer door open.

Damn that little brat.

Dr. Leland sighed wearily and turned back toward her office. She really wanted to give the girl the benefit of the doubt, but her shamelessly inappropriate behavior and surly, insubordinate attitude just wasn't a good fit for a facility like Arkham. There was chaos enough among the inmates, without having the staff contribute to it. She had no choice but to recommend that the girl be let go.

Instead of going back to her office, Dr. Leland took a detour. She walked down to the far end of the hallway, past a series of disused storage rooms and maintenance closets and into a dead end with a barred window that looked out over a gnarled and leafless tree. A quiet, forgotten corner of the facility where she often came to be alone and think.

Putting the apple in her coat pocket, she set her tea on the sill and slid open the window. It only opened a few inches before it was stopped by security blocks, but it was enough for her to reach out and grab the pack of cigarettes she had hidden in the deep sill. Outside she could hear the constant downpour of the rain in the ancient trees that surrounded the estate-turned-institution.

Leland knew that she really should quit. She *had* quit, essentially—except for the occasional cheat, and only when she really needed it. Like now. Pulling a cigarette from the pack, she lit one using the lighter she'd also stashed in the pack, and blew the smoke out the open window.

She couldn't stop thinking about the Joker.

Abruptly the relative quiet was interrupted by a sound coming from the nearest maintenance closet, off to her left. A soft, arrhythmic thumping. Leland frowned, crushing out her cigarette against the sill and flicking the butt out the window.

Stepping over to the closet, she gripped the doorknob, then pressed her ear against the door. It dawned on her how private this forgotten area was. No cameras. No guards. The reason she'd chosen it to sneak a smoke made it a dangerous place to be if an inmate somehow got out of the lockdown ward.

But this wasn't Leland's first rodeo. She'd talked a knife out of a particularly violent patient's hand, thwarted several suicide attempts, and defused a potential hostage situation before it went out of control. Her patients trusted her, and she was a tireless advocate for their well-being, emphasizing compassionate de-escalation over the use of force. Even the most violent offenders still deserved to be treated like human beings, rather than fractious livestock the staff moved from one pen to another.

"Is someone in there?" Leland asked.

The thumping inside the closet increased in tempo, accompanied by a soft, muffled moan.

"It's Doctor Leland," she said, slowly turning the knob. "I'm going to open the door now." Whoever was on the other side, there was no sense in panicking them.

She pulled it open just a sliver, waiting to see what—if any—response there might be to her intrusion. It was pitch black inside the closet and all she got was more inarticulate moaning.

"Now I'm going to turn the light on." She spoke calmly as she slid her hand through the crack in the door, feeling for the wall switch. "That way we can see each other. Would that be okay?"

Nothing. Just moaning.

Leland flipped the switch.

Inside the closet were stacks of cleaning products packaged

in large, industrial-sized tubs. Bleach. Brown paper towels. Powdered soap. A metal roller bucket with wheels and a sad trio of limp, dirty mops. On the floor in the middle of it all, there was a body.

Harleen Quinzel.

"Ohmigod, Harleen!"

She was hogtied and lying on her belly, dressed only in a bra and panties. There was a knotted rag stuffed in her mouth and tied around the back of her head. Black makeup ran down her tear-stained face, mingling with blood from a nasty wound on the right side of her forehead.

"What the hell happened to you?" Leland pulled the door open and moved quickly to the girl's side. She untied the drool-soaked rag. "Who did this to you?" It was a rhetorical question, she realized.

"It was..." Quinzel blubbered between harsh, hyper-ventilating breaths. "Was... the Joker... he... he..." She was seized by a coughing fit, and gasped to try to get it under control.

"Calm down and try to breathe slowly," Leland said, tugging at the stiff rope that bound the girl's wrists and ankles. "That's it. Come on, sit up." As she pulled the bindings away, she saw nasty red welts where they had scraped the skin.

She helped the sobbing intern up to her bruised knees, and took off her own white coat, draping it around the girl's shuddering shoulders as she pressed a handkerchief against the head wound to staunch the bleeding.

"I thought..." Harleen said, lifting her anguished, mascara-smeared eyes up to peer at Leland. Then flung herself sobbing into the older woman's arms. "He said we would be together forever. He said I was special!" The words stretched into a wail.

Something in the girl's histrionic tone tickled the needle on Leland's bullshit detector, but as with the Joker, there was something about this kid that threw her instincts off balance. Besides, this was neither the time nor the place for judgment. She needed to notify security, and get Harleen to the infirmary.

Then it was going to hit the fan, and most likely multiple heads were going to roll. Perhaps even her own. An incident like this would spawn a media free-for-all, with Quinzel in the spotlight. Dr. Leland hated to see any woman forced go through that particular meat grinder in the wake of an assault.

Shaking her head, she figured they would cross that bridge when they came to it. She helped the girl to her feet and led her out of the supply closet, focusing on locating a security phone to initiate an emergency lockdown, and then getting poor Harleen some clothes.

•

Back in her office, Dr. Leland gave the girl her tea to sip, and a bulky brown sweater she kept in her closet for times when the air conditioning was running too high. Sitting at her desk, she was on the phone with the head of security.

"No, Doctor," he said. "The Joker is still in his cell. Batman is with him right now."

That didn't make sense. If the Joker was in his cell, then who did she see leaving the facility? The girl was still too upset to talk about what had happened in the closet, softly crying and staring into the tea cup, looking like a small child as she held it with two hands.

"Then I want a full head count on every ward," Leland said. "Especially Ward A. Make sure you—"

"Hang on, Doc," the head of security cut her off, and she heard someone else talking in the background. "Looks like the baby killer is MIA," he told her. "His cell is empty."

"Kurt Lenk?" Dr. Leland said, frowning. Of all the patients to attempt escape, Kurt was the last one she ever would have guessed. He was so passive, so accepting of his fate, never questioning that he deserved his life sentence at Arkham. There was nothing for him in the outside world. "Are you sure?"

•

"Hold still, Kurt," Quinzel said, gripping Lenk's chin between her fingers as she smoothed whiteface over his flushed cheeks. There wasn't a lot of room in the closet, and the Joker elbowed her repeatedly as he struggled to pull her too-tight pencil skirt up over thick, suntan-colored pantyhose.

"Does this escape plan make my ass look big?"

Harleen giggled and tossed him the long blond wig she'd had inside her massive crocodile purse. She also laid out the size eleven brown leather pumps she'd bought in a specialty store, knowing her own little kitten heels would be worse than useless.

"Don't forget to put the foundation on your hands, too," she said. "After you tie me up, of course."

The Joker nodded, pulling a length of stiff, paint-stained nylon rope from a back shelf while she pulled a spiky green Halloween wig over Lenk's own thinning hair. She wished the cheap wig was curly, like the Joker's own wild emerald green locks, but it would have to do. Hopefully the dim lighting in the cell, combined with the general laziness of the night staff, would work in their favor. All it had to do was buy him an hour or two. Enough time to disappear into the teeming city.

The Joker slipped his lanky arms into the white coat she'd been wearing, and then did a little twirl. Everything she'd worn today had been too large for her, and she'd had to cinch it up so no one would notice.

"How do I look?" he asked.

"You don't look like me," she said, stepping up to press herself against him as she slipped her badge around his neck. "But you don't look like you either." He twisted away from her, pushing her back with his elbow.

"Don't touch me," he said, making a sour face. "You'll ruin it."

Stung but not wanting to show it, she turned her attention back to the faux Joker, double checking her makeup job. Kurt stood in the corner like an unplugged automaton, staring down at his shoes. It was almost too easy.

"He's good to go," she said, waving a hand in front of the man's blank, staring eyes. "Now me. And make it good and tight."

The Joker grabbed her arm and spun her to face away from him, cinching her elbows together, and then her wrists. She arched her body against the knots and issued a small, kittenish purr.

"Knock it off," the Joker said, pressing her down first to her knees and then to her belly on the cold concrete as he looped her ankles with the rope. "You're incorrigible."

"Whatever you say, Mister J," she replied with a wink as he tied her ankles to her wrists.

"Ready?" he asked, holding up a gag made of knotted rags.

Harleen smiled up at him, and then cracked her forehead

sharply against the concrete. Stars danced in her vision and she felt a hot trickle of blood on her temple.

"I am now," she replied.

"Atta girl," the Joker said with a grin, pressing the dusty knotted rag into her mouth and tying it behind her head.

She didn't know what she was hoping for in that moment. That he would pledge his undying love to her, or swear that he would find her on the outside and they would be together forever? But he didn't say a word. He just slipped his knobby feet into the big heels, rubbed the rest of the tan foundation onto his hands and wrists, and then led their doppelganger away.

He kicked the closet door shut behind him. It would take under a minute for him to return the fake Joker to his own cell. Then, using the same electronic badge he'd used to open his cell door, he could swipe through security and walk right out the front door.

In the darkness, she wondered if she would ever see him again.

26

Bruce Wayne set the plate with a seared ribeye in front of Alfred Pennyworth, then sat across from him in the wonderfully appointed kitchen.

Wayne Mansion was grand in the Jacobean and Tudor traditions of dark rubbed woods and stonework, and the kitchen was no exception. From the marble countertops to the Shaker cabinets, brass accouterments, and a spice rack that included a derivative from a plant found only in Nanda Parbat, the kitchen was legendary in architectural circles.

"Let me know what you think," Wayne said, looking pensive. In addition to the steak was a plate of grilled asparagus, but no bread or other carbohydrates. Bruce Wayne maintained an athlete's diet of meat and vegetables. He had prepared this late lunch meal—had even specifically ordered these cuts of meat from the butcher.

"Oh, I shall." Pennyworth cut off a piece of his steak and placed it in his mouth.

When the mansion's "butler" gave a nod of approval, Wayne dove in, as well. Nearby in a built-in cabinet, a portable television showed the midday news, though it was on mute.

There was a report from East Berlin, where police were beating pro-democracy protestors demanding an end to the iron rule of the Soviets.

The two men silently regarded those events, then resumed eating.

"How do you do it?" Pennyworth said.

"What?"

"Not succumb to temptation," he answered, pointing at the screen. The news gave way to a commercial for hair care products. "They're acting under the color of authority—mind you, an authority we would find intolerable here—but we know there are law enforcement professionals who *revel* in the violence. Become lost in the ardor of brutality."

Wayne arched an eyebrow, holding a piece of beef speared on his fork, but remained silent.

"How does one not get carried away, Master Bruce?" Pennyworth continued. "Maintain the wherewithal to use just enough force to defeat the foe, yet not give in to the allure of the righteous vanquisher and beat the living daylights out of an opponent. An opponent—I hasten to add—who would display no such discipline, were the situation reversed.

"What of those who have done far worse, committed far more heinous acts? Who lay awake nights conceiving even more damnable plans of murder and mayhem?" he said. "And for what? At times for profit, but far too often for the sheer sake of, well, evil. You know of whom I speak."

"Two-Face, for example," Wayne said, letting a hint of weariness creep into his voice. "And the Joker." He placed the meat into his mouth.

"Indeed," Pennyworth said. "Yet the righter of wrongs, no matter what uniform he wears, must go 'by the book,' as the Commissioner would admonish." Pennyworth took a bite of the vegetable and wouldn't have minded a dry cabernet to go with the meal. Since the master of the house had prepared the meal, however, they both drank seltzer. Club soda contains too much sodium.

Wayne chewed for a moment, perhaps metaphorically.

"If I really wanted to end crime in Gotham," he said, "why not hire an assassin like Deadshot, pay him to put high velocity rounds through the heads of Jeremiah Arkham or Victor Fries, or rig one of Oswald Cobblepot's trick umbrellas to blow his head off? Wouldn't that solve the problem, on a more permanent basis?"

"Ah, then I'm not the only one to have contemplated such scenarios," Pennyworth commented.

Wayne deferred a response and chewed thoughtfully.

"What *is* it that persuades us not to give in to tactics like those?" he asked finally. "Is it the individual, whatever is inside of them, the raw material, so to speak, or is it a quality instilled in them by their training and experience?"

"I'm no stranger to such a regimen," Pennyworth said, thinking back to his time with MI5. "No amount of training can prevent you from crossing the line, if the strength of character is absent. Indeed, some use their training as an excuse to commit all sorts of heinous acts."

"Ability doesn't always equal ideals," Wayne agreed. "We've seen those who abuse the gifts given to them. A closer look reveals feet of clay."

Pennyworth nodded. Even Batman was subject to such scrutiny, he knew.

Bruce Wayne had received his training from some of the finest the world had to offer, the detective Henri Ducard and martial artist Shihan Matsuda among them. Though Ducard was a man with remarkable skills, the Frenchman's cavalier outlook concerning the use of force had driven a wedge between student and teacher.

"Yet you have to persist," Pennyworth noted, "adhere to your principles even as you thwart these villains for whom death and destruction are both goals and ways of life."

"Death always shadows the work we do, Alfred," Wayne replied. "There's no escaping it."

Pennyworth stared at his food. "I know the dead haunt you, no matter how righteous your actions may be."

Wayne regarded him. "Maybe that's what it is then, Alfred," he said. "No matter what the rationalization, no matter how certain we may be that the fatal decision is justified, there's no taking it back." He paused, looking past the walls. "No matter how clear the evil may seem to be, if we allow ourselves to take the shortcut, to give in to the permanent solution—there'd be no turning back. We'd be no better than those we hunt."

"Then how do you account for your Justice League colleague, the Spectre?" Pennyworth countered. "He seems rather content at bloodthirsty resolutions. Perhaps it's the utterly white face, eh?"

Wayne smiled ruefully.

"Or the Commissioner, for that matter," Pennyworth persisted. "Certainly there was a time when he found himself forced to take lives, in order to protect the innocent. What might he say?"

"We can only choose one path at a time," Wayne replied. "Once we've chosen it, we can't judge the results until we've reached the end. But who can say when our journey is done?"

"Are you quoting Master Chu?"

"A Saturday morning cartoon show," Wayne said, his expression unreadable. "About a mystery-solving dog."

Dryly, "Yes, of course…"

Pennyworth took another bite of steak.

NOW

27

Evening, and Gavin Kovaks sat in his shack leafing through a months-old issue of *Beaver Hunt* while a baseball game played on his portable radio. He paused for the umpteenth time on the two-page pictorial of Suzi Mustang, displaying her assets in the "Girls of Striptease" special section. Man, that chick not only got a rise out of him, but sent him into orbit. What he wouldn't give to spend some time with her.

Not just to get his hands all over her, like some back-alley creep. No sir, wine her and dine her, show the lady a good time. Shit, back in the day he sported fine threads and Italian loafers.

Now look at him, dressing like a stooge.

Wistfully staring off into space, he took a sip of gin from a plastic bottle, and dully noted that the Gotham Knights had loaded up the bases against the visiting Central City Diamonds. The sound of a car cut in, the growl of its engine barely audible at first. It grew louder until he could hear the tires on gravel, then the engine cut. This had to be the prospect one of his old CIs had sent—with the promise of a finder's fee, of course. If he played it right, what with Grissom being out of town, maybe he could get this mark to pony up an advance, and he'd be on the first train out of Gotham.

He looked out the window.

"Aw, crap."

The car was an old 1940s-era Hudson, long and rounded and low to the ground like a giant beetle. It was fully restored and painted a deep purple.

"Shit," he muttered. "The goddamn Joker." Instinctively he glanced around the shack, trying to remember where he'd stashed his revolver. Maybe if he came out shooting...

But no, that grinning maniac had proven too much of a survivor—and frankly, after years of boozing, his aim wasn't what it used to be. So far no one had gotten out of the car, but Kovaks knew there was no avoiding the inevitable.

A wind had kicked up outside, stirring dead leaves and trash. He hunched into his jacket and put on his hunting cap with the ear flaps. Best to act like a simpleton, he figured. He took another gulp of his gin and stepped outside, a shit-eating grin on his face.

"Hello there."

The high-pitched voice came from his left.

"Je-zus," he said, quickly twisting sideways. The Joker stood right next to him. He was dressed mostly in purple, including the trench coat that protected him from the steady drizzle that had begun. Sporting a cane, he wore a flat-brimmed hat, a light string tie, and spats.

Jeez, spats!

Kovaks played it dumb, like he planned.

"Yes, sir," the ex-cop said. "I understand you're in the

market for an investment. Well, let me assure you, this place can bring in the dough—the money I mean. It's a sure thing." Did he sound nervous? "Everybody likes to laugh and have a good time, right?"

"Indeed, I'm all about a good time," the Joker said. His teeth were insanely big, like a hyena's.

"Hey, let's take a look around, okay?" Kovaks said. "Let me turn on the lights, so we can see." He scurried away to the electrical shack, and when he returned to the car the Joker was nowhere to be seen.

Where is he?

Hands deep in his pockets he looked everywhere, jumping at shadows, but there was no sign of the man. As he did, he realized just how much the place had fallen into ruin. He was about to return to his shack when there was movement just off of the midway, and he spotted the tall, lean figure standing there, leaning on his cane. He'd taken off his hat, and didn't seem to notice the pelting drops.

"Ah!" he said, trying not to sound nervous. "There you are! Have you had a chance to inspect the property and decide if it's what you're looking for?"

The Joker peered at the carnival, hand on one hip.

"Well, it's garish, ugly, and derelicts have used it for a toilet," he said, and Kovaks' heart sank. "The rides are dilapidated to the point of being lethal, and could easily maim or kill innocent children."

"Oh," Kovaks said, "so you don't like it."

The Joker turned to him, a look of delight playing across his face.

"Don't like it?" he said. "I'm crazy for it."

They walked along the perimeter, passing old, torn carnival posters advertising the "2-Headed Baby" and the "3-Legged Man." As they did, the Joker seemed to glide along, his feet somehow not crunching on leaves or the hard-packed ground. About half of the lights were lit, casting dark shadows at crazy angles as they passed the carousel and the dilapidated Ferris Wheel with its uppermost gondolas swinging in the wind.

"You...? You really want to buy it?" Kovaks said. "And the price I mentioned isn't too steep?" He followed in the Joker's wake.

"Too steep?" the thin man said with mock incredulousness. "My dear sir, as I look at it, I'm making a *killing*...

"...and anyway, money isn't really a problem," he added. "Not these days."

Yes! Kovaks thought. It was music to his ears. He knew the Joker had to have money stashed away. Maybe *lots* of it. Now if he could just close the deal...

They paused at the entrance to the House of Fun. "How about a walk through?" Kovaks suggested, drawing closer.

The Joker looked down at the shorter man, that damnable grin so wide on his pasty face. His hair ruffled in the stiff breeze.

"Yes, let's." He wiggled his green brows, like a vaudeville comic.

•

When they came back outside, the Joker paused at one of the machines, the "Laughing Clown." He reached out a gloved hand, and a dark look passed over his face.

Oh, shit, Kovaks thought, *he's gonna back out*. He had to do something, so he climbed onto a kids' ride—a googly-eyed pink elephant mounted on a giant spring. Swaying back and forth on it, he tried to sound enthusiastic.

"Y'know, I'm *positive* you won't regret this purchase," he said. "The place isn't *that* dilapidated. Some of the rides are still pretty sturdy…" A smile played across the Joker's features. *Yes!* "Really, this could be one hell of a carnival."

The Joker came forward, putting a hand on Kovaks' shoulder, and he was grinning again. Kovaks was sure he'd just dodged a bullet.

"Oh, you're so right," he said. "Thanks to your smooth salesmanship and your silver tongue you've completely sold me on the place." He clapped a hand on the ex-cop's back and stuck out the other one. "Let's shake on it."

Kovaks looked at the hand. Seeing nothing gleaming in the half-light, he stuck his out, too.

"Uh… well, sure," he said. "It's my privilege." They shook. There was a buzz, and a pinch, and the Joker was beaming like a sophomore who'd just been kissed by the head cheerleader.

"Indeed it is," the thin man replied. "Naturally, I won't be paying you anything." His words were becoming more distant, difficult to make out. "My colleagues persuaded your partner to sign the necessary documents just over an hour ago," the Joker said. He had no colleagues and he had no idea or could care less who owned the carnival. "The property's all mine." He undid the hand buzzer that hadn't been there before, leaning in close to Kovaks' face. "I take it you're happy with that?"

Kovaks' body went rigid. He stopped rocking on the elephant, and his face felt tight.

"I can see that you are," the Joker said, tossing the buzzer aside. "I'm so glad. You know when you see the improvements I've planned for this place, I guarantee you'll be absolutely speechless. And incidentally," he snickered, "that's a lifetime guarantee."

The Joker turned his back and walked away. "Well, I must dash. There's equipment to hire, and workers who'll suit the general tone of the establishment." He put on his hat and twirled his cane as he walked away. "And then, of course, I've yet to secure my main attraction. Do feel free to stick around."

Gavin Kovaks stared straight ahead. There was a rictus grin on his face, a bit of blood trickled from his mouth, his red-veined eyes bugged out, seeing nothing in death.

28

"I still don't know why he chose me to live, and everyone else to die," Zach said. "It's crazy, right? I mean, okay, so like this chip that I'm developing is pretty cool. I mean, it's important. Like big time important, and Professor Stephens knew it—but it's still so sad to think of everyone that died. Survivor's guilt, I guess you'd call it."

Zach knew he was talking too fast, his words tripping over each other like excited puppies, but he couldn't help it.

"I'm so sorry, Zach. This must be so hard for you."

Her name was Lisa MacIntosh. Wild auburn curls and dark doe eyes and the cutest freckles. She was just a little bit taller than him and still awkward with her long smooth limbs. Even though she tried to hide the fact under loose, bulky sweaters, she was definitely at least a C-cup. He spent most of their shared classes wondering if those freckles were all over, and trying to come up with clever things to say to her.

Now she was standing next to him in front of his dorm room door, smelling like clean laundry and secret flowers, and all those clever things just went right out the window. He fumbled around for his key and opened the door.

"Do you want to come in?" he asked. "I mean, I could show you the schematics. I just… I feel like I shouldn't be alone at a time like this. You know, after everything that happened."

She smiled a crooked, awkward smile and looked down, crossing her arms. The move had the effect of pushing those C-cups upward so a little bit of cleavage showed in the V neck of her sweater. She was blushing. That was a good sign, right? Girls blushing? And she didn't say no either. Another good sign. It was working! He figured this was it. His big chance.

He leaned in and kissed her.

Lisa's whole body went stiff, like she'd received an electric shock, and she made a weird noise, a sort of a half-swallowed gasp. Her teeth clenched tight. He pulled back, confused and embarrassed. He was blushing too now. Definitely NOT a good sign.

"Lisa, listen…" he began.

"I'm sorry," she said. "I mean, I'm sorry for what happened to you, I really am, but I just don't think of you that way, Zach."

"But I thought you broke up with Steve," Zach said, hating the way his voice suddenly sounded all high and whiny.

"What does that have to do with anything?" There was anger in her voice now. Her dark eyes went narrow and cold, and he felt pinned and helpless. "You think because I don't have a boyfriend anymore, that I should just make myself available for anyone who comes along?"

"Of course not," he said, offering defensive and conciliatory palms, trying for what he hoped was a disarming smile. "Maybe just me?"

As soon as he said it, he knew it was a mistake.

"God, Zach!" She wiped her mouth with the back of her hand, and he died a little more inside. "You're such a creep. You just don't function right." She turned to walk away.

"Hey, wait," he said to her back as she walked away. "I was just kidding…"

She didn't slow down.

He stood there for a moment in front of the open door, feeling simultaneously hot and cold and more than a little nauseous. The hallway was empty—thank god. His mind was going a mile a minute, replaying every awful moment of the exchange. Why did this kind of thing keep happening to him, over and over?

"Women…" a voice said, speaking from the dark interior of his dorm room. It was high-pitched and strange. His roommate Kevin was working over in the computer lab, so the room should have been empty.

He peered into the darkness, and his desk light clicked on. Someone was sitting in his chair with their back to the door. The desk chair spun around, revealing a leering grin and mad eyes in a gaunt, pale face.

Holy shit, it's—

"…can't live with 'em," the shadowy figure continued, "and it's against the law to kill 'em. Am I right, Zachy boy?"

"How did you…?" Zach looked both ways down the dormitory hall, drowning in shame and wondering if he should just run. "Were you sitting there the whole time?"

The Joker stood, straightening his crooked purple lapels and pushing his fingers through greasy green hair.

"Here's the thing about women," he said. "They're holding

all the cards." He produced a deck of cards from his suit pocket and started artfully shuffling them with his left hand.

"Girls like that will spread it all over campus," he added, "but won't give guys like us the time of day. And why not? Okay, so maybe we don't exactly have teen idol good looks, but aren't we nice guys? Good sense of humor. Always there for them. 'You're such a good friend,' they say, until it's time for a little reciprocity, and *then* what? Then all of a sudden, we're creeps."

Zach blinked. He didn't know how the Joker could claim to be a nice guy, but he did have a point.

"See, the system's slanted in their favor," the Joker continued, cards shuffling hypnotically back and forth now between his slender gloved hands. "Supply and demand. You try to play fair, you try to follow the rules, but they keep shifting and changing, moving the goalposts until the next thing you know, they've run off with some Cro-Magnon whose dick size is greater than his IQ."

"Yeah," Zach said. "It's like you can't win."

"Exactly," the Joker replied, leaning close in the semidarkness, mad eyes twinkling. "So what do you do when you can't beat the system?"

"Um…"

The Joker sharply arched his fingers, causing the cards to fly up and out like a fountain. Like when Zach was a kid, and his older brother used to trick him into playing a game he called "52 Pickup." As the cards fluttered down to the carpet around Zach, he noticed they were all Jokers.

"You *fuck* the system," the Joker said. "That's what you do."

He cocked his pointed chin, gesturing toward the door. "Want to go for a ride?"

•

They stood in a cavernous warehouse space. Zach was still shaking with excess adrenaline from the trip through Gotham City.

Joker's "ride" had been a green-and-purple motorcycle, speeding through traffic, almost colliding with moving vehicles and stationary objects alike. He hadn't wanted to seem weird or gay by clinging to the Joker's waist, so he just clung desperately the edges of the seat until his fingers ached, and kept his head down so he didn't have to see all the times they nearly died. The Joker cackled all the way, the sound sharp enough to break through the noise of the chopper, his iridescent hair snapping in the wind.

Above ground, this secret headquarters looked like a crappy, dilapidated old fun house in an abandoned amusement park, but underneath lay a massive storage space where top-of-the-line equipment had been wheeled in on portable tables, converting it into a makeshift tech lab.

How can he afford this stuff?

"I've had my eyes on you, Zach-boy," the Joker said. "You've been waiting months for a grant proposal, so your new chip can be reviewed." He slung an arm around Zach's shoulders. "Now, with the murder investigation gumming up the works, who knows how long it will be before you receive funding? If you receive funding at all, after all the negative publicity." His face went sad and long, like a theater mask.

The Joker paused, and then spread his arms wide, spinning around like a maniac.

"But why wait, Zach-man?" he said gleefully. "You have everything you could want, right here. Work for me and you can start today—right now! You've got a blank check. Anything you need, just send one of your new assistants down to… I don't know. Computers-R-Us."

As he spoke two stunning, lingerie-clad girls came forward to flank Zach, one running long pink nails through his hair and the other slipping a hand up under his untucked shirt. He tried not to giggle, but couldn't help himself.

"Hi, I'm Tandy," one of them said.

"And I'm, uh," the other one started. "Oh, yeah… I'm Clarissa I guess." She looked nervously at the Joker, whose expression was unreadable.

"Are you our game boy?" the supposed Clarissa asked with a giggle.

Zach didn't know what to say.

"Is this real?" he asked finally. His head was spinning.

"Is *anything* real?" the Joker responded with a lazy grin. "For that matter, what difference does it make?"

Zach couldn't argue with the logic.

•

"So," the Joker said. "How close are we?"

Zach had no idea how much time had passed—it had been a blur. Never had such wonderful resources been available at the snap of his fingers. Hell, the camera alone was top of the line. Once he began, he hardly slept or ate. It was heaven.

All he had to do was ask, and Tandy or Clarissa brought him any equipment he needed, all the while offering sweet words of encouragement. That lent greater urgency to his work. He was pretty sure that, once he was done, another form of heaven would await him.

"Nearly there," Zach replied without looking up from the tangle of the board in front of him. A grey pall of soldering smoke hung over his work station, but he hardly noticed.

"Excellent," the Joker said. "When the module is complete, will it broadcast both stills and video?"

"Broadcast isn't exactly the right word, but yeah," Zach said. "You'll have everything backed up on floppy, too. Easy peasy."

"Easy peasy," the Joker repeated. "That's the way I like it, uh-huh, uh-huh." He danced around, darting in and out of the shadows.

•

The kid had been working around the clock for several nights in a row, fueled by manic energy and sugar. When he wasn't working, he sat there like a wide-eyed and dutiful sponge, soaking up all the toxic rhetoric the Joker could pour into his eager little head.

It was almost too easy.

Whenever Zach seemed to waver, he just called in Candy or Wendy—"Tandy" and "Clarissa." A few giggles, a few wiggles, and the kid was back on task.

Honestly, the Joker didn't care much about women one way or the other. They were fine for stress relief, of course—some more so than others—but he had the voices in his head to keep him company. He had bigger fish to fry. A point to prove. A date with destiny. Or Batman.

Whichever showed up first.

Still, he knew exactly how to get the kid to do what he wanted. Knew how to play on his insecurities and repressed anger. He gave Zach a fake story about Barbara Gordon, that she was this stuck-up librarian who broke the Joker's heart, and then he hard-sold his clever plot to get back at her with a brilliant, comical and embarrassing prank that would make Zach look like a rock star to all his friends. Implying that if Zach helped him with his revenge, then he would *naturally* return the favor. After all, isn't a blow against one stuck-up bitch a victory over them all?

All the Joker had to do was provide the tinker toys and that kid would build a whole fairy tale inside his head. One in which the mean librarian stood in for every girl who ever rejected him.

Because that's what they always did.

The Joker lived his whole life in a near constant ebb and flow of lies, delusions and ever-evolving, self-fulfilling fictions. It was easy for him to allow the people around him to try to make sense of his nonsense, to believe whatever they wanted to believe, to cushion themselves from the truth at the heart of all madness. He believed in breaking eggs to make omelets.

Or just breaking them, anyway.

When he'd first conceived of this plan, back at Arkham, he'd been thinking he'd take photos. He'd dress like a tourist, with a big camera around his neck. Then he'd met the dear Professor Stephens and realized how much more *wonderful* his revenge could be. With Zach's ingenious new technology, he could rip away every last vestige of control and drive his intended victim irrevocably mad.

Even better, the madness would be eternal, reaching

everywhere and lasting forever. Like a malevolent ghost in the machine, replicating endlessly before a captive audience of millions. Pictures could be burned. Negatives could be destroyed. But, what did Zach call it? Cyber-something...

Oh yeah, cyberspace! How Stanley Kubrick.

Yes, cyberspace would be forever.

This caper would be the Joker's masterpiece. Final and incontrovertible evidence that the line between the sane and the insane was nothing but a social construct that could be obliterated at the drop of a hat. Or the click of a keyboard.

It had always been difficult for the Joker to see other people as living breathing individuals, with lives and loves and inner meaning beyond whatever temporary use he might have for them. He didn't *really* care about the pretty librarian or her fine, upstanding father. He certainly didn't care about the angry little nerd. They were tools. Puppets in his grand puppet show.

There was one person for whom he *did* care deeply, though. The person for whom this whole horror show was being orchestrated. His cosmic dance partner, the law to his chaos, the truth to his madness. His audience of one.

After this was done, there would be speculation and discussion and dissection as they tried to figure out what *really* had happened. What he really meant to accomplish. None of that mattered, though. Let them twist and dance and spin. They would never understand his delicious madness. In the end, there was only the final punchline, flawlessly delivered just as the curtain fell.

For him, the end of the show was the end of everything.

Like a kid on Christmas Eve, he could hardly wait.

29

Commissioner James Gordon regarded the chess board that sat on the kitchen table as he and his daughter played a game in his modest apartment. Nearby was the shelf unit that included his wet bar, and held one-of-a-kind curios such as an old-fashioned pocket watch formerly owned by Jervis Tetch, the Mad Hatter. The shelves also held his many scrapbooks, one of which he had taken down and set on the table beside the chess board.

Folded on top of that was the morning edition of the *Gotham Examiner*. The headline announced the Joker's escape.

ASYLUM SECURITY UPROAR
MANIAC ESCAPES AGAIN

Fingers pinching his rook, he glanced up at Barbara's face and wasn't surprised to find an expression of utter calm. This unreadability, which would have been the envy of any poker player, was just enhanced by her eyeglasses—glasses she didn't really need. She'd adopted them when Batgirl had appeared on the scene, thus cementing the public image of the staid librarian.

As a college student Barbara had mastered in library

sciences, at the same time taking many a criminal studies course. Given her dad's profession, no one had questioned her apparently intellectual curiosity. It provided fodder for many a fascinating father-daughter discussion, most recently involving the work of that British professor, Alec Jeffreys, and the use of human DNA to more accurately identify criminal suspects.

It was amazing, Gordon reflected, how far criminal investigation had progressed since he'd been on the job. Since even the appearance of Batman.

"Take your time," she chided, breaking into his reverie. "I know your synapses don't fire as quickly as they used to."

"You young whippersnappers could learn a thing or two from us old war horses," he fired back, weighing a move with his knight. "There's value in patience, and estimating the pros and cons before going off half-cocked."

"Yet some situations call for quick thinking, and even quicker action," she countered. "It's all about the preparation."

"That may be so," the senior Gordon replied. He played his bishop, putting one of her knights in jeopardy. "Yet even if you're in tip-top physical condition, it'll never make up for a lack of experience. You know what they say, 'old age and cunning will overcome youth and skill every time.'" He liked that.

"Still, an unexpected move can catch even the most experienced person off-guard." She sat back, taking in the board. It was reflected in her glasses.

"Lord knows that's true," he agreed, shaking his head.

Barbara smiled.

"He'll catch him," she said. "He always does."

Gordon grunted. "It seems as if the Bat and the Joker

are destined to forever play out their endless game of cat and mouse. He's becoming more driven, if that's possible, and the Joker—who knows what kind of endless loop plays in his twisted road map of a mind. It's as if he hungers for both the chase *and* the capture."

"Perhaps he has no sense of the passing of time," she suggested, "just as he has no sense of morality."

Gordon hunched a shoulder. "He's his own brand of madness."

She nodded and moved her knight. He considered his counter, then huffed and sat back, rubbing his temples. It had been difficult to focus, ever since the incident at the asylum.

"My heart's not really in it tonight."

"That's fine," she said. "We can always pick it up another day. Let's move into the living room."

He nodded and, scooping up the scrapbook and the newspaper, moved to his favorite easy chair. She busied herself in the kitchen. Setting the scrapbook on the glass-and-metal coffee table, he held the newspaper and picked up a pair of scissors.

"I hate this," he said. "Whenever we jail him, I think 'please God, keep him there.' Then he escapes and we all sit round hoping he won't do anything *too* awful this time.

"I hate it," he said again.

"Dad, just *once* could you leave your work at the office and relax?" Barbara joined him, carrying a tray with a pair of steaming mugs. "I made you cocoa."

"Thank you, sweetheart," he replied, holding the scissors up to the edge of the newspaper. "I'll drink it when I've pasted this latest clipping in." This particular scrapbook was devoted to Batman's eternal dance with the Joker. Others were more general, tracking the shenanigans of some of Gotham's more colorful underworld figures, such as the Penguin and the Riddler.

"You know, I found that Catwoman scrapbook you said was missing," Barbara noted, setting the tray on the coffee table. "It was behind the wardrobe. Some day you ought to let me work out a proper filing system, like we used at the library."

"Hmmm…" he responded, applying glue to the back of the clipping and pressing it into the book.

"Look, you used too much paste," she said, scrunching up her face. "It's all squidging under the edges of the clipping. You're going to get it on your pants…" She reached out, but it was too late.

"Barbara, you're fussier than your mother wa—"

He stopped. "Was that the door?"

"Yeah, it'll be Colleen from across the street. Tonight's our yoga class." She walked toward the front of the apartment, still carrying her cocoa. "C'mon, Dad… company! Put your scrapbooks away." As he picked it up to do as she asked, he noticed the oldest clipping in the book.

"Heh, look at this one. First time they met. Now what year was that?"

"Well, I remember you describing the white face and the green hair to me when I was a kid," she said over her shoulder. "Scared the hell out of me."

"I thought you'd be interested."

"Yeah, well, I had some interesting nightmares."

He heard the squeak of the doorknob as she turned it.

•

Zach stood in the hallway on the top floor of a ritzy apartment building, stomach twisting and heart beating too fast.

The Joker was poised in front of an ornate door with two burly henchmen forming a wall of muscle behind him. He was dressed in a weird costume that made him look like a tourist on some sort of tropical vacation. Hawaiian shirt and Bermuda shorts, with a camera on a strap around his neck, but still wearing the usual purple gloves and wide-brim hat.

"You'll see, kid," the Joker had said. "It'll be the best gag ever!"

Cradling his beloved Arpanet module in sweaty hands, Zach was both nervous and excited. Whatever the Joker had in mind, it was going to be *epic*. To hell with the board of regents and their funding. He didn't need it, now. He was part of a cool, edgy crew. He'd show the Lisa MacIntoshes of the world. They'd be *begging* him to—

The Joker pulled out a gun.

"Whoa," Zach said. "Is that real?"

The Joker turned toward him, manic grin blasting him like a klieg light, and the excitement inside him curdled into fear. He suddenly wished that awful gaze would focus somewhere else. Anywhere but on him.

"What do you think?"

"I don't..." Zach stammered. "I mean, what are you..."

"Don't be such a party pooper," the Joker said, rolling his eyes dramatically as he turned and rapped on the door. "It's gonna be a *riot*."

The door opened wide, revealing a well-lit room and a red-haired woman in a yellow blouse, wearing glasses and holding a mug. This was the girl, the one the Joker had told him about, and Zach really wanted to hate her. He needed her to be this terrible bitch to make what they were doing okay, but in that moment, she just looked like an ordinary girl he might see at the campus library. One of her white sneakers was coming untied.

She didn't look scared, she looked furious.

"Hey!" she said, the cup falling to the floor as she lunged for the white-faced intruder.

Then the Joker shot her.

The sound of the gun going off was so much louder than they made it on TV, or even the movies. Zach didn't just hear it, he *felt* it in his whole body as if his skeleton was a tuning fork. It rippled through him and he flinched, nearly dropping the module. The bullet hit the girl in her midsection. She dropped her cup and crumpled, curling inward around her bleeding belly, her glasses flying off and stocking feet coming up off the floor.

She stiffened again, straightening and pitching backward to land on a low glass table that shattered beneath her weight. There was an older guy sitting there, and he looked vaguely familiar. For a split second he just stared down at her, holding a pair of scissors, then he reached out.

"Barb…?" he said.

The Joker stood behind him, smiling and calm.

"Please don't worry," he said. "It's a psychological complaint, common among ex-librarians. You see, she thinks she's a coffee table edition." He walked over to a bar and picked up a bottle of something, pouring it into a shot glass. "Mind you, I can't say much for the volume's condition. I mean, there's a hole in the jacket, and the spine appears to be damaged."

What the hell…? Zach thought furiously, his brain going a

mile a minute as he stared at the ruin the bullet had left behind. There was no way the Joker could tell how much damage he'd done. *Hell, it's a miracle she's still breathing at all.* He didn't think that was likely to last.

The old man got to his feet, one hand still holding the scissors, and started moving toward the Joker from behind. His expression was a mix of shock and anger.

"You, you *scum*," the guy said. "My daughter, I'll—"

Before he could get more than a step or two, though, one of the Joker's bruisers grabbed him and punched him in the gut, causing the old guy to double over with a loud gasp.

"Frankly, she won't be walking off the shelves in *that* state of repair," the Joker continued as if nothing was happening behind him. "In fact, the idea of her walking anywhere seems increasingly remote. But then, that's always a problem with softbacks." He chuckled a little at his own joke.

"God, these literary discussions are so dry," the maniac continued, holding up the glass and staring at it. "When you've finished with the old boy, you know where to take him." As he said it, the muscle-bound thug punched the old dude in the face, causing him to crumple.

"And please... do be careful. After all, he is topping the bill." As two of the thugs carried the gray-haired guy out, he leaned over the fallen girl, his leering grin wider than ever. "You know, it's such a shame you'll miss your father's debut, Miss Gordon."

Wait a minute... is that the police commissioner?

"Sadly, our venue wasn't built with the disabled in mind. But don't worry, I'll capture the moment to remind him of you." With that he glanced to where Zach was standing, just inside of the door. His blood ran cold.

I should run. I should call someone. I should...

He didn't move a muscle.

"Wuh... wuh..." the girl gasped, her face contorted in pain and tears running down the sides of her head. "Why... are you... duh... doing this...?" It looked as if every word caused her intense pain.

"To prove a point," the Joker said. In one hand he held up the liquor. "Here's to crime." With the other hand, he started to unbutton her yellow blouse.

"Set up the transmitter, Zachy boy," the Joker said over his shoulder. "It's showtime!"

Zach started backing toward the door.

"I... I..."

The Joker made an exaggerated face, like a man annoyed by his disobedient poodle. "Don't even think it," he said darkly.

Zach froze, acutely aware that he had to pee. If there had been any doubt that he had made the worst mistake of his life, it was obliterated in that moment.

"You're one of us, now, Zach—no turning back." Then the Joker brightened. "Cheer up! Look on the bright side. This'll put you on the front page! On every television screen in the land! You'll make Michael Jackson look like yesterday's news."

"I need..." Zach swallowed, his throat scratchy and bone dry. "I need a phone."

The two henchmen carried the now unconscious gray-haired guy toward the door. One of them sighed audibly, shifting the unconscious man's lower legs so as to hold those legs together under one massive arm with the casual thoughtlessness of a man adjusting his grip on his grocery bags to open his car door.

He picked up a telephone off a small, ornate side table and tossed it in Zach's direction. It landed in a jangling heap at his feet, the receiver flying off to the full length of its spiral cord and then snapping back.

Zach concentrated on setting up his module on the rumpled, blood-splattered oriental rug. He tried not to think about the gun pointed at him, or the naked and bleeding girl, or what the Joker might be doing to her. He just went through each step with meticulous care, pretending he was back in the familiar, safe Computer Science lab at Gotham University.

Plugging a cord into a wall socket, he booted up the module, fitted the phone receiver into the two rubber-lined holes, and initiated the dial-up sequence. He switched on the camera and tapped the lens. Everything ran perfectly, just like it was supposed to.

"Are we on?" the Joker asked impatiently.

Zach couldn't make his lips and tongue work properly, so he just nodded. He meant to keep staring down at his perfect little machine, obediently doing its job, recording and uploading everything. But then he made the mistake of looking up. Looking at the wounded girl.

All he could see was her head and shoulders. The rest of her was hidden behind the Joker's hunched back. She was looking right at Zach. A tear rolled down her pale, blood-splattered cheek as her body rocked slightly. It reminded Zach of the way a gazelle's body moved while being eaten alive by lions on one of those nature shows.

His hand flew to his mouth and he staggered away, vomit spilling between the fingers.

The Joker's unhinged giggles echoed down the hallway.

Caustic shame burned inside Zach, along with the bile in his throat and tears in his eyes as he ran for the stairs.

What the hell have I done?

30

Barbara faded in and out of consciousness, isolated images and surreal impressions flashing in quick succession like shuffled cards.

A gunshot.

Spilled cocoa.

The Joker, his leering smile and those terrible eyes. White fingers in her mouth. A strange, glittering fish-eye camera lens. A skinny kid with glasses and a pale, horrified face. The intricate weave of the rug beneath her wet cheek.

Was that tears or blood on her face?

Did it matter?

"Why…" she asked, or thought she did. She couldn't tell if she had spoken out loud or not. "Why are you doing this?"

"To prove a point," a warped and distant voice replied as she started to gray-out again.

Terrible things happened to her, but she couldn't feel anything. Just a weird, disconnected sense of fluctuating pressure, like the way you feel at the dentist. Knowing something that should hurt is happening, but numb.

Where was her father? Why couldn't she remember what had happened to him? All she had was this impression of a flurry of violent movement and him calling out her name.

"Topping the bill…"

Then, nothing. The Joker's men must have taken him. Must have killed Carstairs and Badoya parked in their patrol car downstairs, part of her father's around-the-clock detail. If her dad was hurt, or worse, she could never forgive herself for not being able to protect him. After all, what was the point of being a superhero if you couldn't protect the ones you love?

She had to do something. Anything. She had to focus, think, fight. She wasn't anybody's point to prove. She was fucking Batgirl. Her body was broken and her mind jagged and fractured by trauma, but she was still *alive*, and she wasn't going down without a fight.

The Joker was fiddling with some sort of weird machine, laughing to himself like a deranged hyena as he pointed a bulbous lens. Was he taking photos? Filming her? Why?

There was nothing she could use as a weapon, and she didn't think she had the strength to swat a fly, even if there was. She knew she must be bleeding out. Her hands were ice cold and shaking and seemed like they belonged to someone else, but she still had on the watch.

Bruce gave it to her, and she remembered being mildly annoyed when he told her about the tracker inside it. She didn't need him stalking her, even if he *was* Batman. He'd reassured her that it only worked when it was activated, and so she had reluctantly accepted the thing. Just in case she ever found herself in deeper trouble than she could handle, he had said.

She had scoffed at the idea that such a situation would ever occur, but told herself she only wore it so she wouldn't seem ungrateful. The truth was that she really wore it because she thought it looked pretty cool with its matte black finish and sleek, numberless face.

Her hands were slicked with sweat and blood, but she got the watch off.

The Joker was wrapping up what he was doing, pulling a floppy disk out of the weird little machine and tucking it into his pocket. She was running out of time. It was too late for her, but the Joker's men had her father.

Maybe it wasn't too late for him.

It took every ounce of strength she had left, but she reached out to the Joker, weakly clutching at his shirt front and playing the desperate, pathetic victim begging for her life.

"Please…" she whispered through her teeth, pulling him close and willing herself not to pass out. "Please."

"You know I'd love to stick around for more fun, toots," he said, "but a villain's work is never done." She wasn't listening. She was laser-focused on slipping the watch into the pocket of his Bermuda shorts. She just had to push the button.

Abruptly he pulled away from her.

The watch dropped into his pocket, unactivated.

She had failed. Through the despair and anger she could feel what remained of her consciousness slipping away. Her last chance to do something was gone, and she was going to be left alone here to die while god knows what was happening to her father. An involuntary shriek of frustration and fury welled up in her throat, but she clenched her teeth against it.

Barbara wouldn't give that son of a bitch the satisfaction.

His footsteps receded down the hall as she focused her

woozy gaze on the broken handle of her cup lying on the rug a few inches from her nose. It was a sharp, jagged break, raw white porcelain jarringly revealed beneath the rustic brown glaze.

More footsteps.

I tried, Daddy, she thought as she fell away from herself and into the depths of black unconsciousness.

•

Barbara?

A powerful electric shock blasted Jim Gordon back into terrified consciousness. The pain of it was breathtaking as every muscle in his body went into wrenching spasms.

He bit deeply into his tongue without realizing it, his mouth and throat filling with blood until he felt as if he was drowning. When the agony receded enough for him to regain his senses, he became aware of a rough cloth hood over his head, claustrophobic and foul-smelling with stiff stains around the nose and mouth. Someone was touching him all over.

There were lots of hands, slapping, pinching, and inspecting him like he was livestock of questionable value, but there was something very wrong with those hands. Were they… children's hands? They seemed way too small to be adult hands but also felt bony and oddly proportioned with abnormally long, skittering fingers and sharp nails.

"Wake up," a chorus of raspy, lisping voices were saying, speaking in slightly imperfect unison. "Wake up, wake up, wake up!"

Again, the electricity rampaged through his body, whiting out his vision and evoking an involuntary howl.

"He's up," one of the voices said. "See?"

"Are you up?" another asked, patting his face through the scratchy cloth.

"Barbara?" he said. His tongue felt treacherous and too thick, and there was a strange, bitter taste underneath the blood in his mouth. Had he been drugged? "Where is she? *Barbara?*"

"Barbara!" the first voice repeated.

"Where is she?" said the second.

"Barbara!" They all started chanting together. "Barbara! Barbara!"

It was maddening, but he had to pull himself together. His head was throbbing as he made himself focus on small details, to try and figure out where the hell he was. Like the feel of cheap, splintery wood against his back and legs. He was sitting, slouching was more like it, wedged into a corner, and there were a few scattered fragments of what felt like prickly straw beneath him. Was he in some kind of cage or animal enclosure? Like a zoo maybe? There was a slight breeze on his skin, which seemed to imply that he was near an open window or door.

"Time for ups," one of the strange voices whispered, pressing cold lips against his cloth-covered ear and making his skin crawl.

"Time for ups," another voice said, cinching something heavy and way too tight around his neck.

"Ups, ups, ups," the idiot voices echoed. "Ups, ups, ups."

Gordon attempted to get his rubbery legs under him and stand, but all his limbs were weak and swarming with pins and needles. He felt dizzy and sick, suddenly sure that he was going to throw up inside the hood as he staggered and fell back to his knees. He hissed between his teeth as a dozen tiny splinters burrowed into his knees and shins.

"Ups, ups, UPS!" the voices chanted, someone punctuating the final word with a sharp yank on whatever was around his neck.

He resisted, pulling back and twisting his torso, wrists straining against his bonds. The exertion of that struggle brought up a film of cold, clammy sweat to his nude skin, bright spangles dancing under his tightly closed eyelids.

Don't pass out, old man!

He couldn't afford the luxury of oblivion. He had to get free and find Barbara.

That was the only thing that mattered. But why couldn't he remember what happened to her? When he heard the crackle of the cattle prod somewhere to his left, it didn't even need to touch his body to inspire him to leap almost instantly to his feet as he flinched away from the sound. He couldn't get far, as he was still tethered by the neck.

Breathing much too heavily, he gasped for each tortured breath beneath the suffocating hood, and could feel heat surging through the skin of his face as a wave of sickening humiliation drenched him like a bucket of pig blood. He wanted desperately to cover himself and protect his private parts from the unknown assailants that surrounded him, but his arms were bound so tightly behind his back that his hands were swiftly going cold and numb. All he could do was crouch and curve his body inward, cowering like an animal away from the crackling of the cattle prod and the shrill, shrieking laughter of his tormentors.

"Walkies!" the voices screeched. "Walkies!"

Someone yanked on what was clearly a leash attached to his

tethered neck, and he yelped, half-stepping, half-falling forward.

"WALK-IES!" They were chanting in unison again. "WALK-IES!"

He managed one tentative step, then another, when he felt the breeze increase and the wooden floor beneath him start to slant downward. Was he outside now? He knew he must be when he reached the end of the ramp and his bare feet encountered dry, loosely packed dirt. It was colder now, making him shiver and raising gooseflesh across his exposed skin while his face still burned beneath the hood.

"What...?" he said as the relentless pull on the leash led him on a grim and seemingly endless death march to nowhere. "Where am I?"

No reply, just more walking.

"I don't understand," he sputtered. "How did I—?"

There was a sudden wrenching yank backward on the leash, forcing him to stop suddenly, nearly losing his tentative balance.

"Down."

This command issued from one of his lisping captors, and it sounded like it was coming from somewhere very low, disturbingly close to his crotch. Was he right about them being... children? Or worse, was one of them crouching down in front of him, about to do something to him... down there?

"What...?" he started to ask, trying not to cringe away and hating how weak and shaky his voice sounded. The swift reply to his unstated question was the sizzle of the cattle prod kissing the small of his back.

He collapsed into a fetal position in the dust, howling in agony as his muscles seemed to be trying to tear themselves loose from his electrified skeleton and escape in all directions at once. Gordon was shaking and sobbing uncontrollably when he felt another sharp upward yank on his leash.

"Goddammit!" he spat, impotent fury raging through his body as he struggled to his hands and knees. "Will somebody please tell me what the hell I'm doing here?"

"Doing?" This from a new voice. New, yet horribly familiar, coming from up high and farther away. "You're doing what any sane man in your appalling circumstances would do."

He had turned his covered face up towards the new voice when one of the creepy little hands ripped the hood off his head. He was temporarily blinded by a surge of light in a hundred swirling and lurid colors but he was soon able to focus on that familiar pale face and leering crimson grin.

"You're going mad," the Joker said.

31

"Sarge, you need to see this!"

What now? Sergeant Stan Merkle oversaw the crime stats reported in by the dirigible patrols. He was standing at the precinct's coffee machine, breathing in the stale, bitter aroma of the hours-old brew and debating between his freshly blooming ulcer and his existential and seemingly unshakeable weariness.

Judging from the pinched and urgent tone, whatever Officer Tim Carstairs wanted him to see was going to piss him off, so against his better judgment, he went ahead and refilled his chipped GCPD mug.

Reluctantly he followed Carstairs over to their brand-new computer, around which a curious crowd had gathered. Peering between the blue uniformed shoulders, Merkle saw an image on the screen, filling itself in line by line, like a kind of slow digital striptease. It was a nude woman. As her features appeared, she looked vaguely familiar.

"Is this some kind of a joke?" Merkle growled, gulping and instantly regretting a mouthful of lukewarm coffee that both tasted and felt like battery acid going down. "Who's responsible for this?" Other windows appeared on the screen, one by one, and began filling up with similar lurid images.

"We don't know, sir," Carstairs said. "We can't do anything to override the transmission. We've tried everything."

"It's not just us, Sarge." Officer Nancy Payton of the blimp squad was standing at a nearby desk, hand over the receiver of a phone. Her brows were drawn into a worried frown. "I've heard from six different precincts, and they're all receiving these same images."

On the screen, the nude woman's lips appeared in the central photo, line by line. They seemed twisted, teeth flashing in a painful, angry grimace. Around them, disheveled licks of hair became visible, and there was dark blood clotting in her hair and webbing her teeth. Merkle felt a cold twist of nausea in his belly, aided and abetted by the bad coffee. This wasn't some centerfold model.

This was something much worse.

"It looks like Commissioner Gordon's daughter," one of the younger recruits whispered to his buddy.

"You're lookin' at the face?" someone said, and that caused some sniggering.

"Shut up, asshole," Payton said. "That's not funny."

"No, wait," Merkle said, shoving the recruits out of the way and setting his cup down too hard, causing the coffee to slosh onto some nearby paperwork. "Jesus Christ, it *is* her." He tapped the screen, trying not to look at her exposed breasts and focus on the patterned background. "That's Jim Gordon's rug!"

He spun. "I want all available units sent to the Commissioner's place, pronto," he roared. "And I want our best computer man here before this image finishes. Am I making myself clear? And the rest of you knuckleheads, have some respect, willya? This a police station, not a goddamn porno theater."

He took off his jacket and was about to use it to cover the screen when another file suddenly popped up.

"What the hell is this now?" he raged.

"I think it's a... a video file, sir," Officer Payton replied.

"Lord A'mighty," he muttered, covering the screen after all. "Video? Is that even possible? Look I don't want anyone clicking *anything*, is that understood. Where the hell's my computer guy?"

He put his hand over his eyes. Without wanting to, he found himself remembering Barbara when she was a scrappy little girl, back when he'd first started on the job. A whip-smart kid, always with her nose in a book. How she'd essentially grown up around cops. She and Jim had their differences, especially during her rebellious teen years, but he loved the hell out of that girl and there'd be no way something as godawful as this could be happening at his place without him doing something about it.

Which meant he had to be in trouble. Deep trouble. Maybe even the kind of trouble he wouldn't walk away from.

"Do I have officers on the scene yet or what?" Merkle snapped.

"Under fifteen minutes, Sarge," Officer Payton replied.

•

Kevin Lannister was working late in the comp science lab of Gotham University, catching up on some extra credit for his Unix class, when several images started appearing simultaneously on every screen in the room. Just a small handful of his fellow hardcore code monkeys were hanging around the lab, and they all gathered around the monitors, sniggering as the first image started to reveal itself as a nude woman.

"Do you think it might be Tazic?" Lannister asked, taking a rope of red licorice from the packet clutched in the sweaty paw of an anxious freshman named Dave, sticking it into one corner of his mouth like a cigar. "He was all jumpy and cagey, last time I saw him, dropping hints about being onto something big."

"I'll say it's big," Dave replied. "Is that Danielle Embry from Calc-3?"

"In your dreams, doofus," Lannister said. "Nobody with tits like that could get past Calc-1."

"That's a sexist thing to say!" This from a fat kid named Frank, or Fred. Lannister barely knew him. "It's also preposterous to imply any correlation whatsoever between physical endowments and intelligence."

"Fair point," Lannister replied, munching on the licorice. "Anyway, I hear Emmy Noether had an epic rack." He reached up and slapped Frank or Fred's doughy chest. "Nothing compared to yours, of course."

"Um, guys…" someone else said. "Guys!"

"What?" Lannister asked.

The guy pointed at the screen.

"I think that's blood."

Lannister looked closer. "Holy shit!" he said.

Kevin Lannister wanted to look away from the computer screen, but he couldn't bring himself to do so. Whoever was doing this was a certified genius, and most of the logical candidates had been killed.

Holy shit, that's real-time video, he thought, and the realization took away his breath—as well as any doubt he might have had. His original thought had clearly been correct.

It has to be Tazic.

•

Things were quiet in Gotham Central Library, and whenever things got quiet, Cassie Lane got bored. When she got bored, she frequently got into trouble. Barbara always made fun of her, calling her a nymphomaniac, but she liked to say that she was just a healthy red-blooded woman. She had needs that didn't all fit between dusty leather covers. Unlike certain other librarians that she wouldn't name.

So what if she had a lot of boyfriends? She was young and had plenty of time to settle down someday in the ill-defined future. Meanwhile, that cute boy in the philosophy section had been casting lingering gazes in her direction for nearly an hour. Before long the two of them were discussing Kant, passionately arguing the role of reason in morality. Soon they were in a state of partial undress.

Then Mr. Neiderman started calling her name.

What the hell?

There were a couple of reasons this was out of the ordinary. First, the fact that Mr. Neiderman was there at all, when he practically lived in the microfiche catacombs down in the basement. Second, that he was speaking above a whisper. That simply wasn't done. Not by him, nor by anyone.

Something was very, very wrong.

Offering a brisk apology that left the young philosopher looking very chagrined, and a little uncomfortable, she ran back to the main desk. There she found the entire staff crowded around the computer screen.

Holy crap!

•

Greg Grossman, a second-year student, might have missed the transmission if it had come ten seconds later.

He'd been lurking in a chatroom dedicated to a paperback sci-fi series, all about a modern man turned barbarian on a distant planet. He'd also been trawling for new ASCII porn files, but was bored and tired and thinking that he'd just log off and go grab a bite at the Chinese joint down the street. The place had a cute waitress.

Just as he was about to get up a new file popped up, unbidden, on his screen. Then another, and another. In a rush of giddy excitement, he logged onto a private BBS called GROSSNET666. It was a repository for all the most foul, shocking, and outrageous content he and his fellow gross-out enthusiasts from all over the world could find and upload. Car accidents. Autopsies. Tentacle porn.

He typed rapidly.

> 54Filth is this you?
> Gutshot redhead, looks real. Video incoming.
> Y/N?

A reply appeared on-screen.

> Not me dude.
> Upload?

Several others chimed in, and Greg's fingers flew over the keyboard, capturing the images and packaging them for upload to GROSSNET. This was better image quality than he had ever seen, and once he made sure to get them uploaded before anyone else could take the credit, he needed to trace this transmission and figure out where it was coming from.

Because whoever did this had some serious skills—and, in Greg's opinion, excellent taste in content. The last window to open was the clincher.

Holy shit, that's a live video feed!

He was in awe, his mind, already in fast-forward mode, imagining the far-reaching implications of that kind of technology. He could picture a future in which it was possible not only to watch prerecorded porn movies, but to connect with girls performing live, interactive sex shows in the privacy of your own home. All he had to do was figure out how to reverse-engineer this stunning new advance and he'd be in on the ground floor of a priapic empire!

Once he finished uploading the files, they'd be winging their way to at least nine different countries that he knew of. From there, who knew?

His mission accomplished, he opened up the video file and eased back in his chair to enjoy it.

32

When Barbara came to again, she was alone in her father's apartment. Her memory was spotty, but much to her amazement she wasn't dead.

She still couldn't feel anything below her sternum, and her newfound hold on consciousness was tentative at best. She'd been sick all over herself at some point, and miraculously managed not to choke on it.

But where was her father? What had they done to him? Something about *topping the bill*, the Joker had said. What could that possibly mean? Without activating the tracking device, how would they ever find him?

A wave of desperation and panic crested inside her, and she forced it down. Her eyes fell on the glossy, unblinking eye of the camera lens—for some reason they'd left it behind. But why, unless...

It's still on, she realized, rage building inside her. *That sick bastard.* With anger came renewed determination. She might ultimately lose this battle to survive, but she'd be *damned* if she was going to let that thing record one more second of her torment.

It seemed as if it took hours to pull herself three feet to

reach the damned camera. She lost track of how many times she grayed out along the way, but white-hot anger kept her moving, closer to that hateful, unblinking eye.

By the time she wrapped her fingers around it, her fury had reached critical mass. Lifting it as high as she could, she let gravity take over and smashed it against the hardwood floor. There was a satisfying *crunch*, and the telephone receiver was jolted loose from the strange rubber cradle. A glittering, brightly colored chip popped out and she grabbed it, clutching it so tightly that its tiny metal prongs bit into the meat of her palm. It seemed important—a clue of some kind—but she just couldn't think straight.

She felt like a dying animal, rational thought obliterated by pure survival instinct.

The blackness claimed her again.

•

Gordon was surrounded by freaks.

Now that the hood had been removed, he could see his three tiny captors. They were definitely not children, but they didn't seem to have any obvious secondary sexual characteristics either. The thin, patchy green hair on their oversized heads was scraped up into identical topknots adorned with jaunty, feminine pink bows, but their misshapen and humped torsos were bare beneath matching black leather harnesses, revealing concave and undeveloped chests that definitely did not read as adult female.

One was wearing a garter belt and fishnet stockings with high heels on feet that looked far too big for those stubby, knock-kneed legs. Another was sporting a riff on a ragged, dirty tutu. The third wore what may or may not have been women's underwear and nothing else. All three had tiny, crooked bat wings attached to their harnesses. The wings were made of rusted umbrella struts and thin, stained leather that was disturbingly close in color and texture to their own skin.

Their faces were not identical, yet it was likely that they were related as they all suffered from the same unusual genetic affliction. Their narrow and crooked jaws were far too small to hold the number of jagged teeth crowding their near lipless mouths. Their eyes were huge and filmy, oversized pale gray irises barely distinguishable from the whites. Gordon might have believed they were blind if they weren't staring so intensely at him and giggling at his predicament.

They weren't the only ones laughing. In fact, a small crowd had gathered around him, each abnormal and misshapen form stranger than the last, and all of them wearing stark expressions of harsh, mocking cruelty. There was a bikini-clad girl with alligator skin, thick flaky lips drawn back in a nasty sneer. A stooped and emaciated giant in a loincloth was sniggering behind a hand the size of a baseball glove. A smirking strongwoman in a leopard print singlet was holding a giggling, toddler-sized person with webbed hands and feet, and a flat head that sloped back sharply from slitted eyes. Another tormentor seemed to have no lower body beneath the ribs, scooting himself—herself?—around on a rusty old skateboard.

Another was dressed in rags and spattered with blood and feathers, giggling and stroking the limp and headless carcass of a plump white chicken. Twin women, skinny and hunchbacked with choppy blonde bobs parted on opposite sides, shared a single, massive pelvis from which sprouted two thick but normal legs and two narrow, crooked torsos, topped by sharp-chinned and hateful faces howling with vicious laughter.

They were all laughing, laughing at him. The only one who wasn't laughing was the Joker, who maintained an uncharacteristically stoic expression as he watched Gordon try and fail to comprehend his bizarre surroundings.

They were in some kind of derelict amusement park. Above them loomed the warped and weathered bones of the rollercoaster, against which a jumble of old signs had been haphazardly stacked. Some were shaped like what they were designed to sell—a giant hot dog, a carousel horse, or a sexy girl in a spangled pink costume. Others featured strange words and phrases spelled out in chipped florescent paint, dusty dead neon, or broken bulbs. *TEN-IN-ONE* and *BUCKET TOSS* and *ALIVE!*

The Joker's impromptu dais was topped with what had once been a seat on some kind of whirligig ride for children. At first glance, it appeared to be balanced on a massive pile of dead babies, their chubby limbs skewed and dirty, their eyes vacant black holes. That couldn't be right, but he felt like he couldn't trust any of his senses. He still felt like he had been drugged, his mind simultaneously sluggish and hyperaware of every surreal detail.

Without warning, Gordon was hit with a powerful sense memory so pure and intense that it eclipsed everything. It was the first time he held the newborn Barbara in his arms, in the maternity ward. She stopped crying as soon as the nurse handed her to him. He could feel her tiny hand gripping his finger as he smiled down at her, drunk on the sweet smell of her funny little tuft of strawberry blonde hair. In that moment, he could feel his heart opening wide like a previously locked door, and he knew then that he would gladly die for that little girl.

But where was his little girl now?

The present reasserted itself on his reeling senses, abruptly returning him to this twisted reality. It felt like a kick in the stomach.

Barbara? Where is Barbara?

Babies. They couldn't be real…

They weren't babies. They were just dolls. Hundreds of naked baby dolls piled up in some kind of sick mockery of a mass grave. But why? Who would do such a thing. Dead dolls. Dead babies. Dead daughters.

Dead.

His mind reeled, caught in a disintegrating spiral of horror and shattered memory. Was he dreaming? Was he dead? Was he in hell?

A sharp smoky stench of burning plastic pulled him back from the brink. Focus. He had to focus. He fixed his slippery mind on that smell. When he looked up, he found the source. What he had first taken for makeshift torches were actually burning doll heads, hoisted on sticks. Droplets of flaming liquid rubber sizzled on the ground around them while the bland and cherubic faces slowly melted into leering plastic skulls with staring glass eyes.

Focus. He had to focus.

Again unbidden, an intense memory of Barbara flooded his senses. This one of her laying bloody and broken on the floor. Of the Joker, looming over her with cold, crazy eyes and that horrible smile.

"You," he said, fixing his woozy gaze on the Joker lounging

atop his throne of dead dolls. "Oh no. I... I remember."

"Remember?" the Joker replied. "Oh, I wouldn't do that."

•

"If you'd like to make a call..."

No, the voice was real. The black plastic phone handset was right there, just inches from her face. Her woozy gaze locked on the neat little circle of holes in the center of the receiver. The voice was coming from the hand set.

"If you'd like to make a call..."

She *would* like to make a call. Now, if only she could find a way to hang up and try again.

She must have grayed out again, more than once maybe, because it seemed like a really long time passed between her wanting to make a call and figuring out how to make her hand reach over and push down on the cradle. But somehow, she did, and was rewarded with the best sound she'd ever heard.

A dial tone.

She dialed a number she knew by heart. The emergency hotline in the Batcave.

"Alfred," she said into the receiver. "Patch me through to him."

•

"Remembering's dangerous." The Joker shifted from his lazy, insouciant pose to sudden predatory intensity, that razor sharp grin thrust forward like a weapon. "I find the past such a worrying, anxious place. 'The past tense,' I suppose you'd call it."

He snickered between clenched teeth. Gordon raised himself up on his knees and made another feeble attempt to twist his shaking body and pull away from his bizarre captors. He was rewarded with another vicious pop of the leash, choking off his air and making him gag.

"Memory's so treacherous," the Joker continued. "One moment you're lost in a carnival of delights, with poignant childhood aromas, the flashing neon of puberty, all that sentimental candyfloss. The next, it leads you somewhere you don't want to go..."

Gordon couldn't concentrate on the Joker's unhinged monologue. His own mind was lost in a maze of jumbled memories. He remembered watching teenage Barbara sneaking out of her room late one night and down the fire escape—to meet some boy, no doubt—and him lighting a cigarette and thinking he should probably at least try to stop her. Then their eyes met through the rain-streaked window and she flashed that rakish little smile and his heart melted.

His girl, far too much like him for her own good.

Where is she? What in God's name has the Joker done to her?

Why couldn't he stay focused? What was wrong with his mind? Had he been drugged? Poisoned? Was he dying?

Barbara? Where are you, Barbara?

At some point they untied his wrists, though he couldn't exactly remember when or how. He gripped fistfuls of dirt in his tingling hands and ground his teeth, desperate to anchor himself in the here and now. Yet everything around him was so surreal, he couldn't be sure what was real and what wasn't. Harsh, mocking faces. The Joker. This was madness.

Gordon struggled to block it all out and focus on the dirt between his fingers.

This. This is real.

"...somewhere dark and cold," the Joker continued, coming slowly to his feet, bending his lanky body without moving his head so that his smile remained locked in place. "Filled with the damp, ambiguous shapes of things you'd hoped were forgotten." He ambled slowly down the steps from his junkyard dais, kicking a stray doll out of his way.

"Memories can be vile, repulsive little brutes," he said. "Like children, I suppose." He laughed, gestured, and Gordon's captors forced him again to his feet, dragging him away. Above them hovered a tattered, lurid banner with dripping red letters.

GHOST TRAIN

But he could hardly see it. Instead he saw Barbara.

Barbara!

Barbara at two, naked except for a diaper and one red sock, refusing to be dressed and running through the apartment like a tiny demon, drunk on the brand-new power of the word NO.

Barbara at six, holding his hand and pulling him urgently toward the adult section of the library because the books in the kids' section were so boring and she'd read them all anyway.

Barbara at eleven, in front of her school, pulling away from his clumsy attempt to kiss her cheek and rolling her eyes dramatically.

"God, Dad," she had said. *"You're embarrassing me!"*

"Barbara," he cried, unable to stop himself, just as he was unable to stop the gut-wrenching sobs that shook his body as he stumbled toward his unknown fate. "Oh no. Oh no."

"But can we live without them?" The Joker was still talking, behind him but getting closer. It seemed as if he would never stop talking and talking and talking. "Memories are what our reason is based upon. If we can't face them, we deny reason itself! Although why not? We aren't contractually tied down to rationality."

The Joker's voice was suddenly way too close, his hot breath on Gordon's cheek.

"There is no sanity clause."

Gordon was sure for the hundredth time that he was going to pass out, but he didn't. He *couldn't*. The horror just went on and on. The cackling laughter of the circus freaks felt like acid on his exposed skin. His mind swirled, senses reeling and body pushed beyond the brink of endurance. He couldn't think.

Why couldn't he think?

Those terrible little not-children who had been leading him along shoved him forward so he staggered and half fell into a rusty, faded Ghost Train car with a warped and peeling smile painted across its dented nose. Bony, skittering hands far too strong for their size held him down and strapped him in to the ancient ride while his head lolled back in a dizzy swoon.

"So when you find yourself locked onto an unpleasant train of thought," the Joker said, "heading for the places in your past where the screaming is unbearable, remember there's always madness."

The obscene cherubim checked the straps, making sure Gordon was safely strapped in for the ride.

"Madness is the emergency exit," the Joker added. "You can just step outside, and close the door on all those dreadful things that happened. You can lock them away."

With a theatrical flourish he pulled a massive skull-topped lever. The little car lurched forward and smacked into a swinging door embossed with a leering clown face, propelling Gordon into the blackness within.

"Forever."

•

As the Batmobile screeched to a stop in front of the My Alibi bar, the working girls and hustlers who had clustered around the battered front door scattered like cockroaches. He wasn't looking for them. He was looking for a lead and he wanted it quick, no time for subterfuge disguised as Matches Malone. There had to be a line on the Joker somewhere in this waterfront dive bar. He was up to something, something he couldn't name, but he'd known him too long to ignore his instincts.

He'd shown the Joker's wanted poster to a couple of stick-up men jonesing for Giggle Sniff. The damned drug was in short demand thanks to Batgirl busting Python Palmares and the burning of his lab.

Then on to various other bottom feeders, from them up the chain to Junior Galante after knocking out a couple of his goons, and even Oswald Cobblepot—no Joker ally—about to make parole to re-open his damn Iceberg Lounge. He'd come up blank so far, but it was just a matter of whether this low life or another was going to know what he wanted to know.

Inside, the bar was a long narrow room with a low and uneven tin ceiling stained by decades of nicotine and bad intentions. There was a large rusty drain in the center of the floor to allow the blood and vomit to be hosed off after every shift. A couple of crooked old neon beer signs were the only thing that could have passed for décor, and only one of them actually worked, casting a sickly green glow over the hostile patrons. Rough working women. Surly longshoremen and low-rent bagmen. Old men with faces like clenched fists.

None of them were the Joker or any of his known henchmen.

Batman cut a swath through the intoxicated crowd as he strode toward the bar. No one was too drunk to get the hell out of his way. He headed straight for the bar's most infamous patron—at least for this evening.

Sneaky Danton sat in the gunfighter's seat at the far left end, bookended by a pair of salty ladies. They were the best out of a bad crop, which wasn't saying much. A butter-faced pair of bottle blondes similar enough to be sisters, both barely clad in miniskirts and tube tops. As Batman twisted a leatherclad fist in Danton's shirtfront, hauling him up off his barstool, the two women quickly remembered something important they needed to do elsewhere.

The burly, neckless bartender reached for a sawed-off shotgun clipped under the bar, and there was way too much bloodshot white showing around the pale blue irises of his eyes. Without taking his own eyes off the squirming criminal in his grip, Batman pulled a black spiked elongated casing from his utility belt and held it aloft for the bartender to see.

"I wouldn't," he said. "There's enough explosive compound here to bring this place down around that square head of yours."

The bartender offered a shaky smile and raised his hairy-knuckled hands like it was all just a foolish misunderstanding. He also remembered something important he needed to do and shuffled out through the back.

Batman laid the device on the bar. Then he took the rumpled wanted poster from an inner pocket. With unnerving calm, he smoothed it out on the sticky surface.

"Where is he?"

"Wh... what?"

Batman cracked Danton's head sharply against the wood, and then pressed the thug's cheek against the Joker's two-dimensional ruby red grin.

"Where. Is. He?"

"He's not here, I swear!" Danton blubbered, looking like he was trying to tuck his head down into his body like a turtle. "I ain't seen him since he got out, and neither have any of my girls. Nobody has, honest! He usually comes to see his regulars as soon as he's loose, but this time, nothing. He's like gone ghost, man. Disappeared." When the Dark Knight didn't release him, Danton's eyes practically bugged out of his head.

"If knew anything, I'd tell you, man. I don't owe that freak nothin'!"

Batman's cowl communicator crackled. He touched the side of his mask over his ear.

"Yes?" he hissed.

•

"Miss Gordon?" Alfred Pennyworth was saying urgently on the other end of the phone. Had she blacked out again? "Miss Gordon, are you all right?"

"Just put me through to him!" she snapped, then added, "Please."

She bit hard into the inside of her cheek and squeezed

the sharp edges of the little chip in her hand, desperate to stay focused, to drive back the blackness that kept creeping up on her. When Bruce's familiar, gravelly voice came on the line, she felt a shaky wave of relief so powerful it nearly took her breath away.

"Don't ask any questions," she said. "Just listen. There's no time. The Joker's got Daddy."

There was a weighty pause on the other end of the line.

"I'm listening."

"I know you can activate the tracking in my watch remotely," she said. "You told me you couldn't but don't bother to deny it." She paused, fighting a massive wave of dizziness and nausea. "I slipped the watch... into the Joker's pocket... Track him and find out where he took my father."

"What the hell did he do to you?" Bruce asked, genuine concern mixed with anger in his normally steady voice.

"Forget about me," she said. She could feel that she was fading fast. "He's taking it to the limit this time. His eyes..."

"Sir," Pennyworth's voice came back on the line, cutting in to their call. "Sir, we have received an... unusual transmission via the Batcave's main computer."

"Find Daddy," she whispered. "Please..."

She could hear sirens in the distance, getting closer.

When the blackness came this time, she embraced it, swan-dived into it. Batman knew what to do. He would take the reins now. Her father would be saved. She didn't have to fight anymore. She let it all slip through her fingers like the fragments of a bad dream.

If this was death, so be it.

33

Batman pushed the Batmobile's limits as he raced toward the tracer's origin point. A glowing green screen in the center of the console showed a ghostly maze of Gotham City streets, with a pulsing red dot moving along a back alley. Barbara's watch.

As soon as she told him about it, he'd activated it remotely. To his surprise, it was on the move. That meant the Joker might not have found it. There was still a chance.

It wasn't moving fast enough to be inside a vehicle. The Joker had to be on foot. *What the hell is he up to now?*

The big car zoomed past traffic by moving into the opposite lane. An eighteen-wheeler came from the other direction, the driver pounding on his horn. At the last possible second the Batmobile roared back into the proper lane, the wind from the passing truck buffeting the car.

The Dark Knight's eyes flicked back and forth from the street to that red dot on the screen as he circumvented every obstacle and slipped between and around slower vehicles. Time was the enemy. With every moment that passed, the madman might find the watch. If he did, there was no telling what he might do to his prisoner.

Predicting the Joker's insane actions was a waste of time, especially now. He'd gone to a place they never could have expected. Batman had to locate his quarry before the question became moot.

"Alfred," he said, thumbing the car's communicator on. "Any word on Barbara's condition?"

"She's en route to Gotham General's trauma center right now," Pennyworth replied. "They are preparing for emergency surgery."

"Prognosis?" Batman asked, ripping into a hairpin turn and zooming the Batmobile through a red light.

"Master Bruce," Pennyworth replied. "Preliminary indications are it's a spinal injury which, as you know, are very complex. Every case is unique. If she survives, it's next to impossible to predict the long-term effects this early."

"*If* she survives?" Batman felt the muscles in his clenched jaw twitch as he gripped the wheel hard. "Just give it to me straight, Alfred."

There was a pause, faint static crackling in the Batmobile's soundproof cockpit. "It doesn't look good, sir. She may be physically compromised for the rest of her life."

There was a hesitation.

"What else aren't you telling me?"

"Miss Barbara was found in a state of undress. The Joker removed her clothing after shooting her. Uh... I've received a video transmission and, well, certain indignities were broadcast all across Gotham City by some means." He took a breath. "It's all rather sick."

"Yes, sick." Batman went stony. He concentrated on closing the gap between himself and the red dot.

God help anyone who got in his way.

•

He arrived at the location the red dot indicated, an area under a cloverleaf of expressways on the edge of the Narrows. It had become a shanty town for the homeless.

The rain had started again. He leapt out of the car as the canopy slid back, spotting two men dressed in threadbare clothing. They were struggling with each other near an open fifty-gallon barrel in which kindling burned for warmth.

"Gimma that," one of the men said, tugging on the arm of the other with both his hands.

"Let go, he gave it to me."

"But you can't use it."

"You just want it to sell 'cause it came from pasty face."

The one doing the tugging was shoved by the other one, who wore a black watch. The shoved one stumbled backward and collided with Batman. He turned, startled.

"Oh Lordy," he declared, weaving on his feet, obviously inebriated, glaring up. "You're taller than I thought you'd be."

Ignoring him, Batman looked past him to the other one.

"Where did you get that watch?"

"Red lips gave it to me. He was in that old purple car of his, giggling up a storm. He pulled to the curb and called me over, handing it to me. Said it didn't go with his outfit." His eyes were bleary but he seemed less out of it than his companion. Incongruously, he was clean shaven.

"Did the Joker say anything else?" He kept the anger out of his voice. Inducing fear would only make it more difficult.

"He put the car in gear and told the ones in the back seat with the old man slumped between 'em, 'On to the big top,' and laughing like fingernails on a chalkboard, blew out of here."

"The big top," Batman rasped as he turned to head back to his vehicle. The old abandoned carnival? It seemed like the ideal backdrop for the Joker's brand of theatrical black humor.

He thought of Barbara, fighting for her life in the hospital. Her fortitude and quick thinking might lead him to her elusive tormentor after all. He made her a silent promise that her efforts would not be in vain.

At that moment the Bat Signal cut through the night air.

•

Bullock and a uniform cop were there on the rooftop next to the shining klieg light. The stump of a cigar ever present in the corner of his mouth, Bullock stepped forward. For once, he gave no smartass comment as he handed over an invitation-sized envelope. It had a bat on it.

Batman opened the envelope and extracted its contents.

34

The carnival car slammed through the first set of doors, leaving them in utter darkness. Then it slammed through another pair, and Gordon bent forward, his head down and his hands covering his throbbing head.

The tiny grotesque in the tutu grasped his shoulder with claw-like hands, while from behind another grabbed a handful of his sweaty hair, yanking his head back.

"Up, up!" the creature said in a horrifically childlike voice. There above them was a huge screen, filled with the Joker's leering face.

"A-a-ah," the maniac said. "Heads up, Commissioner! No fair hiding your eyes on the Ghost Train, you old fraidy cat!"

It's not real. None of this is real.

It was alternately too dark and too bright, irregular strobe lights flashing as the ride progressed. Crashing through more doors, up and down the rolling track, they traveled from one room to the next, each with its own gigantic screen. They all showed the same image. The Joker's hateful visage, repeated a hundred times.

Gordon twisted in his tight canvas straps, struggling to turn his head away, but the screens were everywhere. Different shapes, different sizes, there wasn't anywhere he could look that wasn't infected with those leering red grins.

"Oh, I know," the Joker continued. "You're confused. You're frightened. Who wouldn't be? You're in a hell of a situation." Over the aging sound system, that voice was even more horrifying, setting every nerve on end. "But, y'know, though life's a bowl of cherries and this is the pits, always remember this…

"Music, Sam…"

What?

There was a sudden blare of tinny, off-key music blasting through rusted old speakers wired to the little car, and pouring out of invisible speakers mounted in the walls. It sounded like a cross between a warped calliope and a child banging on a xylophone. It was coming from all sides at once. Surround-sound of the damned.

The video image of the Joker, repeated endlessly down the pulsing walls of the tunnel, was suddenly wearing a natty straw boater with a green and purple band. He tipped the hat like a hammy Vaudeville performer and, to Gordon's horror, he began to sing.

"When the world is full of care,
And every headline screams despair,
When all is rape, starvation, war
And life is vile

"Then there's a certain thing I do,
Which I shall pass along to you,
That's always guaranteed to make me smile…

> "I go loo-oo-oony
> As a light-bulk battered bug,
> Simply loo-oo-ony,
> Sometimes foam and chew the rug."

The seasick sway of the wobbly ride and the grating discord of the off-key music amplified and intensified Gordon's torment as the straps chafed his raw, exposed skin and the collar around his neck squeezed his breathing down to nearly nothing. His heart pounded against his ribs as if it was desperate to escape from his chest, and he found himself fervently wishing that he would just pass out. But his mind wouldn't stop racing, eyes wide and burning and unable to look away.

> "Mister, life is swell
> In a padded cell,
> It'll chase those blues away.
> You can trade your gloom
> For a rubber room,
> And injections twice a day!"

Why was the Joker subjecting him to this baffling travesty? And where was Barbara?

Barbara!

They slammed through another door, the grip constant on his hair, his captors staring straight ahead with unblinking eyes. The caterwauling continued. The madman was dancing now, joined by several of the other freaks, twisting and writhing in a parody of a classic Hollywood musical.

"Just go loo-oo-oony,
Like an acid casualty,
Or a moo-oo-nie,
Or a preacher on TV

"When the human race,
Wears an anxious face,
When the bomb hangs overhead,
When your kid turns blue,
It won't worry you,
You can smile and nod instead!"

There was the subliminal flash of a blurry, red-and-white image flickering randomly across different screens down the length of the tunnel. Gordon's gut told him that image was something both important and horrifying that he needed to see, but as soon as his woozy gaze could focus on it, it would hopscotch away to another screen, leaving a leering close-up of the Joker in its place.

"When you're loo-oo-ony,
Then you just don't give a fig…"

Again, that awful, twitching flash of red and white raced over the screens, a jarring counterpoint to the Joker's demented Busby Berkeley number. Was that a human leg? Convulsing, bloody fingers? A curtain of sticky, clotted hair? It seemed crucially important for him to focus on that, but all the images seemed to ebb and flow, melding into some kind of unbearable sensory overload.

"Man's so pu-uu-ny,
And the universe so big!

"If you hurt inside,
Get certified,
And if life should treat you bad…"

The jittery, bloody images were more frequent now, and worse, they seemed to rise up off the screens, straining toward him like speeded-up footage of plants growing toward the sun. It was appallingly clear now that these images were female body parts. Every single part.

The rickety little car seemed to be heading right for a large, swimmy and low-quality projection of video footage that looked like something cops might pull off a gas station security camera. At the center of the image was what appeared to be a dead female body, legs splayed at crooked and unnatural angles. A dark figure was crouched over her as its familiar white face turned towards the camera.

The Joker.

His crooning voice continued as his image on the big screen slung an arm around the nude and prostrate woman, lifting her shoulders off the rug.

Is that… is that my rug?

The tunnel of twitching, bleeding female body parts seemed to be closing in around him, each one more appalling than the last, but he couldn't take his eyes off the big screen in the middle. In that rough staticky footage, the Joker was tipping the woman's lolling head toward the camera and lifting one bloody hand to make it wave, silently mouthing the words.

SAY HI DADDY!

It was Barbara.

He could no longer tell if he was screaming inside or out loud, but her name echoed through him like the shockwave from an explosion, shattering everything in its wake.

"Don't get ee-ee-even,

"Get mad!"

"Mad!" echoed the hell-chorus from the freakish non-children clutching at him and shrieking in his ears. "MAD! MAD! MAD!"

He no longer seemed able to control his thrashing body as he threw himself against the straps, sobbing and howling.

"BARBARA!"

He had to get to her. Had to…

"Barbara…" His voice was nearly gone now, just a tortured whisper punctuated by flecks of spit and bile. "Barbara, baby. Oh God, no…" There was silence, then a hint of static over the sound system. It was still on.

"This footage has been broadcast to every computer in Gotham City," the Joker purred from somewhere in the dark. Inside Gordon's head, maybe? "There's no way to call it back. Every cop, every librarian, everyone is watching."

"Everyone is watching!" His chanting captors echoed their master. "Everyone is watching!"

"Everyone knows you failed to protect her."

"Everyone knows!" More chanting. "Everyone knows! Everyone knows!"

"*He* knows," the madman said.

Gordon wanted so desperately for it to go away. To bash his own head against the iron safety bar until it all went away for good. But he couldn't even move. He couldn't escape the atrocities endured by his only daughter at the hands of that giggling monster. They were all around him, inside him, seared into his mind forever.

For a horrible moment, it seemed as if the Joker had the right idea, after all. That the reality of his complete and utter failure—both as a police commissioner and a father—was simply too painful to endure. That the only option was to retreat into madness.

The shameful, cowardly and overwhelming desire for abdication that Gordon experienced in that moment would haunt him until the day he died. With that realization, a flame of anger appeared deep within him.

35

There was a ticket made of card stock inside the envelope. Batman held it in his gloved hands. The ticket read:

BONUS BROTHERS
CARNIVAL AND AMUSEMENT PARK
ADMIT ONE

He turned it over. There was a handwritten note on the back, in loopy purple crayon letters.

With Compliments

Batman's eyes narrowed, fist crushing the ticket.

The big top.

He left the roof, the crumpled ticket on the ledge as Bullock watched him descend on his grapple line toward the idling Batmobile.

36

The Joker stood waiting at the end of the Ghost Train ride when the brightly painted doors flew open and the car came careening out, slamming into the emergency bumper at the end of the track. The Commissioner's head whipped back, and then lolled forward, a string of drool connecting his chin to the sparse white hair on his chest.

"Ah, here they are now!" the Joker said. "My goodness, that's some Ghost Train. When they went in, the chap in the middle didn't look a day over seventeen, and his three little pals were professional basketball stars!"

The three grotesques still clustered around Gordon as the restraining bar lifted, and he rested his forehead against it.

"Look at him now, poor fellow," the grinning man continued, leaning on his cane. "That's what a dose of reality does for you." Gordon's diminutive captors dragged him out of the car. "Never touch the stuff myself, you understand. I find it gets in the way of the hallucinations."

Propelled by his tormentors, the Commissioner stumbled and fell in front of the Joker, one hand sliding in a puddle of water and sending him flat.

"Why, hello, Commissioner," the Joker said. "How's things?" When he got no response, he leaned in close. "Commissioner?"

Still no response.

"Hello?"

Only a ragged panting.

"Anybody home?" he said, louder this time. This was beginning to be *insulting*.

Finally he straightened, letting his disgust show in his expression. The rain was falling harder again, pelting the onlookers and splashing in puddles all around them.

"God, how boring," he growled. "The man's a complete turnip!" He twirled his finger next to his head. "Take him away and put him in his cage. Perhaps he'll get a little livelier once he's had a chance to think his situation over. To reflect upon life, and all its random injustice."

He leaned over, placing his chin on the cane, and stared down into a puddle, reminded of that runoff ditch, all those years ago...

"Hey, c'mon! Quit daydreamin'."

Lifting his gaze, he watched as the pathetic shell of a man was dragged away through the mud like a whipped dog, but as amusing as it was, he quickly grew tired of the spectacle. Turning his face up to the cold rain, he closed his eyes and felt the pulse of a strange radioactive ache burning inside his chest. A sick feverish heat that could never be quenched, like an unrequited crush.

Where is Batman?

What's taking him so long?

•

Gordon thought maybe he was back in that animal cage, but he couldn't be sure of anything anymore. There was something that looked like iron bars casting harsh, film noir slashes across his shivering flesh.

It was as if he had forgotten what it was like to wear clothes. To be warm. To have dignity. To be worthy of a daughter's love. Maybe he'd never actually had those things. Maybe that was all just a cruel dream and this, this was the only reality. Always and forever.

The freaks surrounded him, their shrill mocking laughter like vicious birds tearing into him from all sides. Terrible, unnatural faces distorted by cruelty floated through his blurry vision like creatures in a nightmare. A nightmare that never ended. Gordon curled tighter into a quivering fetal position, but the laughter was inside of him, as well. There was no escape.

"That's so funny," the skeletal man said. "That's *so* funny."

No escape.

There was a barker at this carnival, too. A voice he knew. That voice. That monster.

"Ladies and gentlemen!" the Joker cried theatrically. "You've read about it in the newspapers! Now, shudder as you observe, before your very eyes, that most rare and tragic of nature's mistakes. I give you… the *average man*!"

The freaks oohed and aahed as Gordon tucked his head down under his arms, willing himself to disappear. Yet he remained, and the nightmare continued. With his eyes closed, he saw Barbara. When he opened them again, deformed and mocking faces swirled around him. The Joker was there, in the front, his leering expression only inches away.

"Physically unremarkable, it has instead a deformed set of values," he mocked. "Notice the hideously bloated sense of humanity's importance. The club-footed social conscience and the withered optimism." More than ever, there was menace in those eyes. "It's certainly not for the squeamish, is it?"

He put his head down again, but the voice didn't stop.

"Most repulsive of all, are its frail and useless notions of order and sanity. If too much weight is put upon them... they SNAP!" To illustrate his point, he snapped his fingers. The deformed audience howled. In the distance, there seemed to be the growl of a motor.

"'How does it live?' I hear you ask. How does this poor, pathetic specimen survive in today's harsh and irrational world? The sad answer is, 'not very well.' Faced with the inescapable fact that human existence is mad, random and pointless, one in eight of them crack up and go stark slavering buggo!"

The growl was closer, deep and vibrating up through the ground on which he crouched.

"And who can blame them? In a world as psychotic as this, any other response would be crazy!"

There was a bright and sudden light shining through the cage of his fingers. Moving light, coming from twin sources, washing over Gordon and piercing the iron bars that crisscrossed his broken mind. This wasn't the maddening kaleidoscope of carnival glitter and neon that had come to define his new existence. No, this was a pure, clean colorless light that chased away the shadows. A light that shone on him like forgotten hope.

The *thrum* of the engines ceased, and he wondered for a

panicky moment if it had been his imagination. Then he heard the whine of the canopy as it opened, and the familiar rustle of the cape. No sound from the boots, of course.

"Hello," Batman said. "I came to talk."

37

It could have been a second, it might have been a lifetime, but that clear true light didn't go away. It shone through his eyelids, reminding him that there really was a different world outside this horror. Outside this cage. Outside his head. With that white light came hope. Hope of rescue and return to the real world, and that hope was...

Terrifying.

Slowly, painfully, he opened his eyes again.

The Batmobile really was there, the huge ornament on its prow filling his vision. The piercing headlights sent the crowd of freaks scattering to the holes from which they had come.

Even so, he didn't dare believe it until he heard the voice again. It was deep, the words sounding as if they were carefully measured before he released them.

"I've been thinking lately," Batman said. "About you."

Gordon's attention shifted to the Joker. The madman just stood there, his hair whipping in the wind, a surprisingly calm smile on his face.

"About me. About what's going to happen to us in the end."

The grinning ghoul showed no fear.

"We're going to kill each other, aren't we?" the caped man asked. "Perhaps you'll kill me. Perhaps I'll kill you. Perhaps sooner... perhaps later."

A long pause. Gordon didn't know how Batman could be so *calm*. Finally, his patience must have run out. He set his jaw, and launched himself at his opponent, his cape spreading wide like the wings it was meant to represent.

The Joker grinned all the wider, and pulled a small, round object from an inner pocket. As Batman pressed down, the lunatic used the strange little device to discharge a stream of unknown fluid onto Batman's arm. Uttering a grunt of pain, Batman rolled away from the prone Joker, hissing between his teeth and clutching at the wound.

The Joker clambered to his feet and ran for the nearby fun house, its door painted to resemble the toothy grinning mouth in a clown's face.

Gordon watched this exchange from the space between his folded arms, not wanting to believe that it was real because he was so afraid that it wasn't. Batman looked as if he was going to pursue his foe, but then he looked back over his shoulder.

No! Gordon cried inwardly. *Don't let him escape!*

The Dark Knight approached the bars of his cage.

"Jim?" he said, his voice both guttural and steady. He did something to the lock, and the door swung open. "Jim, are you... are you still okay?"

Something about that simple, ordinary phrase unleashed an emotional flood. What did that even *mean* anymore? How could anything ever be okay again? Okay was for people who had never peeked past the polite curtain of normal everyday life and seen the horrors and madness that lay just behind. Okay was for people who still believed they could protect the ones they loved, who believed there were good people, good cops, good parents.

Okay was for people who didn't know the ugly truth.

"Oh, god," he choked out, wrapping his arms around his rescuer, gripping his cape.

Once Gordon started sobbing, it was like a tsunami, washing over him. It felt like a kind of psychic vomiting, his tortured body and shredded soul wracked with anguish as he felt himself reliving every awful moment of torment, again and again.

"It's okay," Batman said, holding him up. There was that word again. "It's okay. Let it come." Gordon would have collapsed face-down in the mud if his friend hadn't been there to hold him up. He clung to the stiff, unyielding armor of Batman's chest plate like it was a life raft. Like it was the only sure and solid thing left in a whirling vortex of trauma.

Batman helped Gordon settle to the ground, gently this time. Finally the convulsions abated. The fear and the anger were still there, but he could hold them in check. At last his rational mind asserted control.

When he was able to speak, he tried to convey the enormity of what had happened—yet simple, everyday words he'd used for decades suddenly seemed painfully inadequate. Still, he forced his lips to move, forced sounds to emerge. He needed Batman to understand the only thing that mattered.

"He... He shot Barbara," Gordon said. "He... *showed* me. He showed me what he did." He wrapped his arms around his shivering body as guilt and shame and anger and horror and a thousand other dark emotions tried to rise back up. "He tried to drive me mad."

Just saying the words out loud gave his mind a solid handhold, and enabled him to begin pulling himself up out of the abyss. What had happened to him was awful, perhaps unbearable, but it wasn't infinite. He was still here, and it was over... or it soon would be. The Joker had failed, and he would be brought to justice for what he had done.

Had to be.

"Listen," Batman said, pulling a drop cloth off a nearby stack of crates and draping it over his shoulders. "She's been taken to the hospital and has the best team of surgeons working on her right now. The police are following right behind me. I'll stay here with you until they arrive."

What? No!

"No!" Gordon snapped. He took a deep, shaky breath to steady himself, and squared his shoulders. "No," he said again. "I'm okay. I think the Joker gave me something so I couldn't fight back, but I feel like it's starting to wear off now. You have to go after him. I want him brought in... and I want him brought in by the book!"

Batman nodded, eyes narrow and mouth set in a grim, hard line.

"I'll do my best."

As he turned, moving quickly toward the fun house entrance, Gordon called after him.

"By the book, you hear?" he said. "We have to show him!"

Batman hit the fun house door with his shoulder, barreling

inside without acknowledging Gordon's words. But he had heard. Gordon was certain.

"We have to show him that our way works!" But Batman was gone. Gordon put a palm over his eyes and slumped down.

It was out of his hands now.

38

Batman paused for a moment inside the fun house door to let his eyes adjust to the gloom. The place had a sad smell of mildew and neglect mixed with rat piss and a strange plasticky candy undertone that reminded him of those weird fruit-scented markers for children.

There were scattered, uneven fairy lights in mismatched colors running the length of the skewed hallway he'd entered, but no other illumination. As his eyesight acclimated, he could make out a series of distorted, leering faces on the walls that seemed to flicker and twitch. Their eyes followed him as he started down the hall toward a shiny red door.

The floor slanted upward and the ceiling slanted downward, creating a claustrophobic sense of forced perspective as he moved closer to the illusive door. Although it had seemed very far away at first, when he reached it far too quickly, he found that it was really child-sized. Forced to double over, he dropped into a crouch and reached for the coin-sized doorknob.

His broad shoulders barely fit through, and the doorframe scraped painfully against the acid burn on his left arm, rupturing several blisters and causing a new hiss of pain to slip from between his teeth. There was a drop of nearly three feet from the miniature door jamb to the floor of the new corridor.

"So…" The Joker's voice echoed through the fun house, making it impossible to pinpoint exactly where it was coming from. "I see you received the free ticket I sent you. I'm glad. I did *so* want you to be here."

Batman kept moving quickly but cautiously forward while clocking his strange surroundings. The walls were covered with slanting and overlapping screens flickering with surreal images of the madman's face, but grotesquely distorted. All wild, mad eyes and wolfish, cannibal teeth.

"You see," the Joker continued, as the strange stylized faces seemed to mouth his words. "It doesn't matter if you catch me and send me back to the asylum. Gordon's been driven mad. I've proved my point."

Batman didn't bother to contradict the Joker's self-satisfied monologue. He just kept moving.

"I've demonstrated that there's no difference between me and everyone else!" The talking faces on the screens went maddeningly out of synch with the audio, adding to the feeling of distorted unreality. "All it takes is one bad day to reduce the sanest man alive to lunacy. That's how far the world is from where I am. Just one bad day."

There was a stuttering, subliminal flash of something across all the screens, a bright burst of color undercut by a flicker of something bloody. Something too awful to describe, and gone before his mind could register its significance. By the time he realized it was just a distraction, it was too late.

The floor of the corridor dropped out from under him. If not for his finely honed reflexes, he would have plummeted to the bottom of a deep shaft. As it was, he only caught himself with one hand as he fell, grabbing the edge and hanging above what must have once been a ball pit.

Looking down, he could see row after row of thick metal spikes. A forest of shiny metal tubes, each one freshly sliced on a wicked hypodermic angle, their needle-sharp tips dripping and glistening with some oily, iridescent substance.

"You had a bad day once, am I right?" the Joker's disembodied voice asked as Batman twisted his body to pull himself up over the edge of the pit. "I *know* I am. I can tell. You had a bad day and everything changed. Why else would you dress up like a flying rat?"

A fleeting memory flashed through his mind. His mother's arm around his small shoulders, comfort and protection against the chill of that long-ago alley. The warm, gentle perfume drifting from her soft fur coat and her reassuring smile, telling him everything was going to be okay.

And then…

"You had a bad day, and it drove you as crazy as everybody else. Only you won't admit it! You have to keep pretending that life makes sense. That there's some point to all this struggling."

No. He wasn't going back there again. The Joker wasn't going to get to him that easily. He had fought against the siren song of that particular memory loop, every day of his adult life, and wasn't going to give in now. He pulled himself the rest of the way up out of the pit, and continued down the curving corridor toward the sound of the Joker's voice.

"God, you make me want to puke!"

The feeling was mutual, but Batman wasn't going to give him the satisfaction of a response.

When he reached the dogleg twist at the end of the hallway, it led into a new section labeled *BARREL OF LAUGHS*. This was a series of rotating cylinders painted to look like giant barrels on the outside, but all slippery steel on the inside. The steel had been defaced with dripping acid-green spray paint, one short word repeated over and over.

HA! HA! HA! HA! HA!

At the far end of this moving tunnel, the shadow of the Joker was visible. At first it looked as if he was brandishing his walking stick, but then Batman realized it was a microphone.

"I mean, what is it with you?" the lunatic persisted. "What made you what you are? Girlfriend killed by the mob, maybe? Brother carved up by some mugger?" He paused, then added, "Something like that, I bet... Something like that."

Again, the memories of that night tried to force themselves up into his conscious mind. Details leaked out around the edges. Blood on his mother's fur coat. His father's hand—the big strong hand he was supposed to hold so he would be safe crossing the street—palm up and twitching on the crimson-soaked concrete.

He shook his head to keep it clear, and stepped into the first of the rotating cylinders. It was designed to be slick and disorienting, but Batman managed to keep his balance, moving gracefully against the spin and using the textured tread of his boots to prevent him from slipping.

"Something like that happened to me, you know," the Joker

said as Batman made the tricky transition between a cylinder spinning to the left and one spinning to the right. "I... I'm not exactly sure what it was. Sometimes I remember it one way, sometimes another. If I'm going to have a past, I prefer it to be multiple choice."

The Joker's laughter echoed back through the cylinders, mirrored in the spinning graffiti surrounding Batman as he made his way into the final one.

HA! HA! HA! HA! HA!

He kept his focus riveted on the wall of the room ahead—one that wasn't rotating—fighting a creeping feeling of vertigo. Just another few feet and he'd be back on solid ground.

"But my point is..." the Joker continued. "My point is, I went crazy. When I saw what a black, awful joke the world was, I went crazy as a coot! I admit it! Why can't you?"

Nearly there. Just a few more feet. He steadied himself against the spin and then leapt forward, diving out of the revolving barrel and hitting the solid floor with a tight tuck and roll. When he leapt to his feet, coiled and ready to strike, he spotted the jocular bastard ducking through a doorway marked *HALL OF MIRRORS*.

"I mean, you're not unintelligent," the Joker said. "You *must* see the reality of the situation. Do you know how many times we've come close to World War Three over a flock of geese on a computer screen?"

As Batman ran toward the door leading into the hall of mirrors, he noticed that the floor beneath him had become a metal grate, replacing solid wood. Abruptly a loud, whistling jet of stale air shot up from below, smelling like old hydraulic fluid and burning dust. He also noticed a small set of dark, empty bleachers to one side of the grate. Here carnival goers could watch as the compressed air upended loose skirts, annoying the women and amusing the spectators.

"Do you know what triggered the last world war?" the Joker asked. "An argument over how many telegraph poles Germany owed its war debt creditors. Telegraph poles!" That elicited a burst of cackling laughter.

Batman paused for a moment in the doorway. There were two paths from which he could choose, both lined with cracked and dirty mirrors creating the illusion of dizzying gray infinity sweeping vertiginously off in all directions. On the left-hand path, far down the crooked corridor, he spotted a fleeting flash of green and purple.

A thousand fleeing Jokers.

Batman followed, trailed by a legion of his own reflections.

"It's all a joke!" the Joker said, bringing his laughter under control. "Everything anybody ever valued or struggled for…"

Batman reached a series of angled chambers combining mirrors and clear glass, designed to confuse and disorient the patrons.

"It's all a monstrous, demented gag!" Batman followed his voice through the maze and into a dead-end room shaped like an asymmetrical octagon. "So why can't you see the funny side?" Strangely enough, the clown sounded subdued. The question seemed… serious.

Every wall reflected a different distorted, full length image of the Joker. Some angled to the left, some to the right. Some angled up, some down, but off all the reflections, three were straight on, and Batman focused on those. His eyes flicked from one to another and back again.

One of the panels had to be clear.

But which one?

"Why aren't you laughing?" the Joker asked, his long white face suddenly mournful. Was it because Batman refused to participate? Was that betrayal reflected in the eyes?

He made his choice.

Arms thrust forward so his gauntlets would take the brunt of any impact, he burst through. With a sense of satisfaction, he watched surprise—and then terror—sweep over his quarry's features.

"Because I've heard it all before," Batman said, "and it wasn't funny the first time." He grabbed the Joker by the collar, pulling his face nose-to-nose with his own. Distorted reflections mimicked the movement all around, repeated over and over in the warped depth of the fun house mirrors.

The Joker let out a wild howl. It might have been fear or it might have been mirth, but as Batman hurled his foe through another pane, shattering it instantly, the sound most certainly was pain.

Batman followed his adversary through the impromptu exit from the hall of mirrors and into what seemed to be a drab, dimly lit service corridor. A section of the fun house never meant to be seen by customers, allowing access to the wiring and machinery that powered the various moving attractions, it was lit only by two dull yellow bulbs, wrapped in rusted cages and protruding from the unpainted wooden walls. At the far end of the corridor was a metal door propped open with a chunk of broken brick.

"Incidentally," Batman said as he approached his fallen opponent. "I spoke to Commissioner Gordon before I came in here. He's *fine*. Despite all your sick, vicious little games, he's as sane as he ever was. So maybe ordinary people *don't* always crack."

The Joker peered over his shoulder and scrabbled in a pocket for some weapon. Batman stepped down on his wrist like he would on the neck of a striking snake.

The Joker swore and twisted his trapped hand, dropping the weapon. Batman could see it clearly now—it was a rubber wristband fitted with a hypodermic needle. He kicked it out of the Joker's reach.

"Maybe there isn't any need to crawl under a rock with all the other slimy things when trouble hits," he growled, dragging the clown to his feet and pulling him close. Tiny fragments of glass twinkled in the purple weave of the Joker's jacket, falling around them like glitter in a snow globe. "Maybe it was just you all the time."

"NO!" the Joker cried, gouging at Batman's eyes with hooked fingers and twisting the fabric of his cowl so he couldn't see.

"Unngh." Batman had to let go of his opponent to readjust his eye-holes and knuckle the streaming tears from his swollen and stinging eyes.

"Don't," he spat, hearing his foe giggling again behind him. Then bright shooting stars exploded in his head as something hard struck home on one side. He was flung to the side, dropping to his knees. Grasping a railing of some sort, he shook his head, forcing fury to eclipse the pain as a pulsing knot began to form just above his left ear. Struggling to get his mask—and his wits—properly realigned, he heard a familiar sound.

The soft, deadly *ptchik* of a switchblade.

Before his brain had time to fully process this new information, his hand shot out to intercept the downward swing of the Joker's attack. Grabbing the wrist in an iron grip, he used the Joker's own momentum against him, twisting the wrist of his blade hand and pulling him into an uppercut to the midsection.

The Joker doubled over with a comical squawk, blade flying free from his open fingers. He stammered and sucked wind as Batman twisted a fistful of the Joker's tacky shirtfront and raised him so they were face to face. The Joker looked genuinely frightened and almost childlike in that moment.

A stiff right cross sent him crashing through the partially open door, and out into the rainy night.

39

Gordon raised his head when he heard the crash. He had taken shelter from the rain, waiting for backup to arrive for what felt like a cold dark century, and saw the Joker come flying out of a side door in the fun house, landing face down in grass and sliding several feet before he came to a stop.

Batman followed, stepping out through the door to stand over his prostrate foe. Rain dripped from the hem of his rippling cape, providing the only movement in the solemn, silent tableau.

No sound, no movement, until a burst of sudden action broke the moment wide open. The Joker rolled on his back and sat up, throwing off droplets of rain and mud as he pulled a snub-nosed gun from an inner pocket. His expression was wild and manic, eyes far too wide and twisted red lips skinned back from his long yellow teeth, giving him the look of a trapped animal.

For an endless minute, the two of them just peered at each other. Batman still as stone, grim and giving nothing away. The Joker shaking all over as if he was silently laughing. Or crying.

In the space of that elastic eternity, Gordon thought of and dismissed a hundred desperate plans to intervene and save his masked friend. Yet he had no weapon of any kind. Even his fists, upon which he had relied for decades, had betrayed him. They hung dead and useless at the end of his leaden arms.

Instead he lurched to his feet, intending to get between them or draw the Joker's fire. In that moment, taking a bullet for his friend seemed preferable to living after what he had endured. But his body wasn't up to the task. Having shambled a few feet out onto the midway, he dropped to his knees in the mud.

The Joker paid no attention to Gordon's sad little display of crippled valor. Steadying his aim, he pointed right between Batman's eyes, and pulled the trigger.

There was no gunshot. No impact shattering Batman's skull. There was just a jaunty *pop*, followed by a soft fluttering sound as a tiny flag unfurled at the end of the barrel.

CLICK CLICK CLICK

"Goddammit," the Joker said. "It's empty."

The wave of relief that washed over Gordon at that moment was so strong that he almost passed out.

Where the hell is that backup?

The Clown Prince of Crime seemed to deflate in that moment, shoulders slumping, curling inward as his signature grin melted away in the rain. His dripping green hair hung down in his eyes, but failed to hide his bleak and hopeless expression.

"Well?" the Joker continued, letting the gag gun slip from his grip. "What are you waiting for? I shot a defenseless girl. I terrorized an old man. Why don't you kick the hell out of me and get a standing ovation from the public gallery?"

Batman stared down on his defeated opponent, his expression

unreadable. "Because I'm doing this by the book," he replied. "And because I don't want to."

Something in his gaze was different. Where there had been rage, now there was calm. Where there had been a primal force, now there was certainty. Relief turned to triumph as Gordon silently struggled to his feet, clutching the rough drop cloth more tightly around his body. After everything he had gone through, *this* was victory.

Justice was winning.

The Joker twisted away, refusing to meet the implacable gaze.

"Don't you understand," Batman continued. "I don't want to hurt you. I don't want either of us to end up killing the other, but we're both running out of alternatives, and we both know it." He came a step closer, holding out a hand.

The Joker ignored it.

"Maybe it all hinges on tonight," he said. "Maybe this is our last chance to sort this bloody mess out. If you don't take it, then we're locked onto a suicide course.

"Both of us.

"To the death."

A long pregnant pause stretched out between them. The Joker hunched lower, his hands on the ground, fingers interlaced. In that moment, the only sound was the rain.

Batman continued. "It doesn't have to end like that," he said. "I don't know what it was that bent your life out of shape, but who knows? Maybe I've been there too. Maybe I can help."

The Joker turned his head slightly. His eyes were closed, and drops of rainwater fell from his long, hawkish white nose and unnaturally sharp chin.

"We could work together," Batman said. "I could rehabilitate you. You needn't be out there on the edge anymore. You needn't be alone." He paused, as if to let that sink in. "We don't have to kill each other." Another pause. "What do you say?"

Slowly, silently, the Joker rose to his feet, hands still clutched in front of him, shoulders still down. He turned, his face mostly in shadow. His brow was wrinkled in a frown, and for a moment it looked as if he might fly into a rage. Then his features relaxed.

"No," he replied. "I'm sorry but… no. It's too late for that. Far too late." He raised a gloved hand to pinch the bridge of his nose like a man with a persistent headache. His face remained grim despite the clipped giggle that slipped between his teeth. "You know, it's funny… this situation. It reminds me of a joke."

Gordon started to take a step closer to the pair, and then stopped himself. He wanted to hear what the madman had to say, and didn't want to take the chance of distracting him. Although he wasn't sure if either one of them even remembered he was there.

They turned so they were both facing away from him, two black shadows, side by side now and looking off at the distant spires of Gotham City across the bay. Where the hell was that damn backup? What was taking them so long?

"See, there were these two guys in a lunatic asylum," the Joker said, his arms crossed and hugging his body. Then they unwrapped, and he held them out dramatically. "And one night, one night they decide they don't like living in an asylum anymore. They decide they're going to escape!"

Batman stood there, still and listening.

"So, like, they get up onto the roof, and there, just across this narrow gap, they see the rooftops of the town, stretching away in the moonlight…"

The rain picked up, as did the wind, going from a gentle patter to a driving, icy downpour. Gordon was tempted to step back into the shelter, but found he couldn't move. He was riveted.

In the distance, there finally was the sound of sirens.

"…stretching away to freedom. Now, the first guy, he jumps right across with no problem. But his friend, his friend daren't make the leap. Y'see, he's afraid of falling." The Joker's gestures became wilder, more manic. His voice was shaky and tense and starting to crack.

"So then, the first guy has an idea. He says 'Hey, I have my flashlight with me! I'll shine it across the gap between the buildings. You can walk along the beam and join me.'"

At that point, whether from fear or cold or the grip of some unknowable inner psychosis, the Joker began to shiver all over, stuttering and stumbling over the delivery of his convoluted monologue.

"B-but the second guy just shakes his head. He suh-says… He says 'What do you think I am? *Crazy?*'" The last word came out as a shout.

The Joker turned to face Batman, revealing his profile to Gordon. He was smiling again, but this time it was different. His expression was that of a child desperate to be accepted, to please, and knowing full well that it would never be.

"'You'd turn it off when I was halfway across!'" he said, delivering the punchline. Then he began to laugh, and it sounded out of control. Gordon didn't know what to think. The Joker pinched his nose again and covered his eyes, his laughter growing in intensity until his entire body shook.

Baffled, Gordon turned his gaze on his friend, and what he saw was...

Impossible...

A smile appeared. Small at first, barely registering on the granite countenance.

Batman was *laughing*. The smile turned into a grin, more fearsome than any expression Gordon had ever seen on the man's face. He didn't know if he should be afraid.

The Joker continued to giggle hysterically.

As the sirens grew louder, Batman lurched forward and grabbed his enemy. They stood there, their laughter mingling, their bodies shaking. Headlights appeared beyond them, sending a glare through the downpour.

Then Gordon knew.

He's going to kill him, the top cop realized, and his blood ran cold. The Joker's laughter trailed off, the mad trill of giggles turning into choking gasps as Batman pulled him closer.

The laughter died.

The Joker went silent.

"Batman, no!" Strength flooded back into Gordon's limbs, and he started forward, half running, half stumbling. He couldn't allow himself to collapse. Harder than ever, the rain made it difficult to see. As the cruisers came closer, the glare increased. The Dark Knight turned, and his masked face could be seen. In that moment, Gordon witnessed something cold and terrible in his friend's eyes. Something he would never forget.

"You can't let him win!" he cried, staggering closer and struggling to keep his treacherous body upright. "It has to be by the book," he gasped. "It's the only way."

A flight of conflicting emotions chased one another across the masked face, barely visible beneath the cowl. Then he nodded almost imperceptibly and let loose his grip. The Joker collapsed to his knees, clutching his throat. He was silent for a few heartbeats, and then he started chuckling again, between deep wheezing gasps.

Four squad cars pulled up, their spinning red and blue lights spinning, adding to the surreal nature of the moment. They disgorged an army of uniforms, who drew down upon the kneeling villain. More spread out to search the grounds. Two of them ran over to Gordon, placing their hands under his arms. Suddenly he was grateful for their support.

"Commissioner," an officer said.

Dully he acknowledged the man, leaning heavily on his arm.

"There are more of them," Gordon said. "I doubt they'll go far." The uniform just nodded. Gordon squinted in the glare. Once shut, his eyes didn't want to open again.

When they did, Batman was gone.

As the still giggling Joker was cuffed and led away, Gordon wanted to go after his friend, to comfort him in some way. Yet there could be no comfort, he knew, in the wake of this horror show. Each of them would have to find a way to deal with what they'd experienced.

Officers darted through the shadows. In the distance, pitched voices rose and fell, then were silenced. He stared down at the growing puddles.

The rain continued to come down.

The world kept spinning.

40

Barbara Gordon didn't exactly wake up. It felt more like plunging into icy water, trailing tattered ribbons of an ugly dream she couldn't quite remember. The cold shock of reality made her gasp as she tried to sit up, but couldn't.

What is this? Was she tied to the bed? *Bed? Whose bed?*

Where am I?

She did some visual arithmetic, foggy brain struggling to add up clues. There was an IV needle in her arm. Rubber tubes, glowing green screens, ominous machinery measuring various biological values with blips and squiggles.

Hospital.

Metal rails on the narrow bed. Some kind of complex traction bracing her lower body. Oh, god, was that a catheter?

But why was she in the hospital? What happened? Her memory felt treacherous and fragmented. Untrustworthy. She'd been visiting Dad, having a cup of cocoa, and then...

What?

Then she remembered *him*. The sickly sweet chemical smell of him, like bubble gum and formaldehyde. And that smile. That awful, yellow smile.

The Joker.

It all came rushing back to her, causing her to gasp and gulp for air. Every awful detail. Bile surged in her throat and she panicked, struggling to sit up before she vomited. Why couldn't she sit up?

Then there was a nurse beside her, helping her, gentle hands turning her head as she slipped a steel basin beneath her chin.

"It's okay, Ms. Gordon," the nurse said as Barbara shuddered and threw up. "You're safe now."

"Why…" Barbara spat bloody foam into the basin. "Why can't I get up?" Briefly the woman looked nervous, like a deer in the headlights. An instant later she seemed to arrive at a decision.

"You've experienced a penetrating thoracic spinal injury," the nurse told her. "Emergency surgery was required, and you've been in a medically induced coma in order to facilitate—"

"Spinal?" Barbara interrupted. She shoved the basin away and grabbed the nurse's blouse, heart racing as a rush of dizzying anxiety flooded her body. "You mean…" She couldn't seem to find the words. Then she could. "Am I paralyzed?"

"Please try to remain calm, Ms. Gordon." The nurse spoke in a soft, deliberately zen-like tone of voice. "It's best if you wait until Dr. Li arrives to discuss your long-term prognosis."

But her words didn't have the effect she desired. Barbara twisted the scrub top into her fist before she even realized what she was doing.

"Tell me!" she hissed between clenched teeth, dragging the woman's face in close to hers. "Am. I. Paralyzed?"

Then, suddenly there was another nurse, moving silently on rubber-soled shoes and injecting something into her IV line.

The two exchanged a look, sharing weary, wordless understanding and pity.

Barbara wanted to knock their teeth in.

Then everything went muffled and far away. The sound of the machinery. The chatter of the hospital personnel. And finally, the Joker's high-pitched and toxic giggles, chasing her down into the darkness.

•

They'd kept Barbara heavily medicated. For her own good, they said. To ease her anxiety and trauma, and let her body heal. Whatever that even meant.

"Every spinal injury is different," the soft-spoken and serious Dr. Li had told her. "And every patient's body reacts differently over time. It's important to understand that the term 'paralysis' actually encompasses a wide array of functional impairments, each with varying degrees of severity."

Dr. Li was an excellent doctor. She was a straight shooter who didn't mince words, and treated Barbara like an equal who was capable of understanding complex medical terminology, rather than a panicky child who just needed a lollipop and a pat on the head. Yet every time Barbara saw her, she felt a wave of irrational hostility. Like if she wasn't saying all those things—about Barbara's cord contusion, edema, and progressive neurological degeneration—they somehow wouldn't be real.

But the fury was fleeting. Like everything inside her, it was slippery and hard to hold onto. She spent most of her time just staring at the bland white tundra of the ceiling, while people came and went. Doing things and saying things and none of it meaning anything.

Batman had been there, his expression unreadable beneath the mask and mouth set in a hard, grim line. He had gone to stop the Joker, to save her father and when she learned that he had been successful, her relief had been overwhelming. Yet words failed her. All she could do was nod in silence, her face as grim as his.

•

She didn't know how much later it was that she saw her father, standing at the foot of the bed. He was pale and silent, unshaven and wearing an uncharacteristically baggy shirt that made him seem smaller somehow, like a kid in grown-up clothes.

"Daddy?" she said, or tried to. It was hard to tell if the sound made it past her chapped lips.

His hair, normally slick with pomade, seemed dull and unwashed, tumbling down over one eye. There were ugly marks on his neck, a ring of fading bruise that seemed to be the same purplish hue as the sleepless hollows beneath his anguished blue eyes. He looked like he was barely holding back tears, which made her feel as if the underlying order of the universe had been secretly rearranged. She had never seen her father cry.

Not even over losing her mother.

Out in the hallway, there was a noisy metallic clatter. Both of them flinched dramatically as if performing a synchronized dance move. Once they realized what they had done, they shared a rueful smile.

"You okay?" he asked.

"No," she said. "You?"

"Nope."

He moved to her bedside and put his hand over hers, and neither of them said anything else. There was so much she wanted to tell him. She wanted to say she was sorry she couldn't save him from whatever torture he had endured at the hands of the Joker. She wanted to tell him that she was still here for him and loved him and all that nice stuff that you said to a person after they've gone through profound and deeply personal trauma that you will never fully understand. But she knew just how meaningless all those nice words would be, because she hated it when other people tried to say them to her.

More than that, she wanted to tell him, to tell somebody, anybody, about the grief that was gnawing at her bones as she felt Batgirl dying inside her. The secret self she'd kept hidden, reveling in the fearless strength and power of that persona while those all around her were none the wiser.

When a friend or loved one died, there was a memorial service. Old photos were passed around and familiar anecdotes shared, and everyone said how much they'd miss that person. But the best version of herself had been murdered by an erratic, unfathomable maniac who didn't really understand what he had done. No one did.

Everyone saw her naked and tortured body, but no one saw what had really happened.

Batgirl had slipped away in slow, agonizing increments during her drawn-out drugged and broken haze, and now Barbara was the only one who would ever know what had happened to Batgirl. That she had been murdered for no reason other than to prove some mad, unknowable point. Barbara could never tell anyone how much she missed herself.

Looking up at her father, however, she knew in that moment that he too was wrestling with things she would never know or understand. Private demons, perhaps just like hers. In that moment, despite the silent, emotional gulf between them, they shared a profound and terrible connection neither of them could acknowledge.

In a strange way, it made her feel more alone.

•

"Ms. Gordon," the sycophantic social worker was saying. "I understand you've refused physical therapy again."

He was a runty red-headed guy with a relentlessly chipper attitude, and reminded Barbara of a chipmunk in a cheap suit. She turned her face away, staring out the single window at the same dull, rainy slice of Gotham City she'd been looking at for weeks. It seemed as if she'd never see any further. Where once the entire city had been hers, now…

"Please, Ms. Gordon," the Chipmunk said. "Your ability to live independently depends on your willingness to work with our physical therapists. They're only trying to help you."

"Help me what?" Barbara snapped. "Help me roll this stupid wheelchair out into the city so I can watch a thousand strangers pretend not to stare? They already got their big show at my expense. No thanks."

"At the very least, won't you consider talking with our counselor to help work through your emotional trauma." His voice was pleading. "Her name is Mrs. Colbert. She's very nice."

"If she's so nice," Barbara said, keeping her face turned away, "you go talk to her. I'm sure it'd be more fun than talking to me."

"Suppressing your feelings isn't a healthy coping strategy, Ms. Gordon."

"Don't you get it?" She turned back to him, a bitter kind of fury coiling cold in her belly. "I can't feel anything." She pounded a fist against the numb, useless meat of her thigh. "I can't…"

She trailed off, unable to find words to express the hollow, aching loss that had punched a hole in the center of the person she'd always believed she was. Strong. Powerful. Brave. Fighting side by side with Batman as a respected equal. That was all over now.

All that was left of her was this broken body and fractured soul. Just another sad, pathetic punchline to one of the Joker's malicious gags. And what was the point of a punchline after the joke was over? Why bother to go on living?

The Chipmunk went on and on with his platitudes and empty self-help jargon, but Barbara wasn't listening. She was wondering if that window would open, and if it did, how hard it would be to pull herself up onto the sill. If she could get the top half of her body out, gravity would do the rest.

Her heart raced at the thought.

"I said you have a visitor," the Chipmunk said. It might have been the second time he'd said it, but she hadn't been paying attention. "I'll come back later."

"Don't bother," she said.

"Um…" A new, yet familiar voice. "I don't know if you remember me."

She turned toward the door of the room. It was the kid. The kid with the glasses from that night. Her breath caught in her chest, nausea pulsing in the back of her throat. She wheeled her chair over to the bedside table and reached for the phone, gripping the receiver.

"Give me one good reason why I shouldn't call the cops."

"I don't have one," the kid said, looking down at his hands. "You probably should." He shrugged. "I would."

That gave her pause. She relaxed her fingers around the receiver, but didn't take her hand away. She waited to see what would happen next.

For a moment, nothing. They just looked at each other. When he spoke again, his words seemed to come too fast, voice cracking in a shaky rush.

"Look, I'm really sorry about what happened," he said. "About what I did, I mean. It wouldn't have happened without my chip. I never meant for any of this to happen, honest. I thought…" He paused. Swallowed. "I'd understand if you called the police. If I was you, I'd want… justice." Looked up at her and then looked away again. "It was supposed to be a joke."

A hard, dry bark of a laugh escaped before she could stifle it.

"Yeah," she said. "Well, it was a real laugh riot." She frowned. "Wait, did you say 'chip'? You mean the one inside that machine, that broke into all the computers in Gotham City?"

A pained grimace flickered across his pale face. He nodded, and her mind started racing.

"He said he was going to broadcast an embarrassing prank. I had no idea he was going to…"

"Look, forget that," Barbara said, feeling more alive than she had in weeks. She motioned for him to come closer to her. "Can you rebuild that machine?"

"It would take time," he said. "And money. It took me three years to design that prototype. I'd have to start over from scratch."

Barbara's heart was racing again, but this time with a rush of excitement. She reached into the drawer in her bedside table and pulled out the thick plastic bag that contained the one and only thing she'd had with her when she had been admitted. The thing she'd held clenched in a manic death grip so tight they'd had to pry it loose from her fingers before they could operate to save her life.

The chip.

"Look, kid," she said. "What did you say your name was?"

"I didn't say," he replied, looking confused. "But it's Zach."

"Okay, Zach," she said. She might have even been smiling, though it had been so long she almost forgot what that felt like. "I'll make you a deal." She pulled out the chip and held it up for him to see.

His eyes went wider than she thought was possible.

"If you're really sorry, and want to make up for what you did, you can use this to build me a machine that'll give me access to the computers of all the criminals in Gotham City. A machine that will allow me to do it without ever getting out of this chair. Almost like… like a kind of high-tech oracle."

She paused for a moment, looking out over the rainy city and seeing possibilities. Seeing a future beyond Batgirl. The city could be hers once again.

"Look," she said, turning back to Zach. "Forget about revenge and silly sophomoric pranks. This is your chance to do something that really matters with your skills." Her pulse raced, and for the first time in weeks, she felt alive. "We can do it, together. What do you say? You in?"

Zach still looked confused, glancing from her face to the chip and back again. He was wary and nervous, like a street cat that wanted the food she had, but wasn't sure if she could be trusted. Given what the Joker had done to him, she could understand.

Better than anyone.

"Listen, I know what it means to be hurt, and to want to get back at the people who hurt you," she said. "And maybe you can, and maybe that gives you an ego boost, but it also makes you no better than they are. We do this my way, you'll have a chance to really be somebody. To make a real difference in this lousy world."

Barbara picked up the phone.

"You promised you weren't gonna call the cops!" Zach said, backing toward the door. She held up her hand and motioned for him to sit.

"I'm ready for my physical therapy now," she said into the receiver.

41

Light from the setting sun filtered through the wild steel mesh in the windows of Arkham Asylum. The cracked plaster walls, the inmates, and the staff were bathed in comforting hues of orange as if in a Vermeer painting.

Linus Stephens sat in the visitors' room.

"So good to see you again, Noah," the professor said to Noah Kuttler. The young man, along with Zach Tazic, had been one of his prized pupils, but he'd dropped out of school months ago. Noah hadn't resurfaced until this very afternoon.

"I heard about what happened, Prof. Stephens," Kuttler said, "and felt compelled to see how you were doing." The former student was a rangy individual, lean-faced with a hawkish nose.

"Oh, don't be concerned, my boy," Stephens said. "Once I present my evidence at the retrial, they all will understand how the Russians set me up. It's a vast conspiracy, far more so than anyone could imagine. You'll see."

"Yes," Kuttler said. "Of course."

"But please, enough about me, though it *is* my favorite subject." He chuckled for a moment. "What have you been up to? A man with your talents and abilities."

"I've been consulting."

"Consulting?"

Kuttler made a dismissive wave of his hand. "Figuring out strategies, working out scenarios, determining how best to pull off... certain transactions, shall we say."

"Using your profound computer analytics?"

"Oh, yes," the young man said. "Some have even dubbed me 'the Calculator.'" He smiled.

"How colorful," Stephens enthused. "That's wonderful, Noah. Simply wonderful."

They chatted for a while longer, talking computer technology, then discussing the reasons the Russians might want to gain the advantage in what the professor was certain would become the next arms race. Cyberspace, he said—that was where the real war was certain to take place.

Finally Kuttler offered his apologies, and explained that he had a commitment for the evening.

"Of course, my boy," Stephens said. "Not all of us know exactly where we'll be, day in and day out." He gave a wry smile.

Outside the asylum, Kuttler got into a car and smiled at the woman behind the driver's wheel. The freckled Lisa MacIntosh leaned over and kissed him with a smack of their lips. She then put the car into gear, and they drove away.

•

The sky began to darken as Dr. Joan Leland drove her car through the streets. She was returning from a late-lunch fundraiser, and road work forced her to take a detour back to Arkham. She got turned around and found herself cruising through Crime Alley, passing the clinic of Leslie Thompkins—a friend she hadn't seen in some time.

Checking her watch, she decided *what the heck* and parked her car not too far away. She'd drop in to say hello and maybe set up a time for the two of them to get together. Walking along, she passed a boarded-up building. It must have been that way for some time, she figured, as there was a wooden fence erected in front. It was weather-beaten and covered with graffiti, fliers, and posters.

One handbill in particular got her attention.

It was aged and partly eaten away by the elements—a faded image done in German Expressionist style of a man running toward the viewer, his face obscured by shadow. The man's grin was a white crescent in his face, and he had an unruly mane of hair flailing about his head. The man was being pursued by a figure swinging on a rope behind him. This figure wasn't a man in costume, but he had horns on his head and bat-like membranes on either side of the body, running the length of his arms to the middle of his legs.

There was an art deco structure behind the airborne figure, and at the bottom of the poster was a title.

The Mystery of the Monarch Playing Card Company

The poster was for the revival showing of a late 1920s silent film. At least it had been a revival, however long ago it had been. There was no year. It took her several moments to take this in. Unbidden, the Joker's words came back to her.

"Sometimes I remember it one way, sometimes another."

•

As dusk settled in, Harvey Bullock was, not surprisingly, smoking one of his cheap cigars, sitting in his unmarked Marquis up the street from the Gotham Home for Wayward Children. He watched as a beaming Thea Montclair emerged, holding the hand of her nine-year-old daughter, Desi.

Jeez, what a name.

But what the hell. She'd used the cash he'd ripped off from Palmares to get a new apartment in a better part of town, and had proved to Children's Services that her sobriety was here to stay. With the help of Dr. Thompkins, she'd gotten a more upstanding job in a curios shop, one specializing in artifacts gathered from costumed villains Batman had apprehended. This was Gotham after all.

Batgirl had believed his story when she'd cornered him. She'd let him go with the scratch, though she'd warned him that she'd be checking out his story. Bats wouldn't have been that kind of flexible. Sometimes, Bullock reflected grudgingly, you had to use vigilante methods to get past the bureaucratic bullshit to give a person a chance.

Turning the key, he gunned the motor. A familiar shadow flitted across his windshield and he peered up at darkening sky.

"Friggin' bat-eared freak," he muttered. As a doo-wop number played on the car's cassette deck, Bullock threw the smoldering stub of his cigar onto the asphalt and headed back through downtown Gotham.

•

The Nolan-Sprang building, one of the older office structures in downtown Gotham City, boasted Beaux-Arts architecture and an excellent vantage point from which to watch over the entire downtown area.

As night descended, Batman stood on one of its gargoyles—a pitted stone carving of a winged underworld creature said to have been inspired by Dante's *Inferno*. The masked man surveyed his city.

Gordon was safe. The Joker was back in Arkham and had been virtually mute since the incident on the carnival grounds. Yet it wasn't the clown's condition that occupied his thoughts. Nothing he could do would ever explain what went on inside of that head. No, it was his own behavior that mystified him.

Why had he laughed like that?

Had it been gallows humor, of the sort cops used to ease the tension when they secured a crime scene? Had he been releasing the pressure brought on by the shooting, the kidnapping? That didn't make sense though—he'd seen it all before, and much worse.

That led to a more troubling possibility. Perhaps he had discovered his limits. Perhaps the Joker had nearly succeeded in driving him around the bend. How close had he been to letting his worst enemy watch him crumble? How close had the Joker been to the last laugh?

Would he ever know?

His mouth set grimly, Batman raised his arm and shot a line from his grapnel launcher. He had a lead on the two henchmen who'd beaten Gordon, had watched as the Joker shot Barbara. The hook caught hold and he swung down and across the concrete canyons past Crime Alley, where his parents had died. He remembered vividly—as if it had happened just yesterday—kneeling as the moonlight streamed in. He'd said a prayer intended for the wrathful God of the Old Testament.

"I swear by the spirits of my parents to avenge their deaths, by spending the rest of my life warring on all criminals."

He would live by that credo, that night and for many nights to come.

ACKNOWLEDGMENTS

The authors would like to thank Steve Saffel, Nick Landau, Vivian Cheung, Laura Price, Samantha Matthews, Steve Gove, Natasha MacKenzie, Paul Gill, Chris McLane, Lydia Gittins, and Polly Grice at Titan, Josh Anderson, Mickey Stern, and Amy Weingartner at Warner Bros, Mike Pallotta, Doug Prinzivalli, and Michele Wells at DC Entertainment, and of course Bob Kane and Bill Finger, Jerry Robinson, Alan Moore, Brian Bolland, Denny O'Neil, and Mark Chiarello, as well as CDV, Lady V, Django and all the badass Batgirls who are out there fighting back against the Jokers of this world. We see you.

ABOUT THE AUTHORS

CHRISTA FAUST is the author of several hardboiled crime novels, including *Choke Hold*, *Money Shot* and *Hoodtown*, as well as a dozen tie-ins and novelizations such as the award-winning *Snakes on a Plane*. She's written for Marvel and created an original comic series called *Peepland* with coauthor Gary Phillips. She worked in the Times Square peep booths, as a professional dominatrix, and in the adult film industry both behind and in front of the cameras for over twenty years. Faust is a film noir fanatic and an avid reader of classic hardboiled pulp novels, and an MMA fight fan. She lives and writes in Los Angeles. Her website is http://www.christafaust.com.

Son of a mechanic and a librarian, weaned on the images of Kirby and Kane in comics, on too many reruns of the *Twilight Zone*, and on Himes and Hammett in prose, GARY PHILLIPS has published various novels such as *Violent Spring*, the first such mystery set in post '92 civil unrest LA; edited several anthologies including *The Obama Inheritance: Fifteen Stories of Conspiracy*

Noir; and published more than sixty short stories. With Christa Faust, he co-wrote the late '80s-set graphic novel *Peepland* for Titan, about which thefandompost.com remarked, "A damn near perfect comic, hardboiled in all the right ways," and did the *Vigilante: Southland* miniseries for DC Comics.

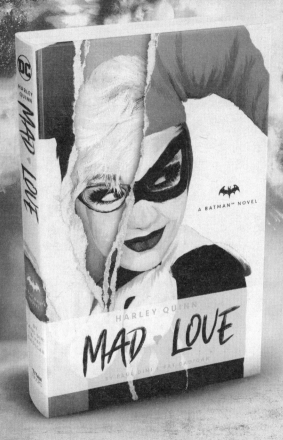

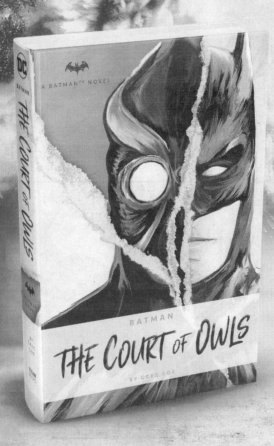